Miss Nguyen's Bodyguard

Rainie Dang

Thank you to my sensitivity readers, Sheina and Jesús, for your tireless work on bringing our hero, and his sexy words, to life.

Content Warnings:
This book is rated 18+ for
sexually explicit content.
The story contains brief moments of assault, gun violence, mentions of childhood neglect, human trafficking, and murder.

Prologue

"Look at me. I want to see what you look like when you come on this cock." I hear him say, but I'm too overcome with pleasure to open my eyes.

I feel myself coming, my walls squeezing his length as my body tenses beneath him, bringing me towards my orgasm while he's pounding into my dripping folds endlessly.

I bury my face into the side of my arm, pulling at the black satin necktie that is binding my wrists to the headboard of my bedroom at my family's cabin.

"*No*, Claire, *déjame mirarte.*" He gently grabs hold of my chin to bring my face towards him so he can watch me. "I want to remember how you look when your pussy is this tight." He slams through my clenching walls, working himself deep into my core as my body threatens to push his cock out. "That's it Claire, keep coming. Fuck, you're glorious." He picks up his pace, pounding into me faster. "You're doing so good. Keep coming. That's it."

His praise is driving me crazy, and before I can come down from my orgasm, I begin again, carried away so quickly, it hits me like a powerful, unexpected wave.

"Oh my god, I'm coming again!" I strain, crying out desperately.

"Come for me, Claire, that's it. You're so good, so hot and wet and *tight*." He leans down to whisper his blazing words in my ear. "Your pussy takes my cock so good, *amor*. Fuck, you're gonna make me come."

He reaches his hand between our heated bodies and rubs his thumb on my clit, bringing me all the way through my pleasure until I'm coming down.

With his final, ragged pumps, he pulls out and comes all over my soft stomach.

In my pleasure-filled daze, I open my eyes, but my bedroom is dark, and I can't see the man who has just fucked me out of my mind.

I can't see him, but I can never forget that voice... even as my world fades away, and I start to wake up.

Chapter One

Club Masque is giving me a headache. I hate going out. The loud music, flashing lights and idiot drunks annoy me.

But I would basically do anything for Jenny Kar. Her long legs, glowing, rich dark skin that screams "I'm an Indian woman and damn proud of it" and her passion for finding resources for refugees and immigrants, makes her the perfect best friend, muse and personal cheerleader. She also models on the weekends.

We met in a Humanities class in graduate school, and have spent the last five years being practically inseparable.

Tonight is her birthday, and she never asks for anything. But she just went through a bad breakup and wanted a night full of sexy dresses, sky-high heels, great food and dancing.

I could never deny her anything.

So here we are, smack dab in the middle of the dancefloor at Club Masque, one of the most exclusive institutions in Manhattan. One of Jenny's model friends knows the owner, so she pulled some strings to get us both in tonight.

4

My feet are sticky from the various drinks that have spilled on me over the course of the night. Jenny is looking hot in her silver mini dress, and I'm looking great in my gold dress with spaghetti straps that are barely holding in my overflowing chest.

I'm in my head, not paying attention to the people around me, trying to block it all out. The music is too loud and there isn't a beat to be found.

How do people dance to this?

Our attempts at dancing continue when suddenly, Jenny flashes me a wide-eyed, horrified look before yelping and jumping to my side.

"That guy just grabbed my ass!" She screams in my ear, and I'm on guard immediately.

I search for the perpetrator, ready to fight, my defenses up. I'm a whole head shorter than Jenny, but I'm already gearing up with a can of whoopass.

I lock eyes with the man who was dancing behind her, a stout, chubby Asian guy with gaudy gold chains around his neck. He's wearing a completely matching yellow tracksuit.

Behind him is a handful of large men dressed in black suits. I spot earpieces attached to wires going down their jackets. They must be his bodyguards or something, which means he must be someone rich. Or someone's son. Or someone's rich son. Either way, I can already tell this is not going to end well.

He's dancing toward us, and I immediately put myself between him and my best friend.

"No thank you!" I shout over the music, hoping he hears me. From what I can see behind his yellow sunglasses and him spilling rum and coke, he's drunk as hell and doesn't hear a word I'm saying.

"Hey baby, you and your friend wanna-"

"No thank you!" I scream again, moving away from him while he dances towards us, invading our space. "We aren't interested!"

"Oh c'mon baby, I could show you a good time. You and her." He slurs. I can barely hear him over the music as I try shoving Jenny off the dance floor.

He reaches out and grabs my boob. One, singular boob, with the hand that isn't holding his gross drink.

I slap him before I have the thought to stop myself. One loud *thwack* of my palm against his jiggling cheek throws him to the floor.

"You mother*fucker!*" I yell, reeling my arm back to hit him again. I feel Jenny grab my forearm to stop me, but I wiggling free.

"Fuck you, you old bitch!" I hear him whine as we're being swept away by the crowd.

"Hey, that guy just groped her!" I heard a girl shout somewhere nearby.

"He grabbed her! Her chest!" Another guy says.

"What's your problem, man?" A broad, androgynous person screams, going up to our assailant and kicking him while he's down.

The idiot's entourage swarms around him right away, but this crowd is rallying behind us, moving the pair of us off the dance floor.

"You okay?" Shouts a lovely dark-skinned girl with glimmering crystals dotting around her eyes.

"Security!" Another blonde girl calls. "Security, this dude is groping girls out here!"

If they removed that disgusting pig from the club, I'll never know. The crowd ushers us off the dance floor and Jenny is already pulling me towards our table, grabbing our coats. I respond to our saviors with various "we're fines" and "thank yous."

"Let's go." Jenny huffs. "I've had enough of living out our old college days." She slips on her coat and helps with mine.

"Tell me about it." I yell, sliding my arms through my long tan peacoat just before we head out the door.

"I can't believe that guy!" Jenny shouts, the cold air hitting us as we leave, momentarily blinding me.

"I should've kicked his ass." I say, still seething from the interaction.

Jenny smiles. "You basically did." She tightens her coat around her thin frame to keep out the chill. "Everyone was so nice though, coming to our defense."

"Yeah, that was great. They had our backs." I nod.

Our heels clack on the wet concrete as we walk towards the subway. It's a chilly night, but thank God it's not snowing.

We pass by one of our reliable pizza places and I slow our pace to peer inside. "You wanna grab a slice before we head down?"

Jenny shakes her head. "You know I'm not doing gluten anymore."

"Get two slices and just eat the cheese and pepperoni." I shrug.

"Nah, I have some leftover beef and broccoli at home, I'll eat that." She says.

"Okay, I'll just be a sec."

We pop into Two Joe's Pizza and I order my usual dollar slice, tossing the loose coins from my pockets in the tip jar. The guy behind the counter shoots me a smile in thanks and eyes us while he heats up my slice in the oven behind him.

He's in his mid thirties with a slim build, and he has gauges in his ears. Kinda cute, if I'm honest.

8

"You two pretty ladies heading out for a fun night?" He asks, leaning onto the counter across from where I'm grabbing a handful of napkins.

"More like heading home." I smile at him, feigning an eye roll. "We're too old for this."

The guy chuckles. "Aw, c'mon, the night is still young! You can squeeze in at least two more bars before the Oober surge gets crazy." He quickly pivots in his spot to grab his pizza peel, opens the oven door and grabs my slice to put on two white paper plates. I take it happily, flashing him a smile.

"Not for this lady." I point to myself. " I'd take pizza and a movie night over the club, anyday."

"Well you're easy to please." He leans forward again, ignoring the other people in line behind us in the small shop. "You got a boyfriend to do that for you? I could show you a good night in, no doubt." He winks.

I laugh at his pretend-flirting as I sprinkle a generous shake of parmesan and chili flakes on my slice before turning to leave with Jenny. "Have a good night, thank you!"

"Hey I'm serious! What's your name?!" He shouts after us, but I wave him off with a smile and take my first, and favorite, bite of pizza.

"He really liked you." Jenny teases as we head a few blocks towards the subway entrance. She's holding my purse while I try not to burn the roof of my mouth.

"Please." I dismiss, my mouth full. "He just thought *you* were hot."

"No way, he barely looked at me. His eyes were all on you, baby."

I scoff, taking another bite. "No one was looking at me." I wipe my mouth from the grease dribbling down my chin.

"Oh stop it. You're hotter than you think, and you know it."

I sigh, but nod at her unyielding support.

"Say it." Jenny demands. "Say 'I, Claire Nguyễn, am hot as hell.'"

I sigh again, but oblige. "I, Claire Nguyễn, am hot as hell."

Jenny smiles, pleased. "And don't even get me started on your sparkling personality." She says, walking in front of me to bust out her infamous jazz hands, a skill she's perfected from her days as a dancer.

"Alright!" I laugh, finishing off my crust in a few bites. "You love me and I'm incredible and beautiful! I get it!" I find the nearest trash can and toss my grease-splotted plates.

"And I'll never stop saying it!" Jenny laughs.

I dust off my hands of any remaining crumbs and take my purse back, bringing the strap over my head to wear it safely across my body.

"Did you have a good birthday?" I ask as we descend down the subway steps. We're both fishing out our subway cards while we walk.

"It was perfect. Thank you. I barely thought of Jeremy at all." She smiles, but there's a little sadness in her voice.

"Ew." I say, pretending to spit at the mention of his name. "He's gross. He looks like a foot, and he's a cheater. Good riddance." I add before we swipe our cards to walk through the turnstiles.

"I know, I know..." Jenny sighs, trying to keep the smile on her face, but her brows are furrowed together and I can see she's getting worried again. "But I keep thinking if I was more patient, more attentive, more *anything*, then he wouldn't have done that to me."

"I'm almost certain he wasn't thinking of you at all when he was screwing his secretary on his desk." I tell her, sternly. "This has nothing to do with you. You're perfect. He's a disgusting pig. Plus, were you even ready to be a step-mom if he proposed?" I ask as we sit on a few open seats on the platform.

"I couldn't be a mom, yet. I know. You've told me countless times. But he had a doctorate!" She cries.

I scoff again. "Yeah, in Business Administration. He couldn't be any more boring if he tried!" I affectionately tap Jenny's hand to comfort her. "You'll find someone better. Someone who is just as educated as you, but also as passionate and artistic, and will make you a priority. You deserve the best. Hell, you deserve someone who treats you as well as I do!" I tease.

Jenny laughs, appreciating my efforts to lighten the mood, sniffling a bit and reaching up to wipe away her tears. "You're right." She concedes. "You're always right."

I dramatically shrug. "It's a curse."

"Have things gotten better with your parents?" She pivots.

"It hasn't gotten worse, so I take that as a good sign. I just wish they were a little less... intense with their work. My dad is gonna work himself to death if he doesn't take some time off soon." I say in a more hushed tone than before. I feel myself lying, and I hate the feeling.

During all the years of our friendship, I've never told Jenny what my parents actually do for work. She's safer not knowing, so I told her they run a chain of nail salons.

I wouldn't know what I'd do if she knew the truth...

"Plus, my mom keeps trying to marry me off. There hasn't been one time we've met for tea this year that she hasn't had a stack of files filled with eligible bachelors."

Jenny nods, resting her head on my shoulder. "It could be a good thing. It could save you from having to slum it out here in the dating world. It's slim pickings, you know."

I nod. "I know, but I've never cared about status, and that seems to be the only guys she's picking. Plus, my mom is convinced that I should *only* marry a Vietnamese man."

"Isn't your dad half black?"

"Exactly." I nod, completely astounded by the fact my mom conveniently forgets she married a man who is Vietnamese *and* Black.

The C train arrives and we hobble on, our feet numb from our heels. I was hoping the late night would mean the train would have some free seats, but all the cars are packed, so we're forced to stand. We ride the few stops in silence before Jenny hugs me goodbye at 72nd street. She demands I text her when I get home before she gets off and heads to the apartment she shares with four other models.

I ride the next few stops alone before getting off at my station on 125th.

I walk as fast as I can to the penthouse, my shoes killing me. I'm cursing myself for not bringing a pair of sneakers to change into, but I didn't want to be weighed down all night.

I put my headphones in, not wanting to deal with any catcallers tonight, and play the music on my phone. Turning up my k-pop mix and flooding my senses with a lively beat makes me feel like all is right in the world.

My street takes me away from the busy station, and a few more turns brings me to my apartment building. The entrance is gated, a blessing on nights like these, and I tap my wallet on the sensor to allow me in.

The curated, grassy courtyard has a neat brick path connecting the front gate to the front door.

Juan, my doorman, sees me clopping my way up the path and stands to open the door for me.

"Late night for you, Claire." The older man says with a hint of surprise.

"Don't start with me, Juan. My feet feel like they're about to fall off." I breathe, peeling my heels off so my feet hit the cold marble in the lobby.

He raises his hands in surrender. "Just surprised. Not judging." He flashes his every-friendly smile. "Hot date?"

I smile back, leaning against the front desk as he rounds to the other side and takes a seat.

"Yes, but not in the way you think." I wiggle my eyebrows. "It was Jenny's birthday."

Juan's eyes light up. "Ah, Jenny! Great girl! How is she?"

"She's fine. She just went through a tough breakup so I tried making tonight special for her."

"You're a great friend." Juan nods with a smile. "What about that guy your mom wanted to set you up with?"

I dramatically pretend to gag. "Ew, he was such a mama's boy! Seriously, Juan, the men out here are giant babies. Especially if their parents spoil them *well* into adulthood!"

Juan dismisses my lamenting. "You'll find someone. A woman as beautiful as you? You should have no trouble."

"Ha. Thanks." I sigh. "Well, I'm heading up. I'll see you tomorrow."

"Goodnight, Claire." Juan calls to me as I push the arrow next to the elevator. It's already in the lobby, so the gold doors open immediately.

"G'night, Juan!" I wave before stepping inside and tap my wallet on the sensor to allow the elevator to take me to my level.

I remember the first time Jenny came to my place. She couldn't believe I could afford the entire top level, but I told her my uncle works in real estate and the place was his. He's letting me stay here while he's out of the country on business for a few years. She doesn't need to know my parents own the building, or they kept Juan employed here because of his loyal service to the job for over 26 years.

The mirrors covering the walls of the elevator normally don't bother me, but I'm so cold and grumpy, my own reflection is offensive to my overstimulated senses.

My mascara has traveled down under my eyes, making me look like a racoon. My supposed "long lasting" lipstick is now a flakey ring around the edges of my mouth, making me look like an absolute clown.

How Jenny let me walk around looking like this, I'll never know.

I snap a quick selfie and send it to her.

> **WTF? I look like this and you let me walk around all night looking like Bozo?**

The elevator brings me to the top floor. I've never been happier than tonight to live alone because I cannot deal with explaining how draining the club was to anyone, and if Mom was here, she'd want to know all about it.

I hang up my coat and purse in the closet by the front door, enjoying the satisfyingly slow way the door closes flush against the wall. All of the storage in this place closes this way, making clean, modern lines.

I head straight to the kitchen and grab my water glass from the white marble countertop that matches the floor and backsplash. I tap the gold faucet on my sink that flows filtered water into my cup and chug the first few gulps, parched from the pizza.

The bathroom is calling to me. I eagerly shed my clothes before warming up the white marble tile on my shower floor with a steady stream of water that will eventually come up to temperature.

I stand at my sink and make a sloppy attempt to remove my eyeliner and mascara with a cotton pad smeared with cold cream. I'm exhausted. My eyes can barely stay open, and I feel a headache coming on.

The bathroom echoes with my sigh as I toss the cotton pad into the small gold trash can that sits underneath the countertop.

I check myself out in the mirror. I look like hell. My round face is blotchy from the alcohol we drank at the club and I'm breaking out from the makeup my skin isn't unused to wearing. My boobs, though bigger than I'd like, still sit pretty above my soft belly.

My legs are my favorite feature, the muscles I've worked to grow in the gym and at pilates are forming nicely, and I admire the way the shadows in the hollow of the muscle contrast with the plump softness of the rest of me.

I turn away and step into the lava-hot water, allowing the heat to wash over me. I run my scalp under the stream and sigh, washing away the curls I spent hours putting into my hair earlier tonight. I'm slowly warming up, but I still feel the night chill in my bones, so I move the knob to be slightly hotter and slowly turn in place to get every inch of skin under the water.

My soaps are various mixes of citrus and lavender, and the smells instantly calm me. My mind wanders to the events of the night while I lather up my white loofah.

I remember Jenny and I getting ready in my bathroom, us meeting up with a few of her model friends for dinner, and then her and I at the club before that asshole groped me. Just the memory has me fuming, but I'm satisfied I got in a good slap before being rushed away.

I turn off the water and grab a white towel from the gold warmer rack just outside the shower. I dry off quickly and wrap the towel around my body.

18

Brushing my teeth feels like the greatest feat to my aching body, but I force myself to give my mouth a quick pass, feeling the night's events weighing on me.

Flossing is an ever bigger nuisance, but I do it anyway before throwing on my pink satin pajamas and head to bed. The king size is a little too big for me to fill alone, but I don't mind the extra space.

I grab my laptop and settle in the middle of my white pillows and duvet. I can't seem to break my habit of searching for apartments I can't afford. Sure, the luxury of this place is a privilege many wish they had, but relying on my parents as a grown 34-year-old is leaving a very sour taste in my mouth.

But the paycheck from my current, low paying dream job at The Strande bookstore barely covers my groceries, let alone any sort of rent. I'd be destitute out there on my own, and despite my parent's success in their business ventures and the fronts they put up to conceal them, I still hold on to the desperate possibility I can make it on my own.

I don't agree with what they do, so I stubbornly look for my own apartment every night before going to sleep and fantasize about building a new life away from their complicated world.

But when I used to work for my family, I was really good at it. I coordinated schedules, payments, events, kept all the plates spinning, and my parents loved it. They told me it would all be mine one day, but the future they have planned since my childhood scares the living daylights out of me.

So for the last year, I've been working at The Strande, on my own, and visiting them in their empire on the weekends I have free.

Even though I'm exhausted, my mind won't slow down, so I spend the better part of the next hour looking at apartments, some I can afford, and a lot I can't, before my phone buzzes with a message from Jenny.

**If you're a clown, you're the cutest one I've ever seen! LOL goodnight. Text me tomorrow.
Jenny**

I "like" her message and place my phone on the charging dock that sits on my white marble nightstand.

I turn on the TV and pull up my favorite British baking show as background noise while I move my cursor to various high-rises surrounding Central Park. I should be more realistic and look at apartments in Brooklyn, or Queens. I ponder typing in New Jersey, but even I'm not that desperate.

It's a habit to check the social media pages and websites I built for the nail salons, breweries, jewelry stores, and other small businesses I used to manage for my family. They seem to be updating their pages frequently, so I'm relieved to see they can function without me.

The baking show on the TV soothes me, and I feel my eyelids getting heavy. I close my laptop and plug it into the charger on my nightstand before burying myself under the covers and finally falling asleep.

Chapter Two

I'm barely into my workday, but can already feel my breakfast latte wearing off. As I'm straightening the poetry section, I'm considering heading down the block to Boba Gals for a matcha latte to tide me over before lunch. My cranberry, goat cheese and chicken salad can wait until after the afternoon rush.

I decide against the drink. Considering I already had a boba the last time I worked, getting another one seems too self-indulgent.

I wander through the fiction section, slowly brushing the various spines with my fingertips.

I love it here. My family can't fathom *why* I'd want a job that pays so little when they've been able to cater to my every whim since birth.

I want to make a difference in the world, the way Jenny does with her work housing refugees. I want to put the work in, pay my dues, and be proud of the woman I see in the mirror at the end of the day. My dad instilled that work ethic in me. He never took a day off, and I want to work just like him.

Maybe not *exactly* like him, though...

But with so many of my past jobs never holding my interest for longer than a few months, from a barista to a personal assistant to a nanny, I was forced to consider putting my time toward something I *loved* because I couldn't commit to anything else.

And I love nothing more than books. I'd love to open my own bookshop one day. One that caters to diverse, queer folks that could raise money to help the unhoused community. I could run a soup kitchen out of my store after hours, and begin a program that donates books.

Until I can make that happen, here I am, working at my favorite bookstore in the city, learning how a business like this is run so I can take notes and put them towards my own plans. I'm going on a year and a half now, the longest job I've held so far.

I decide to do my coworkers a favor and reshelve a cart full of books. I make quick work of the Drama section before rolling the cart to the elevator up to the cookbooks.

Ever since a popular TV cook was canceled recently after a photo of him in brown face wearing a sombrero was leaked from a few Halloweens ago, we've had an influx of returns on his barbeque cookbook, so I have to rearrange the display to make room.

I stick these towards the back, hoping the managers will mark them down soon.

As I stand back to take a wider look at my handy work and make sure the display looks nice, my favorite cookbook catches my eye, and I can't help but smile. I circle towards the front and grab our best-seller in cookbooks this year, Laura Phan's *Dessert for Dinner.*

I flip through the pages, enthralled with the bright pictures of her decadent and easy recipes. I remember attempting her eclairs for Jenny's birthday last year and royally screwing them up.

I'm a better cook than baker, but the first time I flipped towards the back of her book and saw Laura's face, round and chubby and Vietnamese, like mine, I was filled with a false sense of confidence, and I went home to attempt, and fail, almost every recipe in this book.

Turning the thick, glossy pages now fills me with a renewed determination, and I decide to try her fruit tarts again tonight. I can stop by the Hole Foods around the corner before heading home.

I put down the book and straighten the stack before heading downstairs to return the cart.

As I'm organizing the graphic novel section towards the rear of the store, I look up and catch three broad men entering the front doors. They are all dressed in matching black turtleneck sweaters with thick, silver chains around their necks.

I can already tell they aren't our run-of-the-mill customers. None of them had a tote bag in sight. They look as if they run in the same circles as my family, putting me on guard. Their uniforms are different from what my dad requires his employees to wear, so I know they aren't ours.

They are Vietnamese. I can tell immediately by the shapes of their noses and their rich skin tones, and the fact they look like some of my cousins who live in Texas.

The group stands by the door and scans the place, all three of their gazes locking with mine. They all stalk towards me, as if they're wolves finally laying eyes on the lost bunny they were sent to find.

This has happened before. One of Dad's enemies tries to leverage his hand by finding me and either kidnapping me or holding me for ransom, but I never feel unsafe because good ol' Pop is usually three steps ahead of them.

Before I can panic, before I can run, before I can pull up the hem of my white sweater dress and reach for the knife in the waistband of my thick leggings, someone grabs my hand, pulls me through the rear employee door and walks me down the back alley.

25

I'm hit by the chilly morning air but try to keep my feet moving. I look down at the hand holding mine as I'm being pulled to wherever we're going.

He could be here to kill me. He could be here to save me. I don't know which, but I know I need to get away from here.

I don't feel unsafe in his large, warm hands, which is a good sign. I look up to see if I recognize him.

He's a stranger. The cuff of his black suit has a gold embroidered "NN" on the sleeve. He has curley, dark hair that is longer on top and buzzed short on the sides, revealing a tattoo behind his ear with "NN" in the center of a triangle.

My dad's logo.

One final look at this man's all-black suit shows he's sporting slightly satin lapels and a black necktie, my dad's signature uniform for his employees, and I'm reassured I'm safe.

"My dad sent you."

"Yes, Miss." The man's voice is gruff, but he turns to me when he says it and I'm taken aback by his face and voice.

My dad only hires our own people, so I'm surprised to see this man. He's older than the usual henchman my father hires, with a strong, cleanly-shaven jaw, even stronger brows and a prominent nose that makes him indescribably handsome. His rich olive skin makes me think he might be Latino, or mixed.

"Your name?" I huff, slightly winded by our brisk pace. He is a lot taller than me and his strides are much bigger, so it takes an awkward extra half-step to keep up.

"They call me Cage, Miss." He answers obediently with a slight nod as an introduction.

He keeps my hand in his while we quickly walk to wherever he's ushering me. I take every moment I can to measure his features.

The sprinkle of gray hair at his temples and throughout his curls makes me curious about where he comes from, and why he joined Dad's team so much later in his life? Dad usually hires his goons when they're barely out of high school, so how did this...gentleman... end up working for my family?

We turn a corner and arrive at a parked black SUV. Cage opens the passenger door and helps me in, finally letting go of my hand.

"Thank you. You're very...surprising." I admit honestly.

Our eyes meet, and his are the most gorgeous brown, like the warmest molasses mixed into sparkling sugar. His handsome face is a little weathered, but the lines by his mouth make it seem like he laughs easily, and his serious scowl does funny things to my stomach.

"I'd say the same about you." Cage gruffs, his gaze burning into me, his heat making me blush.

I see another one of Dad's henchmen coming down the sidewalk dressed in the same black suit with satin lapels. He gives Cage my purse and coat, having snatched them from The Strande's employee break room. Before I can register what is happening, the man disappears out of sight just as quickly as he emerged.

Cage hands me my things and gently tucks in my coat under my thigh to keep it from getting caught in the door, an oddly tender gesture from a man I expect has probably killed a few people this week alone, and it's only Monday.

Cage rounds to the driver side and climbs in, the sheer size and weight of him jostling the SUV. He snaps his seatbelt on and quickly takes off before any of the bad guys can catch up.

I feel like I should be panicking a bit, but I'm not. This is typical of Dad. Any sign of friction and he sends a swarm of his goons to take care of it. This is the third time this year I've had to be swept away from my day, so I'm used to it by now. I assume those three men in the store are after me, but Dad had his men on the ground before they could get close.

I haven't been tuned into the business side of my parents for a while now, so I don't know the latest on their employees, but who is Cage? Where did Dad find him? And why is he so...hot?

I'm normally not attracted to the hitman, bodyguard type. My last few boyfriends were lanky bookworms, but something about this man is making me a little more excited than when I'm usually around the boys working for my dad. It could be that he's strikingly handsome and hot as hell, but I still need to figure it out.

"Thank you. For saving me." I say cooly, peeking up to look at Cage while we sit at a red light, heading towards Chinatown and Dad's headquarters.

Cage grunts in acknowledgement. "Sorry we were late. Business across town kept us longer than usual." He flashes me another half smile, staying serious. "We didn't mean for those men to get anywhere near you."

"Who were they, anyway?" And what was this all about? I had a sneaking suspicion it was a business deal gone wrong, and the jilted party is trying to retaliate against Dad by targeting me, but the ploy is getting old, and I'm getting bored.

"Your father will explain when we arrive, Miss."

"Call me Claire, please. *Miss* makes me feel so old." I scrunch up my face to try and dispel the formal air between us. I want him to be familiar with me, despite only having just met the man. Any other nameless goon, I'd be happy to be sitting here silent, but with this large, quiet force, I want to know more about him.

Cage attempts to stay professional again, but a little smile creeps onto his plush lips. "Right. Claire."

I smile when he obliges, content with getting the formalities out of the way.

Titles and rank are ingrained in our culture and language, but I hate how Dad's position in his work has everyone addressing me much higher in social rank than I normally would be considered, and it always has made me uncomfortable.

"So, Cage. Where do you come from?"

"Oh, many places, originally Florida. I worked in New Zealand for a few years before coming back here."

"How many years?" I ask lightly, trying to decipher his age.

"More than I care to admit." Cage's voice rumbles. When he speaks, he sends tingles down my spine, and I like the feeling.

"What did you do in New Zealand?"

"Many things." He dodges my question as we make the tight turns heading into Chinatown. "Special ops." He's a little more sly when he looks over to me. "Nothing for your pretty head to worry about."

"Oh, so you think I'm pretty?" I tease, knowing very well the men who work for my family are contracted to never lay a finger on me. They're dead, otherwise. But I can't stop myself from pushing the boundaries with this man.

Cage's eyes sparkle with a hint of mischief. "You are *hermosa*, but I'm not taking your bait. You'll get me in trouble." He gives me a side-eye. "Little flirt." I hear him mumble under his breath as he fights another smile.

I try to hide my laugh while I pull out my phone. I want to know what he just said in Spanish, so I type in 'ermosa Spanish' and the result says 'Did you mean *hermosa?*' I discover it means 'beautiful,' and my stomach flutters.

"So, are you one of the killing guys?" I ask, trying to keep the conversation going and distract myself from the warmth growing on my cheeks.

"Sometimes." Cage nodded slightly, turning his attention back to driving. "I'm the head of your surveillance. We're short staffed, so I've been assigned to bring you to the compound, Miss."

"Claire." I correct him.

"Claire." He repeats, slightly bowing his head in apology.

My dad has many teams of many people who work for him. Some negotiate, some are pure muscle, and some kill.

I wonder if Cage is asked to kill as part of his job?

Sitting in silence, I manage to steal a few glances in Cage's direction. His arms are huge, like massive tree trunks, and he looks as if he's about to burst out of his suit.

He also smells incredible, like clean cologne and fresh orange.

We begin to approach a narrow alley that descends into an underground garage. Cage taps his pass on the sensor and the metal gates open for us to enter.

Cage parks in one of the few empty spots in the expansive garage filled with luxury cars, motorcycles, and other large, drivable toys my dad has accumulated over the years.

"I'll get the door for you, Miss." Cage offers as he's turning off the motor and taking off his seatbelt.

I toss my coat in the back seat before putting my purse strap over my head.

"I've got the door, Cage, but call me 'Miss' one more time and I'll have to show you these fists." I turn to him and put both of my hands up in a pathetic attempt at a boxing position, stopping him in his tracks.

Despite my plump waist and chest, my hands and wrists are disproportionately smaller than the rest of me. They are my downfall everytime I try push ups, but in this instance, they look like two little dough balls hovering over the center console near Cage's face.

He huffs a chuckle and gives me a quick fist bump with one of his clobbering hands. Both of mine can fit into one of his, and it makes me feel so entirely encompassed by his presence.

And I think I like the feeling.

"My apologies. I'd hate to get on the other end of these slammers." Cage teases.

I laugh before he fist bumps me again. I'm smiling as I climb from the SUV and close the door behind me when I hear Cage lock it with a few quick *beeps* from his keys.

Before we can make it to the elevator, Helen, Mom's right hand woman, meets us by the doors. She's tall and thin with long, straight black hair that goes down to her lower back, making her look like a stroke of thick ink on parchment. She's always dressed in an áo dài, the traditional Vietnamese dress with billowing, satin pants.

"It's great to see you, Miss." Helen coos in her quiet, docile tone. "Welcome back."

I smile in acknowledgement, but don't respond. I'm mentally preparing myself for the onslaught of pampering that always comes when I'm here.

The three of us ride the elevator up to Dad's office in silence. I'm a little on edge, not having been here in months, and I don't know what to expect. Are they disappointed in me? Will they be happy to see me?

The elevator doors open to Dad's onyx office. The floor and walls are all covered in black marble. On one end of the expansive office is a large desk carved from one singular chunk of black marble. On the other side is where a long, glass meeting table stands with black office chairs surrounding the perimeter.

The office sits on a small city beneath it. In the compound, there's housing, a cafeteria, a gym, a barber, a tailor, storage, and everything else my parents could think of to keep their work efficient. These amenities are for those who work for us, and since they can't leave unless they're on an assignment, it feels a lot more like a prison than an all-inclusive workplace.

Dad sees me from the head of the meeting table filled with men from his squads. He stands and rushes to me.

"There she is. It's been too long!" Dad gushes, wrapping me in a big, warm hug.

I'm immediately embarrassed, especially in front of Cage. I don't want him to see me as a helpless, frivolously spoiled woman, even though that's how I've been treated since childhood.

But Dad's oozing affection has always been my biggest savior in times of trouble. His ability to provide a flawless plan paired with a bright kindness is what granted him his success. At least, that's what I always believed. So I hug him back, taking in the comfort of home I feel in his arms.

Mom hears Dad's excitement and enters from the break room, decked out in an all-white power suit with pointy white heels to match.

"Claire, you're here." She says cooly, kissing me on both cheeks before going to grab Dad's hand, taking her rightful place by his side.

If Dad is the sun, Mom is the moon. He's all sunshine and warmth, and she's all coolness and calmness. Together, Noah and Angel Nguyễn built an empire worth billions, and seeing their affection for each other, even after all these years, gives me hope I'll find love like theirs someday.

"What's going on?" I ask them both as I'm ushered to his office. My dad gives one motion of his hand and the goons exit immediately, leaving just the three of us to talk.

"Oh, nothing." Dad brushes off casually. "I've handled it. It's old news. Tell me, how is your job? Are you coming back to work with us again soon? How is Jenny?"

"*Anh*, ah." Mom chastises him affectionately, using her term of endearment. "She needs to know."

Dad's ever-present smile falters just a bit. "*Em*, she doesn't. She did nothing wrong. We saw the surveillance videos."

Mom turns to me, her face steeled in a firm expression. "You were receiving death threats, and your dad has taken care of it, but there's no knowing if they'll come back. We're suggesting you leave the city for a few days until we can put the matter to rest."

"But what happened? What did I do?"

"Nothing, *con*, you didn't do anything wrong." Dad reassures me, patting my hand gently and calling me child, an affection I've always loved hearing in our language. We all sit before continuing, but Mom ignores him.

"Our main competitors, The *Lê* family, are claiming you nearly murdered their one and only son, and we've been... investigating." Mom explains, gently. "Do you remember being at Club Masque last night?"

"Yes, we went out for Jenny's birthday."

Mom nods. "Well the *Lê's* are saying you assaulted their son, but we watched the videos the club gave us and you were only defending yourself."

My mind immediately flashes back to the dumbass who groped me. "That dough-faced moron is a *Lê*?!" I scream, standing in my outrage. "Oh Mom, you bet I hit him. I would've done it again! And harder, too!"

Dad stands to calm me. "We know, *con*, we know." His hands float to my shoulders to gently coax me to sit again.

"Dad, you should've seen him. He was disgusting. And I only slapped him once." I sit, stewing at the memory. "I wish I could've gotten another swing at him before we were pulled away."

He nods in agreement. "I know, *con*, and we're proud of you."

Mom jumps in. "We sent the video to his parents but still haven't gotten a response. We're waiting it out, but we still think you should take a few days at the cabin and wait for all of this to blow over."

Mom suggesting the isolated, secret cabin in Pennsylvania means this is far more serious than they want me to believe. The last few times something like this happened, I just slept at their place for a night and everything was resolved in the morning.

"Why is the *Lê* family freaking out so much?" I ask them both.

My parents exchange a look, silently agreeing Dad should take this question.

"They've been trying to encroach on our territory for a while, and they think this is the perfect time to strike, so they're going all in. They didn't just try to kill you at your job. They've been trying to infiltrate our organization for a while now, but we're countering enough that it's not a problem. Our only concern now is your safety."

I consider this, seeing a possible solution to my biggest problem with the family business. "Dad, isn't this the perfect opportunity to let them have it? Just let them take over, step back, and you can focus on the legitimate businesses that are making perfectly good money on their own."

Mom sighs. "We've talked about this a thousand times, *con*. You know the work we do is the most profitable compared to all of the little things that make a few measly million here and there."

"But it's human trafficking, Mom."

"It's not, and you know it." Mom says, a little more sternly. "There's nothing wrong with connecting young women to eligible, wealthy bachelors."

"It's a problem if they're in Vietnam and are trying to come to America. And if you're putting them on a pedestal to auction them off!" I lay out, knowing my explanation is futile, the same way it was the first few hundred times I disagreed with their 'matchmaking.'

"That's nonsense." Mom shrugs. "The parents pay what they can, and the women don't complain."

"That's even worse!" I shout, dumbfounded by her lack of understanding.

Dad chimes in, almost on cue. "They want to be here, *con*. We aren't forcing anyone to work with us. They want a better life, and we help them get it."

"But Dad, have you ever considered these girls only want this because they don't know any better? What if we offered them scholarships to college in America, allowing them the chance to make a life for themselves without having to rely on marriage to make it happen?"

"You will never have to make the decisions these girls do, Claire." Mom says firmly but gently. "I know you don't approve, but you come from a wealthy family. These girls have nothing. If you're ever in a situation to have to make the choice to leave your entire family, your home country, everything you know for the chance to be in possession of enough money to save your starving family, then you'll know more about what's best for these girls." Mom stands.

"That is what we offer them. We set them up for it, and they take it."

"Do you need to kill the men who don't pay, though? Or the people who try to stop you?" I hear myself repeat the question the same way I've asked it a hundred times before, sounding like a broken record.

"Would you rather we killed the girls?" Mom counters in the same way she always has.

"I'd rather you didn't kill anyone." I say, knowing they'll both respond with how their reputation is solid with their clients knowing they have such a high success rate thanks to their extreme methods.

But Dad doesn't respond like he always does. We sit in silence before he puts on his figurative business man hat and keeps the plan moving.

"Well…" He begins. "We'd feel better if you were safely out of town. We've made sick calls to your work and have taken care of everything." Dad pats my hand reassuringly. "A few days away and everything will be back to normal."

"Yes." Mom smiles, if a bit forcefully in the wake of our little tiff. "I can go to the cabin with you. Dad can handle things on his own for a while. We can paint our nails and watch those Korean dramas you like." They both stand.

"Fine." I resolve, standing to meet them. "But I still need to go back to the penthouse to get my things."

"Cage has been assigned to take you while Mom packs." Dad offers, buzzing the intercom that sits on the table. "Cage to my office, please." He speaks into the small microphone on the intercom system. It's how he gets the word out in this huge place.

"Cage is your dad's new favorite." Mom says quietly to me, teasing him. "He's been the first one called since this all began."

"Yeah, what's the deal with him, anyway?" I ask, trying to be nonchalant but internally dying to know everything about him.

"He's very good at what he does. He'll keep you safe while you get your things." Dad smiles at me, ignoring my question and Mom's taunts.

Cage quietly comes into the office and waits by the door for his orders. Dad walks through the giant open space to meet him and explains in hushed tones that Cage needs to take me to the penthouse so I can pack my things, and then drive me back here.

"Are you sure you don't want one of my ladies to go with you?" Mom asks, holding my hand. She's really asking about my safety. If Cage attacked me, I'd need reinforcements to fight him off. But that goes for every man working for us, and Dad would never put me in a dangerous position.

"No, I'll be okay. I trust Dad. And I trust Cage." I don't mention I find him wildly attractive.

Some things are best kept to yourself.

"Okay, *con*. Keep your pepper spray nearby, just in case. I'll see you when you get back tonight."

I nod, grateful to always have her looking out for me, even after the tension between us.

Dad gushes and cries, as if this is our last goodbye for the rest of my life, just like every other goodbye we've had since I was a kid. I reassure him I'll be fine and I'll be back within an hour or two.

I blow a kiss to the both of them before it's just Cage and me going down the elevator alone.

We're walking towards the SUV, Cage rounding to the passenger door and opening it for me again. I don't usually ask for my door to be opened, being capable of doing it myself, but I'm feeling a little mischievous being alone with him, so I hold out my hand, indicating he should help me up into my seat the way he did when we were coming from the bookstore.

It takes half a second before I feel his firm grasp on my fingertips, his arm tensing as he practically lifts my entire body into the car with one hand. I almost gasp when I step up and sit in my seat, feeling like I'm floating into place.

He doesn't let go. His warm hand sends shivers down my spine when he steps forward, closing the already short distance between us. He's trying to call my bluff, facing my flirting head-on and possibly trying to make me regret asking for his hand.

I don't back down and try to hide my smile.

Cage's eyes lock with mine. Being propped up so high, I'm closer to being eye-to-eye with him, and his gorgeous face is just inches away. I watch his gaze roam my face, linger on my lips, then flash back up to my eyes.

"Feeling snug?" He asks, slowly loosening his grip on my hand.

"Like a bug in a rug." I breathe, swallowing the urge to lean in and kiss his full lips.

"Do you want me to help you every time you get into a car?" He asks, his thumb gently stroking my knuckles. The question is simple, but I can hear the meaning behind his words. If I keep asking him to touch me, he will. If I ask him to stop, he will.

I'm feeling daring, meeting his burning eyes with my own. I don't break eye contact as I nod.

The faintest smile pulls at the corners of his mouth. "Okay. From now on, you never touch the handle of this door. I'll open and close it for you. Understand?"

I nod again. "And you'll hold me?" I ask, gently squeezing his hand. "It's a tall climb for a woman so small." I feel myself playing the helpless maiden, but he's giving me the chance to be taken care of, and the prospect of being a passenger princess is enticing.

He huffs a small laugh before leaning in to whisper in my ear. "I'm sure you're very small."

"Do you wanna find out?" I counter unexpectedly, my boldness coming from somewhere unknown.

Cage shakes his head when he pulls back. "I'm a dead man if I try. You know that." He gives my hand a gentle squeeze. "But I'm here for you, whenever you need."

Cage lets go of my hand completely, and the coldness he leaves behind is much more enveloping than it has a right to be.

Before I can respond, he abruptly steps back and closes the door, leaving me a blushing mess while he crosses the front of the SUV and climbs into the driver seat.

We sit in silence as he pulls out of the garage and onto the streets of Chinatown. We drive a few blocks, the tension in the car so thick, I can cut it with a knife.

Cage breaks the silence. "Do you make it a habit of teasing your employees?"

"Only you." I shoot back with a smile, meaning to be playful but from seeing his reaction to my words, his body tensing and breath hitching, I might have made a mistake.

His grip on the steering wheel tightens. "Lucky me." When I don't respond, he continues. "I have to apologize for what I said. It was inappropriate."

"I liked it." I admit, feeling a little out of my depth with my teasing. It turned so serious so quickly, and I'm beginning to regret testing the waters with this man.

Cage shakes his head with frustrated laughter. "You're killing me, woman." He shoots me a look of wonder while we're stopped at a red light. "You sure are making it hard to work when you look at me like that."

"And you sure are bold talking to me like that." I counter, though I love the way he speaks to me. He sounds almost like he can't believe I'm here, and his gruff, low voice shoots right to my core.

He shrugs. "Every man makes mistakes." He gives me another pointed look. "Again, I apologize. Strictly professional from now on."

"What if I ask you not to be?" I push, trying to keep things light, but I'm learning quickly that Cage isn't someone who takes being teased lightly.

He shakes his head. "You know I'm dead otherwise. I can't lose my position just because I fell for your taunts, no matter how beautiful they are." He shakes his head again, as if to loosen his thoughts from his mind. "You're precious cargo, nothing more."

"Gee, thanks, you make me sound like a pallet of durian." I huff, backing away from the idea of pushing Cage past his limits. I can be civil, for now.

"Many people have done a lot more for a lot less than a pallet of durian." Cage says matter-of-factly.

I nod in agreement.

We're turning down the street leading to the penthouse. I'm gathering my things, prepared to tell Cage where to park and wait for me before I see his eyes lock on something that sends him into high alert.

"GET DOWN!" Cage shouts, his hand flying to the back of my neck and pushing my head down between my knees so I'm staring at the floor mats.

A half-second later, gunfire pummels the SUV.

It sounds like hail. The unrelenting pops overwhelm my senses, and I cover my ears as Cage speeds down the street and out of the area in a matter of seconds.

A bullet shatters the window of the back seat behind me. I scream at the noise, the shattering glass falling onto my back and into my hair.

Cage pulls a gun, aims through the broken window and fires three rounds.

I have no idea if he hits anyone, but he seems satisfied enough to bring his hand back to the wheel and turns his focus on the road.

I'm scared. Shaking. I can't figure out what's happening. It's all so fast, so dangerous. I thought I wouldn't be phased by any of this, but I feel my heart about to leap out of my chest.

I hear bullets hit the rear end of the SUV, and they slowly dissipate as Cage speeds away calmly, not one hair out of place, not one breath catching. He's as cool as a cucumber, and I'm grateful to have someone here who is grounded and I can gauge my breath against.

I watch his massive chest inhale and exhale. I try to match him, to calm myself, but I'm still crouched down, too afraid to sit back up, and my breath doesn't come as easily as I want.

I feel his large, warm hand on my back.

"It's okay, we're outta there."

Cage calls Dad through the Bluetooth in the car. I hear him say "ambush" and "not safe" but I don't register the conversation.

I hear Mom. She's calm and collected, as always. She says it's too dangerous to keep me in town and tells Cage to take me to the cabin without her. It's too risky to come back to the headquarters, so Cage has new orders to take me to the cabin and Mom will join us tomorrow morning after she ties up some loose ends and wraps up her late-night meetings.

They continue discussing their plan, but I don't listen to any of it. I'm too shaken, and my ears are ringing.

I feel so helpless, and I hate the feeling. Wasn't I always the brave one? The smart one? The one who could handle anything? I never let a rowdy night at a bar phase me, and I always managed to keep my wits about me when my friends forced me to go out.

I've dealt with my parent's business for most of my life.

So why is being the target of gunfire so jarring on my nerves? Why can't I handle it? We didn't even get hit. At least, I didn't.

I assess Cage's body and he doesn't seem hurt either.

I feel tears pricking my eyes and I move quickly to wipe them away before he can see.

Cage hangs up the phone call and immediately, his hand is on my back again, brushing the remaining glass off my sweater.

"You're safe now, Claire." He says softly, his voice rumbly and low. "Whoever they were, they're gone."

I slowly sit up, wiping away the tears I can't stop falling down my face. I'm covered in glass, so I use the sleeve of my sweater to carefully brush the shards onto the floor.

"I'm sorry. I should've known they'd be there." Cage says.

I sniffle. "It's okay. How could you have known? It's not your fault."

"Yeah, well. I should've." He reaches into the backseat and grabs my coat, shaking off what he can of the glass and hands it to me. "Put this on. It's about to get cold, and we've got a long way to go."

"Can't we trade out the car? And stop to get some things? I don't have any of my clothes, and-"

"Sorry, Claire, but it's too dangerous to stop. Maybe when we cross the state line and find a small town, but I'm not chancin' you getting shot at again."

I can only nod. He's right, of course. I can slum it for a few hours, but with the whipping wind coming in from the broken window and the high speed we're picking up on the interstate, it's starting to freeze in the SUV.

After about an hour, I can't take it anymore and ask Cage to stop at a small gas station in the middle of nowhere. I hop out and brush as much broken glass as I can from my seat and the floor mats while he's filling up the tank. He crudely tapes up the broken window with a piece of cardboard and duct tape just before a light snow flurry begins to fall.

Cage is acutely aware of everyone and everything around us. He won't let me out of his sight, and it takes some extra convincing for him to come with me into the gas station to buy some snacks and the bare necessities.

He begrudgingly follows behind me, his hand never leaving the gun he now has strapped to his hip. I load up on chips, canned soup, soda, bottles of water and snack cakes for the road.

I head down the tiny aisle with travel-sized items and grab us both toothbrushes, toothpaste and floss. I know we have soap and shampoo at the cabin, so I don't bother with that, but there isn't much to eat there, so I toss a few cans of Spam onto our pile before Cage whips out his card and pays without a word.

The nice lady behind the counter hands me our two full bags, and I wave a friendly goodbye as Cage stalks out ahead of me, making sure it's clear before we head to the car.

"Honestly, Cage, is anyone going to be all the way out here besides us?"

"Y'never know." He grumbles, and leads me back to the SUV.

We snack and drive, and it's a little warmer with the window covered up, but my fingers are numb from the cold, so I do my best not to complain and try keeping warm while we head through Pennsylvania.

I don't know how I manage to fall asleep, but one moment, I'm warming my hands on the heater vents, and the next, I'm waking up in my bed at the cabin.

Chapter Three

The two-story, giant wood cabin is fortified with the latest security system. All of the windows are double-paned with bullet-proof glass. Dad mentioned something about steel in the walls to strengthen the structure when he first had it built, but I don't remember the details.

My room is upstairs. I'm warm and comfy in my bed, which means Cage must have carried me up here in the middle of the night when we arrived. How I didn't wake up is a miracle, but the events of yesterday must have knocked me right out.

My parents were living out their rustic cabin fantasies when designing this place, because every room is decorated with polished wood to really drive home the humble mountain retreat experience, except we have the newest technology when it comes to our electronics and security system, all hidden away in hand-made looking wooden cabinets.

My custom log headboard creaks as I stretch. I grab my phone to check my notifications.

Just a few missed calls from Dad and Mom and a few texts from Jenny. Nothing I can't handle.

I reply to Jenny, saying my parents took me on a spontaneous trip this week and I'll be back next week, so she wouldn't worry about me missing our Wednesday lunch dates.

Then I call Mom to talk to Dad, since he rarely answers his phone.

She picks up after three rings.

"Claire?"

"Mom!" I sigh with a smile, happy to talk to her.

"Hold on, *con*, let me put you on speaker."

"*Con*!" I hear Dad shout. "Are you okay? Cage said you're at the cabin already."

"Yeah, we must have gotten in late last night. I fell asleep." I tell them, rubbing the sleep from my eyes. "But why isn't Mom here already? I thought she would've left by now."

"We can't get there." Mom says calmly. "Cage said that huge snowstorm last night snowed you in? The roads are buried, we can't drive in. And the copter can't fly with the winds howling."

"What? What storm? There wasn't a storm..." I roll out of bed and I'm immediately hit with the cold air in the room. I move the blackout curtains to the side, blinded by the bright, thick blanket of snow stretching as far as the eye can see, the trees surrounding us capped with lumps of white.

"Holy shit..."

"You slept through the whole drive?" Dad asks, his voice sounding far away from the phone.

"I must have. I don't remember anything past our first gas stop."

"*Con.*" Mom says firmly, taking me off speaker and putting the phone to her ear, making her voice clearer. "If you feel unsafe with Cage, we can send someone in. I don't know how I feel about you being alone with him."

"He saved me, Mom. From the shootout in front of the penthouse."

"I know, I just don't want you to feel we abandoned you there."

"I don't feel like that. I feel safe. Don't worry. We'll wait it out here. There's plenty of books, and I can always watch K-dramas in my room. I won't let him do anything. Don't worry." I don't have the guts to say that he should be the one worried I'd do something to him...

She releases the smallest of sighs, but I can still hear it. "Alright. But keep your weapons near you at all times. Your dad may trust him, but I trust no one."

I fidget with the knife I keep in my waistband, twirling it on my nightstand. "I know, mom. I'll keep myself safe. I promise."

"Okay. Call me later. I have to go, I have a meeting."

"I will. Love you, Mom. Tell Dad I love him."

"Love you, con." Mom says.

"Love you, Claire!" Dad shouts from afar, and I hang up with a smile on my face.

I look around the dark, cold room. I'm freezing, and I'm still in yesterday's clothes.

I head to the en suite bathroom and flick on the switch, but the lights don't come on. I flip the switch back down, up, then back down.

Shit, the power is out. That explains why it's so damn cold in here. I figured it was impossible the water heater kept any water warm before the outage, but to my delightful surprise, the shower water warms up right away. I strip and rush under the hot stream to wash my hair and body before the water can run out.

My towel is clean, but old. It feels a little crusty, but I'm grateful to be clean so I put up with the discomfort.

I realize I don't have an old toothbrush or toothpaste, so I'm relieved I had the sense to buy them at the gas station. They're probably still downstairs, and if Cage is down there, I have to make myself decent to look for it.

It's freezing in my bedroom, so my only option is to put on my old, crusty blue robe that hasn't been washed since our trip here last year.

It's scratchy, but does the job. I find a pair of slippers under the sink and wrap my hair up in a towel before bracing myself for the cold, opening the door, and heading downstairs towards the kitchen.

The dark gray marble of the counters and island are my favorite part of the kitchen. The rest of the cabin is cold, too, so at least I know the whole place is without power instead of just my room.

I listen for Cage, but don't hear anything. It's like I'm alone.

Our gas station haul is on the wooden dining table, the contents spilling from the plastic bags. I rummage through the chips and snacks to find the toothbrushes, grabbing the essentials and rushing upstairs to the warmth of the bathroom.

The sun creeping through the window is giving just enough light for me to see my ragged face in the mirror.

I brush and floss before rushing back to my bedroom and rummaging through my drawers for any clothes I might have left from our last visit here.

I have no extra socks. No underwear. Just a giant sleepshirt I bought from a famous broadway show about our country's forefathers.

Well shit...

I toss on the black t-shirt and grab my only pair of socks and underwear from yesterday before filling my bathroom sink with water. I use some shampoo to make suds and wash them all before hanging them up on the shower rod to dry.

I could wait until the power comes back on to use the washing machine, but who knows when that will be, and I'm not about to walk around this place without any underwear.

Not with him here…

My stomach flutters. It could be that I'm hungry and very thirsty, or it could be the idea of being in this place with Cage makes me excited.

Before my mind can run away with the thoughts of possible shared meals, slow touches, warm caresses and soft kisses, I shake those dirty scenarios from my head, not allowing myself to go there.

Who was this man, this *stranger*, anyway?

I bet he wouldn't be firm to touch. No way could he be tender and warm. He would be the worst to cuddle in bed, all big and hot and hard and…

I gently smack my cheeks, trying to bat away these sexy, intrusive thoughts.

Pull yourself together, Claire.

I need to tell myself he wouldn't want me, anyway. Otherwise, I'd jump his bones and then we'd be in *big* trouble. Maybe two years of being single really was taking a toll on me…

Suddenly, the power kicks back on and the cabin comes to life. Heat begins blowing from the vents, the various TVs, speakers and other electronics beep and buzz on, and I'm immediately relieved.

I rush to grab my clothes and robe and toss them into the washer. The large, neat glass jars holding detergent and fabric softener have convenient spickets, making it easy to measure out the tiniest amount for my mini load of laundry.

I'm still freezing and can't feel my toes, so I grab my coat and throw it over my t-shirt, grateful to have my slippers at least, before heading back downstairs to the kitchen.

Tea is the quickest way to warm up. I grab the electric kettle and fill it under the tap before turning it on. A quick pass through the cabinets finds our rice dispenser completely full, but we don't have much in the pantry besides a few cans of pinto beans, an open package of rice noodles and a slew of seasonings. In the back of the corner cupboard is a canister full of Jasmine green tea and some organic black tea bags.

Dad's ceramic tea pot is in the next cupboard over. I gently place it on the counter and spoon some loose green tea leaves into the pot.

I check the fridge while I wait for the water to boil, hoping for a miracle and to my surprise, I see a carton of eggs, a leftover tub of butter from our last trip, and a gallon of 2% milk in the otherwise empty shelves. I look around and see a loaf of cheap white bread on the counter.

Cage must have gone out for some essentials while I was sleeping. The gesture is so heartwarming, even if he is just following orders and doing his job.

I always fought against my family's insistence to do everything for me, forcing myself to be fiercely independent, but having our bases covered in this emergency is a nice feeling.

I don't drink dairy milk and I swore off white bread years ago, but considering the circumstances, I'll take what I can get.

Having milk changes the tea game, so I pivot from green to black tea and pour the loose leaves back into the canister, tossing a black tea bag into a mug.

The water is finally ready and I gratefully pour the steaming water into my mug. I grab the milk from the fridge and pour in a splash before wondering if Cage would like a cup as well.

I err on the side of caution and make him a mug, just in case, but realize I don't know how he takes his tea, so I leave the bag steeping in the water, for now.

I rummage through the mostly empty cabinets but don't find any sugar. I huff, but know you can't win them all, I guess, so I settle for just milk and warm my hands as I sip away.

I hear Cage come through the front door, which is down a long hallway. He stamps his feet to get the snow off his shoes.

"Fuck." He curses from the cold. His massive frame fills the hallway as he makes his way to the kitchen, and he sniffles and coughs as he enters.

His eyes land on mine, and he softens immediately.

"Ah, Claire, you're awake." His rough, low voice goes straight to my core and I have to fight the blush threatening to crawl up my cheeks.

I clear my throat. "Um, yeah. I made you tea, if you like?"

"No coffee?" Cage asks while he removes his gloves.

I shake my head. "Our luck ran out with coffee, unfortunately."

"I should have thought of grabbing some." Cage smiles and takes the mug from me, gently. "Thank you."

"There's milk, but no sugar."

"Just milk is great."

I grab the jug from the fridge and pour a splash for him while he goes back to the front door to shed his coat and boots.

"I got the power back on." Cage calls to me down the hallway, and when he returns, I push his mug towards him. "Thanks." He says before sitting across the kitchen island and taking a sip. "That's good."

I shoot him a small smile. "I saw you got some eggs and bread, too. Thank you."

Cage nods. "Last night. Bad news though, we're snowed in. I tried heading to the nearest town for more supplies but the snow kept coming and now the roads are impossible to drive. Good news though, no one will be able to get to you, so you're safe."

"That's good, at least." I smile before taking another sip.

And, slowly, comfortably, we are surrounded by silence as we both enjoy our morning tea. I try not to notice his curls coming down on his forehead, accentuating his handsome face. His nose is a little red from the cold. The droplets of water on his hair sparkle in the morning sun, and I stop myself from staring at him before he notices.

"I, uh, got the security system up." He says gruffly. "I'll be keeping a close eye on the cams, so you should be safe inside the house. But maybe don't go outside, just so I can keep my eye on you."

I shudder at the thought. "I'd rather die than *recreate* in the snow."

That makes him smile. "Not an outdoorsy gal?"

I lean onto my elbows across the kitchen island, cradling my warm cup in both of my hands. "Let's just say while my family was skiing in Park City earlier this year, I was sitting by the fire at the resort lodge with a hot chocolate and a romance book."

"I didn't take you as the type." Cage rumbles as he takes a few more sips.

"Type of what?"

"Woman who reads those kinds of books."

"You mean the fiercely passionate, highly educated, extremely detail-oriented kind of woman who reads unabashedly smutty, sexy books? Why yes, I am." I wink at him, putting him in his place.

He smiles and puts his hands up in surrender. "My mistake, truely."

"Damn right." I smile, knowing he doesn't mean any harm. "You could learn a thing or two from those books, y'know. You'd be able to keep your wife satisfied for much longer if you took some notes."

Cage shakes his head. "I'm not married."

I feel my heart skipping a beat. "You're single?"

Please don't say you have a girlfriend who's probably tall and thin and blonde.

He nods. "Kinda have to be, in this line of work."

"Ah. Right. Killer bodyguard turned babysitter." I head to the fridge to begin an attempt of scrounging up some breakfast. "Sorry about this, by the way. I'm sure you have more important things to do than be trapped here with me."

"Not much more important." Cage says lightly, coming over to peer into the fridge with me. I feel myself stiffen from his proximity, but hold my ground. "Are you hungry? Want me to make you something? He offers.

"Oh no, let me handle breakfast, please." I say, shooing him back to his seat. "You've done more than enough." I take another look at our measly options. "How do you feel about congee with eggs and Spam?"

"Sounds delicious." Cage nods, going back to his tea, but keeping his eyes on me.

I flash him a smile, happy to see he's a good sport. "Alright."

I find the metal bowl insert of our rice cooker and get to work, washing the rice and measuring out the water to start on the porridge. I close the lid on the rice cooker and hit the start button.

Cage quickly goes into the guest room on the first floor to grab his laptop. He folds up the screen when he returns to his seat in the kitchen.

"The cameras in this place are all good to go, except the feed from the front reading room looks to be connected to the ones upstairs, and I haven't been able to get those online yet."

"Those ones have always been finicky." I reassure him. "Don't worry if you can't get them up. I seriously doubt anyone is trudging through all that snow to get to us."

"You're right, but we can never be too careful." Cage flashes me a small smile. "Precious cargo, and all that."

I roll my eyes at him. "Yeah, yeah. I'm very important." I dismiss as I walk to the wooden dining table and grab the Spam. "So what does a normal day in your life look like?" I ask, making small talk while I cook. It's one of my favorite things to do, and I'm happy to hear Cage oblige.

"I specialize in surveillance." He sips his tea. "I watch the cameras. Fix them when they go down. Chase after the people we're looking for. Boring, really."

"Sounds like you're a pretty important guy." I say, heating up a skillet on the gas stove, which is miraculously working. "We just recently got access to every major surveillance network in the world. My dad wouldn't let just anyone do that job." I suddenly realize. "Wait, is that because of you?"

Cage tilts his head a little sheepishly. "I may have had a hand in developing the program they all run on."

My jaw drops. "Cage. That's amazing." I praise as I'm slicing up the Spam. "Why are you working as one of the muscle men if you're so brilliant? Stay in the office."

"I like being out." He says, walking over to make himself another cup of tea. "I wasn't built to be behind a desk."

"I understand." I say before bringing my cutting board over to the stove to brush the diced Spam into the skillet. It sizzles nicely and I only need to turn the heat down a smidge for it to begin browning evenly. "I need to be on my feet. I worked as a receptionist for about a week before I developed back pain from sitting so long."

"Why do you work at that bookstore anyway? Are you trying to get out?" He asks, referring to the illegal, criminal lifestyle we both find ourselves in.

I nod, opening a nearby drawer to grab a pair of wooden chopsticks. "Easier said than done."

"I know what that's like." Cage says knowingly.

"Are you trying to get out?" I ask, surprised.

Tearing yourself away from the mob isn't easy, and I can't even fathom what it's like getting tangled into a world that traps you for life, especially if you owe them money.

For me, they're my family, so it's difficult in its own way, but getting wrapped up in the way my parents do business is not a good way to live, and I can only imagine the horrific circumstances Cage must have been in to end up working for us.

His answer is very direct. "I'm fine staying, for now. But it would be nice to be free."

This breaks my heart to learn. This means Cage owes Dad something, and he'll spend the rest of his life trying, and being unable, to pay it off.

"What did Dad do for you?" I turn to face him while I'm moving the Spam around the pan.

"Nothing to worry your pretty little head." Cage tries to lighten the mood, but I'm sticking to my guns.

"Cage, I'm serious, maybe I can help." I walk over to face him head on. "No one should live this life-"

"I'm better off now than I was, Claire." He interrupts me, sensing my savior complex, most likely, and letting me down gently. "I promise. You don't need to worry about me."

I think of Dad's compound. Of all of his goons, the young men in debt, in trouble with the law or at risk of homelessness. All of the men he employs, he buys, and they work for him and live at the compound, with all of their freedoms stripped away.

They must loyally serve Dad and his business, and maybe, after a decade or so, they can buy their freedom with the money they've collected throughout the years. But Dad pays them pennies, and with the compound providing all of their food and necessities, it's almost impossible to save up enough to leave.

I think of Cage, so much older than the others, and wonder what kind of hard times he must have fallen on to have to work for Dad now.

"Besides..." He continues. "I'm supposed to worry about you."

"Pshaw." I dismiss, satisfied with the browning on the Spam and putting a paper towel onto a plate before transferring the cubes from the pan, draining the rest of the fat into a mug to use for later.

I grab the carton of eggs from the fridge. "I'm nothing but a princess living in a plush mansion. I'm fine."

"You're unhappy enough to try to leave."

"And you know how impossible it is, even for someone as privileged in my situation." I say while checking on the rice. There's still a few minutes left on the timer, so I'll hold off on frying up the eggs until it's closer to being done. "If I had my way, I'd open a bookstore." I beam.

I pummel Cage with my ideas, my hopes to open a soup kitchen for those on the streets, to raise enough money to give away free books, to somehow fund an education course that will get them off the streets and into jobs.

"I basically want to do what Dad does, just in a more ethical and creative way." I say, bringing over the plate of diced Spam and snacking on a few cubes.

"Forgive me if I'm overstepping, Claire, but don't you think you could make more of a difference if you worked with the resources your parents already have?" Cage asks while he takes a few cubes for himself.

I shake my head gently. "Blood money is still dirty, even if I try to use it for good. Plus, they're too greedy to do anything I want anyway, so for now, my plan is to try it all on my own."

"I hope you do get out." Cage's eyes are intense and hot, drilling into mine. "It's practically impossible, but I hope you do it."

"Thanks." I say, staring back. "The only other option is to take over the whole operation. Then I'd be your boss, and you wouldn't want that." I wink.

He smiles, and there's a hint of mischief behind his twinkling eye. "I wouldn't say that."

"Oh?" I'm intrigued. "Would you work well under me?"

"Too well, most likely." Cage says a little too quickly. He brings his hand up to cover his smile, the boyish move giving me a glimpse into a softer side of him, and the sight makes something inside me come alive.

I can already imagine him under me in my bed upstairs, my legs straddling his waist, his massive body filling every one of my senses. He would be so easy to bounce on, so easy to rock against...

"Sorry..." He continues. "I didn't mean anything by that."

"I think you did." I smile, unable to stop myself. I feel a blush coming on.

Cage only laughs and shakes his head. "You'll be the death of me, woman, I swear."

"Hey I'm innocent here. You're the one with your mind in the gutter."

He gives me a knowing look, as if to say *you're one to talk*. "I should stop. Again, I apologize." He says, his face returning to a stern, neutral look.

The rice cooker beeps and I'm grateful for the interruption. I feel myself getting in over my head with this man so I'm happy to tear my eyes away from his striking features.

The congee is cooked well, even in such a short amount of time. I'm thanking Dad silently for being so obsessed with this rice cooker. Between this and the

Japanese toaster, the kitchen is streamlined for maximum efficiency. I give the porridge a quick stir with a large, bulbous ladle and close the lid to keep it warm while I fry a few eggs.

I throw together a piping hot breakfast bowl within the next several minutes, and Cage and I are tucking in as the sun begins to fill the entire kitchen and living room.

"This is great. Thank you." He says between hot bites of comforting, salty goodness.

"Anytime." I smile, but even after a few mouthfuls, I feel like something is missing. The porridge is a bit bland, and even though I know our resources are low, I rummage through the kitchen drawers in hopes of finding something to give it some oomph.

I finally see a few stray packets of soy sauce in a drawer full of loose pens. "Success!" I grab a handful and toss a few over to Cage before sitting back down. "I don't know about you, but this needs some flavor." I tear off a corner of the packet and splash it around my bowl.

"None for me, thanks. It's seasoned perfectly. Just enough salt."

I nod. "The Spam really is doing the heavy lifting here. If we were back home, I could make you a *real* breakfast. Bacon, pancakes, the works."

Cage flashes me a smile. "We'll get you back in no time."

"Let's hope by tonight. I need to water my plants."

We finish our breakfast while talking about a whole lot of nothing. I tell him about my favorite books, ones I'll happily revisit in the front sitting room while we wait for the all-clear to return back to town, and he tells me absolutely nothing else about himself. When I ask what his favorite books are, he says he doesn't read. When I ask what music he listens to, he says he prefers looped tracks of white noise.

"It helps me concentrate." He tells me while he's washing the dishes.

It takes all of my effort not to drool over the sight of him elbow-deep in the sink with a sponge in his hand. The sleeves on his black button-up are rolled up, showing the veins on his thick forearms. The soap glistens on his rich skin, and I wonder what other veiny parts of him look that good covered in slick, shiny wetness...

I ignore the impulse to tell him what I'm thinking...

"Wait, you don't listen to any music? What do you sing at karaoke?"

Cage scoffs. "I don't go to karaoke. I work."

"I work too, but that doesn't stop me from belting out "Living On A Prayer" on Friday nights."

"Maybe you're just more fun than I am."

"C'mon Cage, you don't do *anything* for yourself? On your days off, what do you do for fun?"

"Nothing. I don't take days off. I go to work, eat, sleep, repeat."

"Well since we have nothing to do for the next few hours, how about some karaoke?" I offer, the excitement oozing from my pores. I beeline to the living room and turn on the karaoke system that was installed a few years ago. It's connected to the large flat screen above the fireplace, and it all whirls up without a hitch.

The microphones also all have batteries, too, thank goodness.

"C'mon, Cage." I say through the mic in a deep voice, mimicking a popular musical theater character based on a Greek god. "Sing us a song."

He's smiling while drying his hands on a rag, but shakes his head. "You sing all you want. I've got a job to do."

"What could you possibly be doing all the way out here in the middle of nowhere?" I ask him, keeping the mic up to my lips and stalking forward, attempting to intimidate him into singing.

"There's a certain woman in a safehouse being hunted by a rival mob family." Cage picks up his laptop and brings it over to the wooden dining table, plugging it in with a few other gadgets and wires I don't recognize. "So I'm going to sit here, watch the cameras, and do my job."

"Fine, you'll just have to put up with my squawking for the rest of the day." I say over my shoulder before selecting one of my favorites in my repertoire.

Shania Twain's "Whatever You Do! Don't!" ripples through the house, and since Cage is the only audience member, I sing directly to him.

"Deep in Denialville, tryin'a fight the way I feel. I go jello when you smile, I start blushing, my head rushing."

I climb onto the couch as if it's the bar of my favorite karaoke spot in the Lower East Side.

"If you stand too close to me, I might melt down from the heat. If you look my way one more time, I'm gonna go out of my mind!" I croon, climbing over the couch and dramatically falling to my knees, clenching my heart and singing right at him.

"Don't even think about it. Don't go and get me started! Don't you dare drive me crazy. Don't do that to me, babaaay!"

Cage is amused, watching me with a small smile on his face.

I'm crawling towards him now as I sing the next verse.

"You stop me in my tracks. My heart pumping to the max. I'm such a sucker for your eyes. They permanently paralyze!" Being this close, I can take in the sparkle in his brown eyes, and they really do dazzle. I turn away before I get too lost in them.

"Don't even think about it. Don't go and get me started! Don't you dare drive me crazy. Don't do that to me, baby!"

I end my routine back in the living room, right in front of the TV. As the song fades out, I dramatically bow, and Cage is courteous enough to applaud.

"Thank you, thank you." I say to the room, as if it's filled with adoring, drunk patrons and friends. "I'm here all week!"

"God, I hope not!" Cage calls, playing along and pretending he's shouting over a crowd.

I cackle with laughter. He's such a good sport. I'm searching around the room for the remote to pick the next song, but I can't seem to find it. Maybe it fell between the couch cushions?

I'm busy digging my hands behind the pillows and the cushions, so I don't see Cage come closer.

He startles me, standing so near, making me yelp with laughter. He's holding the remote in his hand, offering it to me silently.

"Thank you." I breathe a little harder from laughing. I take the remote from his large, warm hands and begin scrolling. "You wanna sing? There's like, thousands of songs on this thing." I beam up at him.

His melting, sweet eyes glimmer at me. "No thanks. You keep going."

Cage doesn't pull away immediately. He's hovering, closely, as if my face has its own gravitational pull and he's drawing closer and closer.

He's studying me. I can see his eyes roaming my features, slowly in some instances, darting in others. I don't know exactly what he's doing, but I let him.

And I do the same.

I look.

At him.

I like looking at him. His tall nose, the smattering of gray hair growing at his temples, and a thick five o'clock shadow dusting his jaw makes my palms itch to touch him.

I wonder what he looks like with a beard? If he's grown this much facial hair in the few hours we've been stuck here, I bet he could grow one easily.

I never really liked the look of beards, but if Cage had one...I *could* be convinced it might be nice to kiss...

I look at his lips, full and soft. They almost look like velvet, the way their smoothness dully reflects the light of the room. I think they would feel nice on my lips...

He stares at me, intensely. He's making my neck feel hot from being under such close inspection and attention.

I want to make him feel the same way. I want my eyes to make him feel like he's the most interesting book I've ever read, or the most handsome man I've ever seen.

I want him to know I want him.

Because, deep down, I think I know he wants the same thing.

We aren't touching...

I want to touch him.

But I don't.

I'm the one who breaks away first, turning my head away from his face and back to the TV screen.

I ignore the pang in my heart telling me I've made a mistake by not leaning in and pressing my lips to his.

"How about "All Star" from Smash Mouth?" I say, trying to sound nonchalant and unaffected by the silent moment we were sharing.

Cage keeps looking at me, his eyes practically burning a hole in the side of my face.

"Great choice." He grumbles, and after a few more stretching seconds, he releases me from our mutual orbit of each other, and returns to his seat.

Cage somehow keeps one eye on the cameras and his entire attention on me as I belt out "All Star," "Don't Stop Believing" by Journey, "Suddenly, Seymour" from Little Shop of Horrors (with me singing both parts) and "My Heart Will Go On" by Celine Dion.

As I'm singing, having the time of my life, I can't help thinking this would be a typical night out if Cage and I were together. He'd be sipping on a dark beer, snacking on some loaded cheese fries and watching me rock the crowd. Depending on how many drinks I've had, He'd be shaking his head and laughing at me making a fool of myself, too.

But he wouldn't be embarrassed. He'd be happy to spend the night with me. He'd take me back to my place, take off my clothes, and...

I stop my fantasy right in its tracks and don't let myself go there. Sure, we'd make a great couple. Sure, he's probably an excellent kisser. Sure, he'd probably fuck me until dawn, but that doesn't stop me from thinking there's some other woman out there, probably tall, thin and tan, who would excite him more than me.

Someone he would lose control for.

Instantly, I've hurt my own feelings. No song can cure this. I need to stop.

I toss the remote on the couch. "I'm tired. I'm going to take a nap." I say over my shoulder, not looking at him.

"Why? You okay?" He asks lightly, a hint of concern in his voice.

I shrug. "It's lonely, being the only one singing."

Cage shakes his head, a small smile pulling at the corner of his mouth. "Trust me, you don't want to hear me sing."

I don't answer. I make my way towards the kitchen.

"Hey, what's wrong?" Cage asks, and I'm annoyed he can read me so easily. He feels the immediate change in the room, but doesn't have the decency to let me stew over my self-inflicted heartbreak.

"Nothing, I'm just tired. Are you sure you don't want to move to the couch? It's comfier there."

Cage shakes his head. "The table is more centralized. And these chairs will keep me alert." He slides the stiff, wooden chair closer to the table.

"Fine, but don't complain to me when your ass falls asleep because you've been sitting there for who-knows-how long." I say before I can stop myself. The biting tone in my words is unintentional, but it spills from my lips all the same.

If Cage is surprised, he doesn't show it. "I never complain."

"I'm sure you don't."

I trudge towards the bookshelves lining the far wall of the front sitting room. I grab the familiar blue cover of my favorite book and plop into one of the plush, white reading chairs facing a small glass coffee table. A soft, fluffy white blanket is hanging on the armrest. I unfurl it over my legs.

I want to dive into the smutty story of a woman hiring a male escort to show her how sex works as she navigates the world as a woman on the autistic spectrum, but I'm stewing over Cage's refusal to open up even a fraction of an inch to me, and my insecurities of him not finding me attractive.

I'm sure he's hiding something, but to give me absolutely no insight into his life is annoying the hell out of me. I try flipping open my book to the first page, but I'm seething with irritation along with some burning curiosity.

Before I can march back to the kitchen and demand all I want to know from Cage, Mom calls me.

I answer immediately.

"Hey Mom."

"Hi, *con*. How are you holding up?"

"Pretty alright. It's cold as hell here, so I'm ready to leave this place behind me." I say as I curl deeper into my seat and pull the blanket around me. "What's the latest? Can we head back tonight?"

"About that…" Mom hesitates, which is never a good sign. "Things aren't ironing out as smoothly as we hoped. You might need to stay there a few more days."

"*Days*?!" I cry, sitting up. "No, Mom, I have to get back, I have to water my plants!"

"Give Dad some more time." She attempts to calm me down.

None of my excuses are enough. I'm suddenly a teenager again, arguing with my parents about letting me stay late after school for theater practice or grabbing ice cream with my friends. I'm unrelenting, begging for them to let me come home.

I haven't had this much energy in ages to argue, but still, after hearing my ranting attempts, Mom doesn't budge.

"We don't have any food. How do you expect us to live for days here without food?" I point out, hoping to have backed her into a corner.

"We have that emergency pantry in the basement, next to the gym. Did you forget?"

Oh that's right, we did have a small closet downstairs full of various canned goods and non-perishables.

"Fine." I cave. "But call me tomorrow and keep me in the loop."

"Alright. We love you, *con*. Bye."

"Bye." I hang up and climb out of my seat, ready to break the bad news to Cage.

He's just hanging up his phone as well, looking up when he sees me.

"We have to stay-" I begin.

"For a few more days, I know." He motions to his phone. "Your dad."

I point to my phone. "My mom." I'm defeated, slumping into one of the dining chairs next to his computer setup. "What do we do?"

"Whatever you like." Cage says softly, sitting back down in front of his monitor. "I'll stay here. Keep watch. Make sure you're safe."

"You'd rather sit here than watch a K-drama with me?"

He playfully winces at the idea of having to sit through hours of cheesy, romantic dramas. "No thanks, I'll keep an eye out." He turns his attention to the laptop. "Feel free to go wherever I can keep my eye on you."

"Gee. Thanks." I roll my eyes before heading upstairs to check on my laundry, abandoning the notion of befriending the disinterested bodyguard in the kitchen.

I swap my clean underthings to the dryer before suddenly realizing my parents might have left some clothes behind.

I check their bedroom on the other side of the second floor. I come up empty, except for one set of cream sweat pants and a matching hoodie Mom left behind. I thank my lucky stars and throw off my coat to put on the set over my large t-shirt.

Mom is a bit slimmer than me, so the set clings onto my hips and chest tighter than I'd like, but at this point, I'm grateful for anything.

I double-check for extra socks and underwear, with no luck. Now that the house is warmer than it was this morning, I no longer need my coat. I hang it up in my room before heading back downstairs.

"Hey, I think the food storage closet downstairs might have more options." I say to Cage as I'm rounding into the kitchen, conveniently leaving out the fact I completely forgot about it.

Cage looks over to me and freezes where he sits. His eyes are wide for a long moment before he slowly combs my body. His gaze rakes over my curves, lingering on my breasts.

The attention is like a chill through my body, and I feel my nipples harden at the sight of him staring at me.

His eyes shoot back up to my face before tearing away and he turns back to his laptop.

"Oh, good." Cage says quietly.

It's all he says. He doesn't look at me again, even as I heat up the kettle for a cup of tea.

I'm annoyed. I don't know what to think about him clearly checking me out, and me clearly liking it.

I first think he likes what he sees, but suddenly getting the cold shoulder from him is reminding me of how I used to feel when Mom forced me to go to charity events, where all the eligible men stuck up their noses at me for being heavier, softer, and curvier than the other women from other wealthy families.

Fuck that. I'm too old to be worrying about what some *man* thinks of me, especially one who means nothing to me.

I pour the boiling water over my tea bag and leave it on the count to cool. I walk past Cage with as much dismissive energy as I can ooze and storm through the living room to reach the stairs leading to the basement.

I make quick work of gathering an armful of canned beans, soup, baby corn and other vegetables from the storage closet. I make a mental note to take advantage of this gym later.

I can hide from Cage down here if he annoys me even more. I think as I head back upstairs.

The cans clatter loudly when I dump them onto the kitchen island. I no longer wish to tip-toe around the man, so I'll make as much noise as I want.

Is this immature and childish? Maybe a little. My feelings aren't so much hurt, but maybe a little stung. I'm too proud to talk to him about it, though, so I leave him alone and go back to the front sitting room to wrap myself up in the fluffy blanket and read my book.

Chapter Four

The next day passes in a steady, hazy blur. I come downstairs in the morning after having an intense dream I cannot remember, to find Cage sitting vigilantly at his computer, keeping watch of the house. He hasn't moved from his perch since I last saw him last night.

I'm finally feeling rested, catching up on some much needed sleep, but after a boring brunch of rice and beans, a silent afternoon of reading and an uneventful dinner of rice and sauteed vegetables, I'm beginning to feel a little stir-crazy.

Mom calls late in the evening to update us both on the status of the whole "*Lê* family trying to kill me" situation and says they need one more day to wrap things up. I fall asleep disappointed, but lack the energy to fight back.

I wake up early this morning with a headache and a bad mood. I need to workout, or I'm gonna lose my mind.

After getting myself ready, I pull up my hair and throw on the cream sweat set, glad to have a spare outfit while my others are in the wash.

When I come downstairs, I'm surprised to find Cage isn't at his usual seat at the kitchen table. His laptop is gone, but all of the wires and connectors are still on the table. I check the garage and see the SUV is still parked safely from the snow, so he must still be in the house.

I don't bother spending any more time looking for him. I grab a tall glass of water before heading to the gym in the basement. The light is on, and it takes me too long to realize Cage is there before I'm hit with a sight too overwhelming for one woman's eyes.

Cage is shirtless, sweaty, and glistening. His rippling muscles are covered by a beautifully deep olive tone to his skin, and the thickness in the air is made more apparent by the size of him compared to the many machines throughout the room.

His chest, taught and bulging, has a smattering of salt and pepper hair that gently curls. As he pumps his biceps, the veins in his arms look as if they're about to burst, and the hair on his forearms is thick and masculine. My eyes barely make it to his expansive back before his eyes lock on mine through the mirror. He quickly finishes his last rep, returning the weights to the rack behind him.

"Sorry, Claire." Cage huffs, out of breath. "Didn't see you there." He turns to put on his black sleeveless undershirt, and I already miss the sight of him, though he's barely covered up. He's wearing the only pair of pants he has, but it's somehow even hotter seeing him in a black tank with black dress pants.

"I didn't mean to interrupt." I flush, backing up the stairs. "I'll come back-"

"I'm done." He breathes, grabbing his laptop, which was perched on a bench in front of him.

Cage must have been keeping watch of the cameras during his workout. That seems excessive, but I'm touched he's working so hard to keep me safe. "I need to charge this, anyway." He flashes me a quick smile as he's passing me near the door.

His proximity to my body warms my skin and I can't stop the blush from crawling up my cheeks.

Cage stops, towering over me. His eyes are liquid heat, burning into mine, and a delicious warmth unfurls at my core. He looks as if he wants to say something, his gaze now hungry for my lips, but he abandons the thought, his voice gruff.

"I'll be upstairs." Cage grunts.

I can only nod and rush into the basement before I do anything foolish.

I'm blushing. Like a schoolgirl. My mature, collected self has gone out the window and in her place is a simpering, horny, mess-of-a-woman.

I can't do this. I can't lose control over a man who doesn't even know me. What would Jenny say?

He should be groveling at your feet for your attention. You should be his sun and moon. His first thought in the morning and last thought at night. If not, he's not worth it! Any of it!

I'm missing Jenny now while I warm up and stretch. I wish I could talk to her as I'm walking on the treadmill for the next hour, running through the events of the past few days and trying to figure out what advice she'd give me.

I'm halfway to calling her by the time I finish a pilates video I pull up on the large TV, but decide against it. She can't know about Cage, or any of this, for that matter. She's safer this way.

So I'm alone with my feelings as I gulp down my water, turn off the TV and lights, and head upstairs to rinse my cup in the kitchen sink before going back to my room.

I'm distracted by the memory of Cage's glistening muscles while I peel off my clothes and turn on the water in my shower, but after a few minutes of the temperature staying the same frigid, cold stream, I curse at the ongoing problem of hot water not reaching the upper level of the cabin at a decent pace. With how much money my family has, you'd think they could fix this.

I wrap a towel around myself and pad downstairs to the bathroom on the main floor. I'm freezing, so I rush to pull open the bathroom door and smack into what feels like a brick wall.

"*Ay dios mio-*"

Large, hulking hands grab my waist as I fall backwards and yelp in surprise. Thick arms wrap around my shoulders to pull me up to standing before I even register what's going on.

I look into stunning, warm brown eyes that are wide with surprise, but are sturdy and constant. I eventually get my feet under me and steady myself.

Cage is wrapped in a towel at his waist, but everything else is bare for me to see.

He has those pelvic lines and a fuzzy happy trail leading down towards his towel. I wonder what it feels like to touch, and if it's as soft as I think. He also smells amazing. Clean and manly, like bourbon and cinnamon, with a hint of orange he can't seem to wash away. He feels so easy to cling to, his sheer mass a comforting presence in my hands.

I feel my towel begin to slip and I'm shocked out of my thoughts. I scramble to keep it closed around me.

"Oh my god, Cage, I'm so sorry, I-" I stumble as I try to tighten the betraying cloth around me.

I... What? didn't mean to attack you? Jump on you? Assault you? "There's no hot water upstairs and I was rushing to make it in here so you wouldn't see me-"

"Sorry." He flusters at the same time as my apology. "You okay? My clothes are in the dryer. Let me go out and-"

"Oh my god I'm so sorry, really, no, I'll go, I-" I'm mortified. I need to get out of here as fast as possible.

Cage puts his hands on my shoulders and tries to move me towards the shower. He's leaning his back against the sink in order to get my body past his, but I trip over his feet and fall face first into his hard, built chest. I feel his arms wrap around my back to keep me steady.

"Jesus." I wince, rubbing my nose from the sting of hitting my face on his pec. "Sorry, I..."

Looking up to check if he's offended, I'm met with Cage's eyes hooded with warmth. He's taking me in, his gaze roaming slowly around my face. His hand comes up to caress my cheek before moving a stray piece of hair behind my ear. I feel the heat rising in my face, and the steam from the bathroom isn't helping.

He gently nudges my nose with a knuckle, assessing the damage.

"You hurt?" He grumbles lowly, his voice melting and delicious.

I can only shake my head in response.

Cage huffs a quiet laugh of relief, but doesn't push me away. He leans back to get a better look at me. His eyes are fixated on my breasts spilling over my towel, and I watch his Adam's apple bob as he swallows and his tongue comes out to wet his plush lips.

Being this close, I get a more intimate look at his thick, five o'clock shadow beginning to dust his face, and the flecks of gray on his jawline sparkle in the sunlight.

Cage suddenly comes to his senses and stands, gently moving me a safe, arms-distance away.

"Shower. I'll go." He breathes, avoiding my eyes and turning to stalk from the bathroom.

I run the water in a daze, relieved to find it hot and steaming. I shower as fast as I can and dry myself in a fury, desperate to get to my room and solitude.

I peek into the hallway, and with no sign of Cage, I bolt upstairs and close the door behind me.

Jesus Christ.

Devastating humiliation runs through my veins. How could I be so careless? In this entire, gigantic house, why did I have to *literally* run into him? I'm mortified.

I hang up my towel and wrap my robe around me, burying my face into my pillows as I squirm at the all-too-recent memory. Smacking into Cage's body, the yelp, the stumble, his skin, his smell, his shoulders, his strength...

And his kindness. As I'm replaying the scene over and over in my mind, I realize he had every opportunity to make me feel horribly embarrassed about the situation, but he only made me feel his tenderness and care. He's a protector, and he protected me, and I should feel grateful instead of humiliated.

Putting it all into perspective is really helping me get over this. I won't be able to avoid him forever, so the sooner I can come to terms with my mistake, the better I'll feel.

I mean, sure, he was looking at my breasts, but I was looking at his abs, and I'm sure he noticed, too. He didn't hold it against me, so I won't hold it against him. It's a natural thing to do for anyone thrown into that situation, so it doesn't mean anything.

It doesn't mean he finds me attractive, and although I can admit to myself he's definitely hot, I don't know a thing about him, so therefore, I don't have any sort of strong feelings towards the man.

Right. Exactly, Claire. Keep your wits about you. You got this.

I go to grab my clothes but realize I forgot to wash my other set, and now both are dirty.

Fuck.

I check the dryer to make sure Cage got his clothes, and it's empty, so that's a good sign. I quickly throw in both sets of clothes and start the washing machine on the fastest setting.

I scroll through my phone in bed for the next few hours but when the sun sets, I realize it's dinner time, and I'm too hungry to hide out in my room any longer. I wrap my robe around me, too lazy to fetch my clothes, and head downstairs.

When Cage sees me, he doesn't say anything, probably to spare my feelings. I'm grateful for his lack of attention.

To my dismay, scanning the pantry in the basement for what feels like an eternity doesn't magically conjure up different cans, so I settle on a tin of soup. I'm about to head upstairs when I see a bottle of rosé wine in the corner, and I nearly sob with delight.

I make my way upstairs and flash Cage my treasure.

"Want some?" I ask, beaming.

"No thanks. I don't drink on the job." He smiles from his station, clearly happy for my find. "But you have all you want."

"Don't have to tell me twice." I say, popping open the cork and pouring myself a glass before heating up my soup. "What do you want for dinner? I found some more cans of chicken noodle downstairs." I offer, emptying my can into a bowl and warming it in the microwave.

"I'll have the leftover beans and rice." Cage says, joining me in the kitchen and taking out the leftovers from the fridge.

"You're abandoning your post?" I gasp, teasing. "What if some ghouls or goblins come our way?"

Cage smiles, shaking his head. "One of the other guys is watching while I go on break. I'll need to sleep for a few hours, and then I'll get back on." The microwave beeps when my soup is done, and he places it on the counter for me before putting his plate in.

"Wait, you didn't sleep last night?"

"I haven't slept since we've been here." He says while sitting at the island, waiting for his food to warm up.

"What?!" I shout. "Cage. That's ridiculous!"

He just shrugs. "I'm working."

"Yeah, working to watch cameras on a house *no one* can get to!" I pull my phone out of my robe pocket. "This is unacceptable. They are working you to the bone." When his food is ready, I take the plate from the microwave and set it in front of him. "That's it. You sit and eat."

"Claire, really, I'm fine-"

"Eat!" I growl. I'm calling Dad as I walk to the front room. He answers after a few rings.

"Claire! You okay, *con*?"

"Dad, did you know Cage has been watching the cameras ever since we got here without taking a break?"

"He's good at what he does."

"That's completely unacceptable, Dad! That would exhaust anyone, no matter how good he is! How do you expect him to watch over me if he's too overworked to keep his eyes open? Plus, don't you think this is pushing it a little too far? Just turn the motion sensors on and the alarm will let us know if anyone passes onto the property."

"What if they fly in?"

"You seriously think we won't hear a helicopter flying above the house?"

"Hmm...alright, *con*. Let Cage rest for an hour or so and he can get back to watching the cameras."

"No, Dad. Give him a day. Have one of your other guys do it, if you insist on keeping watch. But I'm telling you, it's not necessary. No one is out here. And they physically can't get out here, so it's a waste of time."

"Alright. I'll see what I can do."

"Thanks, Dad."

"Mm-hmm. I gotta go. Love you, *con*."

"Love you, Dad."

I march back to the kitchen just in time to see Cage finishing up his food. "You haven't been using the guest room?" I demand.

"No."

I sigh in frustration and walk through the living room to turn on the guest room light. Sure enough, the hunter green bed sits perfectly made, not a pillow out of place.

I turn down the covers and move the decorative pillows to the green seat in the corner. I'm angry with myself for not noticing Cage isn't taking care of himself.

He reminds me of myself. When I used to get caught up in problems with my parent's business, I'd forget to eat or drink water.

Cage leans against the doorway to watch. I can hear him behind me, but I don't turn to face him.

"You're upset." He says, quietly.

"Yes, I am."

"Why?"

"Because, while I've been...*annoyed* at this whole situation and distracted by my own selfish existence, it didn't occur to me that you'd be tired. Or hungry. Or uncomfortable." I feel tears betray me, but I wipe them away quickly, not allowing him to see it. "I'm sorry."

"No need." Cage walks into the room, and I turn to see he really doesn't look tired or put out at all. "It's my job."

I try to smile, but I'm internally kicking myself. "I know. But you don't need to work this hard." I look up at him as he stops in front of me. "This is no way to live. It's not worth it." I say to him with a pathetic smile.

"For you, it's always worth it." He says softly.

A small laugh escapes me, disregarding his words. "Promise me you'll sleep?"

Cage looks around the room, disapproving. "Not here, it's too far back in the house." He reaches for a few pillows and tucks them under his arm. "The living room?"

I smile. "I can work with that." I grab a few blankets and together, we make up a bed on the plush, deep white cloud couch.

Before we can finish putting the pillows down, the power goes out, the house plunging into darkness.

"You're shitting me." I snarl, looking at the ceiling as if my fiery glare will scare them back on.

"I'll be back." Cage says while throwing on his coat, grabbing a flashlight and heading outside to check the breaker.

I'm already getting cold, but I rummage through the cabinets and drawers for any candles and matches before the chill permeates my bones.

I only find one 3-wick lemon candle and one tall pillar with the image of Pedro Pascal depicted as a patron saint printed on the label. No luck on a lighter or matches, but the gas is still on, so I light up a wooden chopstick on the stove and place the orange flames on the candles before blowing out my makeshift match.

My soup is lukewarm by now, so I quickly gulp down the spoonfuls while chugging my wine, irritated at our loss of power.

I'm either imagining I'm freezing, or the insulation of the house is nonexistent. A shiver runs through my body.

I take one of the candles to the front room to grab the plush blanket before returning to the living room and curling up on the loveseat across from Cage's bed. I curse myself for forgetting my wine, quickly standing to grab both the bottle and my glass and setting them on the coffee table. No way was I going to be upstairs in the dark by myself. What if I freeze to death?

Cage returns with bad news. "No luck. The electric company website says outages are all around us. Must be the weather."

I nod with a frown, but curl further into my seat. "Do you mind if I stay here? It's awful up there in the dark." I ask, sipping my wine.

Cage shrugs. "No worries." He looks around, a bit awkwardly now. Since he has no cameras to watch, he doesn't quite know what to do with himself.

"I'll, uh, I'll be in the bathroom. Think you can hold down the fort while I'm gone?"

I salute him dramatically. "Yes, sir."

He chuckles. "That's my girl." Cage turns and heads down the hall, but his words echo in my mind.

That's my girl.

Heat rises in my cheeks and a nagging pressure between my legs forces me to close them together. Just those three words have me irreversibly hot.

I didn't think I had a kink, but if it was Cage saying those things to me, I could get into some dirty talk...

Cage returns in his black tank and dress pants, unfazed by how uncomfortable I think he looks, and climbs into his couch-bed.

"Will you sleep there tonight?" He asks, fluffing his pillows, already looking more comfortable than he ever has since I met him. "I like the idea of having you close. I can keep my eye on you."

I nod, happy to stay. "At least until the power turns on." I take the last sip of my wine and return my glass to the table. "Does the candlelight bother you? Should I blow them out?" I ask.

"I have a hard time sleeping, either way." Cage says.

"You sure you don't want a drink? Take the edge off?"

"No thanks." He shakes his head. "It won't help, anyway. I've tried."

I nod, understanding. It usually takes me hours to fall asleep, as well, and alcohol usually makes me feel sick, not sleepy.

"Cage, can I ask you something?"

"Sure." He says, turning his head to face me.

"What did you do to end up working for my dad?" I expect him to deflect the question, but he turns his body to face me now, looking right into my eyes.

"I killed one of your clients. For beating his new wife." Cage says, directly. Unflinchingly. "Except I didn't know he was one of your clients at the time. I just thought he was some piece of shit beating on a woman I saw on one of my cameras. By chance. I wasn't even looking for him."

He sat up then, putting his feet on the plush white carpet and leaning his elbows on his knees. "Instead of jail, your dad brought me to the compound. And now I work off what he paid for me, plus the money he lost from that client."

"Cage…that must be…millions…"

"6.7 million, to be exact." He breathes an unamused laugh. "I've barely made a dent."

"Oh, Cage…" I try to fight the tears welling in my eyes, but I can't stop them. I make my way towards him and sit on the sturdy white coffee table that separated us, grabbing his hands. "I'm so sorry." I sniffle, the alcohol in my system softening my defenses.

I know, from the way the contracts are drawn, he'll work the rest of his life for Dad and never be free.

"Hey, it's okay." Cage says, consoling me. "Really, it's alright."

"No. No, it's not alright." I shake my head, the tears falling freely. "Nothing about any of this is alright! The killings, the girls, the money, the *death threats*?! None of this is okay!" I sob in front of him, and Cage pities me so badly, he scoops me up and places me on the couch in front of him.

It's cozy. Warm and soft from the blankets, hot and sturdy from him. I kneel and reach up to wrap my arms around his neck, crying into his shoulder.

Cage's arms lock around my waist, holding me tight.

"Why couldn't I belong to a normal family?" I lament, wiping my tears on the sleeve of my robe. "One where my parents just work in a nail salon and pressure me into becoming a doctor? A family that doesn't hold your freedom from you?" I pull back to look at Cage's face, searching for an answer.

"I think you're meant for more than that, I'm afraid." He says softly. "You were born into a family like yours to make a difference."

I shake my head as I sit back on my heels. "I can't seem to do more than make a mess of things around me." I give into my urge to touch his hair, and the curls falling on his forehead feel so soft between my fingers. "What if I could have helped you? What if I could have released you, all this time, and instead, I've been playing bookseller and trying to ignore this part of my life?"

"You were trying to leave. Escape. Anyone would do the same, in your situation." Cage says, caressing my bottom lip with his thumb. "I knew you were beautiful, but I had no idea you were so hard on yourself."

A small laugh escapes me. "You'd feel the same if you were as stuck as I am. I'll be 35 soon and will have never lived a life of my own. Except for a pathetic attempt at a retail job. I don't even know if it'll still be there when I get back."

"From what everyone says at the compound, with how many businesses you were keeping tabs on, I'd say you've accomplished more than you give yourself credit for."

That pulls a genuine smile from me. "Thank you." I sniffle. "I can't help but think about you." I lean in closer. "You can't leave. See your family. Do anything for yourself. It's got to be torture." I feel the tears start to sting my eyes again.

A half-smile pulls at one corner of Cage's mouth. "I've got all I need." He says simply, his hands pulling me closer into a hug. "Don't cry for me, *hermosa*. I'm fine. Really."

I look up into his eyes to gauge if he's lying, if he's secretly asking me to let him escape, to flee from this place and never look back.

But Cage's eyes pierce me with the most heart-melting heat. His warm, sturdy frame envelops my senses, and I can see, hear, and smell nothing but him.

I look at his lips, thick and plush, and I can already imagine what he tastes like.

Cage licks his lips and swallows, no doubt feeling the heat from my gaze. I watch his Adam's apple bob at the action, and I fight the urge to lean down and kiss it.

I sit up closer, looking in his eyes for any sign I should move away, but when he leans into me, ever so slightly, I take the plunge and bring my lips to his.

He's soft, warm, and delicious. I kiss him once, slowly, gently, and pull back slightly to see if I've made a mistake and he wants me to stop.

We stare at each other for seconds that stretch on for what feels like a lifetime, both of us understanding the cameras are down. No one is watching. This is our mistake to make, and it's up to us to end this now.

Or keep going.

Cage growls, grabbing my ass and lifting me up to straddle him, moving his legs to stretch out wide so I can nestle my core comfortably onto his thighs.

He gives my ass one good squeeze before letting go. "I'm not supposed to touch you, but you..." His eyes are burning with heat, locked with mine. "Do you want to stop?" He huffs, giving me a genuine choice.

I'd rather watch the world burn around us than stop. I shake my head.

"Then kiss me again." Cage snarls, and the sound of his gruff demand shoots straight to my center like a bolt of lighting. I take his face into my hands and kiss him again, hungrily, the way I've always wanted.

His tongue slips into my mouth, wet and wanting, and I moan at the delicious feeling. His hands aren't on any part of my body now, but he lets me roam his face, down his neck and to his sturdy shoulders. I love the feeling of him.

"Mmm." My fingers come back up to tangle into his hair and the feeling of him in my hands is intoxicating. I'm grinding down on his bulge, the sweet friction of my pussy on his pants feels much better than it has a right to be.

"Fuck." Cage breathes, bucking his hips up to meet me. "That's it, *hermosa*, give it to me."

I push down firmer than I dared before, and the pressure brings a wash of pleasure over me. My hips, of their own accord, begin rocking back and forth as I start grinding harder, chasing my pleasure.

"I'm sorry, Claire." Cage says, pulling back slightly and bringing his hand under my robe, up my leg. "I gotta know."

His large, warm fingers reach my core and he strokes my folds, drenching himself. I gasp at the contact as he flattens his hand, rubbing me slowly.

"You're so wet." He breathes, a smile on his lips. "I'm sorry. I had to know what you feel like."

"That feels amazing." I say, hoping to encourage him to continue.

"I gotta stop, Claire." Cage huffs, staying exactly where he is and continuing to rub my folds. "I can't touch you."

"You're not touching me." I say, mewling at the feeling of his thick hand and gasping when his thumb comes to rub my clit. "I-I don't know what you mean. I don't feel anything." I smile, grabbing his wrist and moving his hand so his fingers are circling my folds faster.

"Right. Not touching." Cage plays along, slipping a single finger inside me and almost making me come at the fullness alone.

I brace myself on his shoulders, overcome by the pleasure. Cage slowly pumps one finger inside me, and when he inserts another, I gasp at how far he's already stretching me.

A few more pumps and I'm brought over the edge, my pleasure washing over me. My thighs shake as I ride out my high, melting into him while I'm coming down.

That's the fastest orgasm I've ever had, and I'm limp with pleasure, leaning into Cage for support.

He is burying his face into my breasts, inhaling sharply.

"Fuck." He growls, wrapping his arms around my back and laying me down gently. He hovers over me and takes his fingers, brings them to his mouth, and tastes me. "Fuck, you're so sweet."

Cage kneels onto the floor, hooking my legs over his arms and pulling me to the edge. I yelp at his strength.

"Let me taste you?" Cage asks, a hint of demand in his grumbling voice.

I look down and see him waiting for my answer. In the glow of the candles, his stunning face looks even better between my legs.

I nod at him, smiling.

"Thank god." He says, and his warm breath and tongue are at my core, licking, kissing, and feasting on me.

Cage's thumb comes up to my clit and I'm overcome. Jolts of pleasure shoot through every nerve. I'm squirming, chasing my orgasm while also feeling it's all too much and I need to wriggle free of him. He's giving me a beautiful symphony of contradictory urges and taking over my senses.

It feels amazing.

Once he slides two fingers inside me while his other thumb is rubbing my clit, I'm reaching my peak, another orgasm tensing my muscles and shooting through me like lightning, hard and fast. I'm seeing stars in my peripheral vision as I'm both lost in the dark around me and the brightness from Cage's attention between my thighs. My moans nearly shake the cabin with their intensity.

As I'm coming down and my breath slows, Cage crawls up my body and hovers over me, one hand continuing to rub my folds slowly.

"Fuck, you're gorgeous." He breathes, kissing me hungrily. "I could listen to you all night."

I can taste myself on his lips, all slippery and hot, and Cage's enthusiasm is riling me up again.

"Hell, if you let me..." He says, smiling. "I'd eat you out for breakfast, lunch and dinner and never need to eat again."

"Ha!" I shake with laughter, my hands coming up to his cheeks as he buries his face into my neck. The rough prickle of his facial hair against my palms is so very masculine and effortless, I can see myself getting lost in the details of his face easily.

"We can make that happen." I say, bringing his face up to look at me. "Not only would I let you, I'd feed you a proper meal, too."

"Mmm, you are an excellent cook." Cage nods, slipping a finger back into me.

I gasp. "The best." I try to joke, but the pleasure running through me is taking away all of my focus. "Wait until we're back in town, I'll make you a full meal."

"You're already a full meal." He whispers, now using two fingers to slide in and out of me languidly.

It feels incredible, but now that I'm hot and wet beyond comprehension, I want more.

I reach down towards the bulge in his pants. "I think it's your turn-"

Cage grabs my wrist to stop me faster than I thought someone his size could move. In half a second, he has my hand pinned up over my head.

"No, Claire." Cage is serious. "I can't. I'm a dead man already, giving into...you." He kisses me. "My temptation." He playfully accuses. "But I can't let you-"

"If you're fucked for all this anyway, why not just give in?" I ask pointedly, ready to take the lead. "I can protect you. Plus, I want to feel you in my hand."

I try to reach for his zipper, but before I can lift my arm, he has them both pinned above my head.

"No." Cage warns, sternly. "I'll give you anything you want. Make you come as many times as you want. But I can't fuck you."

"What if I just want to give you a blow job?" I challenge, playfully.

Cage huffs out a laugh. "No can do, beautiful."

"But I want you." I smile, and it's the truth. No man has gotten me so hot and bothered, and made me come so quickly, as this force above me. He is everywhere and everything, and I want to get lost in the world he's created for me.

I also want to feel his cock stretch me out.

"If I could..." Cage begins. "I'd give you all of me. Every breath, every cell, every thought I have, I'd give to you."

"Every thrust?" I wriggle beneath him, hooking my legs around his hips and pulling his pelvis down, grinding up into him. "Every fuck? Every chance I could bounce on that cock, you'd give to me?"

Cage growls as he grinds out one long thrust against my core before pulling away.

I let him go, releasing him from my legs.

"If I could, I'd fuck you until you came so hard, you'd see fireworks." Cage kisses me feverishly. "You'd *scream* my name."

I nod quickly. "I would. We could do that. Right now. So easily."

Cage shakes his head, looking pained at the idea of saying no. "This is still salvageable if I keep my cock in my pants, so let's keep it that way, for now."

He releases my hands and straightens onto his knees between my legs. "Now, what do you want, princess? A break? Another orgasm?"

I pretend to gag dramatically. "Don't call me princess. It's too close to what I want to get away from."

Cage huffs a small laugh. "Apologies, my mistake." He puts his hands up in defense.

"What I want is to keep this going, but you're really not gonna budge on me giving you any sort of pleasure or fun?"

"Don't get me wrong, I'm having a *lot* of fun." Cage smiles. "But it's a hard no on this." He gestures to his cock. "No matter how hard it is."

I roll my eyes. "Ha. Ha. Very funny. It's just killing the mood, you know?"

"I know." He says, moving to lay down next to me. "I'm sorry. But I can't jeopardize the job by being selfish."

"It's not selfish if I'm asking you. Technically, you'd be doing your job by following orders." I wink at him, but already feel like I'm fighting a losing battle.

I roll on my side to face him. "Thank you, for all…that. It was incredible. And I'm sorry for pushing you to do something we definitely both want but your obligation to your job keeps us from being close." I joke, but it rings true, and I'm suddenly fearful it's too true, and I misread the whole thing. "You did want to, right?"

Cage smiles, attempting to swallow a small laugh. "Yes, definitely."

"And by want to, I mean you wanted to have sex with me, right?"

"Among other things, yes." He chuckles.

"What other things?" I ask, practically holding my breath waiting for his next words.

Cage sucks in a large breath, taking his time choosing his next words. "I don't know if I want to tell you, but considering we might not see each other again after this, I don't see the harm." He turns onto his side to face me. "I want to know what you sound like the moment I push my cock into your tight, wet pussy. How you sound when I'm pounding into you. How you look when you get lost in an orgasm while riding me. How it feels to take you out to dinner, wearing a dress you picked just for me. How your hair looks in the morning after I've fucked you all night. How you sound when you call my name. And a lot more. Countlessly more." Cage sighs, a hint of pain on his face.

"But...why?" I ask, genuinely baffled by such a thorough, beautiful description of a life I can already imagine sharing with him. "How could you come up with all that after meeting me just a few days ago?"

He only shrugs. "You're the Ruby of Chinatown. I've known about you a lot longer than just a few days."

I prickle at the nickname. "Don't call me that, either. I hate when our community calls me that."

With my parent's reputation comes recognition, and the people we do business with have called me The Ruby because I'm so precious to my family.

"Sorry, I won't say it again." Cage apologizes, gently caressing my cheek. "I just can't have sex with you. I won't be able to redeem myself later. Especially if I'm only in this situation to fill your whims."

"What?" I ask, taken aback by Cage thinking this is casual for me.

"I can be here to pleasure you, no problem, but if you can get by without having sex, then we don't need to get into the fact you're only pursuing me because I'm the only man around right now."

"What?" I ask again, stunned. Does he think I'm just a horny freak that takes all she wants and gives nothing in return?

"C'mon, do you really think you'll even look in my direction after we get back?"

"Cage…" I begin, not knowing where to start. "Where is this coming from? This sounds like an explanation to a stranger, like you're talking to someone else, not me." I sit up. "Look at me."

His eyes began to wander to the blankets underneath us, and he has to look up to meet my eyes.

"You're one of the most amazing men I've ever met. And when we do get back, I would like to go out on a date with you, just like you said. In a pretty dress and everything."

"Be real, Claire." Cage says, his tone distant and dismissive. "They wouldn't let me anywhere near you."

"Unless I told them to."

"You can't even tell them you want to leave."

"You don't know what I've told them!" I shout, enraged.

How dare he. He doesn't know how much I fought for the little freedom I have. I crawl to my feet, seething.

"I know that this..." Cage gestures between us. "Needs to stop. Before one of us gets hurt."

"So you really think I want to fuck you because you're just convenient, not because I like you with any sort of degree of depth or clarity?"

"All I know is there's no future for us."

"How can you be so certain without even giving it a chance?!"

"Because men like me don't get chances! Not with women like you!"

"And what exactly is a man like you?"

"A poor man!" Cage shouts, standing, squaring up with me. " A man with no choices! A man with no life! A fucking... servant! Slave! I have nothing to offer you." He huffs, his chest rising and falling from his outburst.

"Are you only those things? Or are you a brilliant programmer? A man who saw a woman being beaten by her husband and saved her? A brave man who saved my life after we were ambushed by gunfire?" I search his face to see if my words land, but he avoids my gaze.

Despite Cage's outburst, an endearment unfolds for him in my chest. His vulnerability and exposure of insecurity shows a raw, wounded part of him that reflects the same parts I see in myself.

But his words still hurt, and I'm too tender from the fresh emotional lashings to continue.

"You're more than your circumstance." I say defeated, wrapping my robe closer around my body and grabbing a candle to retreat upstairs. "I know it. Maybe you'll see it, too."

As I'm halfway through the kitchen, the power kicks on. If anyone were watching the cameras, they'd see Cage getting under his covers on the makeshift bed-couch, and me passing through the kitchen to head upstairs, turning off the lights as I go.

What they won't see is the moment I close the door to my room, I let the tears I've been holding back, fall.

Chapter Five

Our isolation is all over the next morning.

I'm brushing my teeth when I get the call. Dad tells me all is resolved and I can finally come home. He's ordered Cage to drive me back to the penthouse, and before Dad can finish his sentence, I'm throwing on my clothes, packing what I can for car snacks, and rushing downstairs.

Cage is ready to go, all of his wires and electronics already tucked away in the SUV.

He still opens the passenger door for me. I climb in without meeting his eyes.

We spend the next 4 hours in silence.

When we're finally making our way over the bridge into town, I'm pulled by a feeling in my chest to apologize, reconcile, and ask him on a date. I want to take him to a place that serves his favorite food, whatever that may be, so I can watch him let down his guard a little and open up. I want to uncover what it is about this man that has me so intrigued.

But his little outburst still leaves a bitter taste in my mouth, and I don't know if it's up to me to apologize first, so I bite my tongue.

He has me acting like a strung-out teenager, and this is the first time in a while I'm not embarrassed to feel young and nervous.

Cage makes me excited, and I haven't been *this* excited about a man recently, if ever.

Damn it, I might have a crush.

I think about all I want to say to him. That it's okay to be insecure, I still think he's hot, and we should leave this all behind us and start again.

I settle on staying lukewarm. "For the record, I'd still like to go out on a date with you. Despite everything." I shrug, trying to play it cool, hoping he doesn't hear my heart pounding in my chest.

Cage pulls up just outside my building. "You know they'd never allow it." He says quietly. So quietly, I almost don't hear him. I realize he's probably trying to avoid the microphones that are undoubtedly throughout the entire vehicle.

A shooting pain bolts through my heart when I hear his words.

I know he means he'll lose his job, his *life*, if he continues this. I know he's being the mature, responsible person here. I know he's protecting himself, and me.

But all I hear is *you're not worth the risk*.

The dam breaks in my heart, and all of my insecurities drown me.

I grab my things and leave without another word.

I'm sprinting across the courtyard and almost make it to the door when I hear Cage call my name.

Do I turn around and face him? Do I allow him to reconcile, clear the air and make things better between us?

Or is he just going to tell me I left my lipgloss in the cupholder?

I can't deal with the rejection, or supposed rejection, from him, so I ignore Cage and rush past my doorman Juan to take the elevator upstairs.

I'm numb as I make my way to bed, fighting a dreamless sleep.

The next day, I'm re-stocking shelves at The Strande as if I never left. My co-workers ask how my vacation was and I say it was great spending time with Mom, doing our nails and watching K-dramas, like we originally planned.

I meet my parents for dinner at an omakase restaurant that is one of the more recent fronts added to our properties in the city. While it functions as a specialty chef's choice restaurant, in the back, they cook and deliver food for the young girls who are kept in our luxury apartment buildings, waiting to be auctioned off to the wealthy men on our roster.

I try not to think about it while I'm eating some of the freshest sashimi in town.

"You weren't annoyed with us by being out there on your own?" Mom asks before taking a sip of her green tea.

"Your mom doesn't want you resenting her for not being there with you, but doesn't know how to ask." Dad clarifies, enjoying his miso soup.

"I'm fine, Mom, really. I had a good time. Lots of resting, lots of episodes of Crash Landing Onto You."

"Oh, that's one of my favorites." Mom smiles, pleased I'm not upset.

I think about asking them to let Cage go and the approach I would use.

Would appealing to their empathy work? If I asked them to release Cage from his contract because they should care about his well-being, would they consider my plea?

Of course that's not going to work. Why would they care about him over any other goon? I don't think they care about any of them at all.

What if I asked them to release him because I wanted to be with him? They would take my happiness into consideration...

But they'd never approve of me dating someone they consider so beneath me. That would never work.

I should just tell them he died so he can run away and be free forever.

No matter what angle I think of to approach my parents, I can hear their voices in my head shooting all of them down.

So I sit and listen to them apologize again and again, swearing they'll make it up to me, and we plan a trip to Paris that will undoubtedly end up with Mom and I shopping and Dad having to stay behind to work, as always.

I head home, sleep, wake up, go to work, head home, sleep, wake up, go to work. This routine continues for the next week and a half and still, my mind can think of nothing but Cage.

I miss his smell, his strength, and his warmth, in the way he holds me, but also in the way his attention seems to comfort and envelop my senses. The world melted away when I was with him, and now, the world doesn't seem to be enough without him.

I'm reminded of the last time a man plagued my mind. Back in graduate school, Alfonso Martinez bought me a bottle of pink moscato for my birthday after I mentioned it once in passing while we were chatting before class began. We dated for 7 months after that before my family found out and, of course, I had to call it off.

Now, having had just a taste of what my days could look like with Cage by my side, I'm hooked on the fantasy... and I hate it. I hate how inaccessible he is to me, and what I hate more is that he was right about the whole thing.

I haven't seen him once since we got back to our lives, and the pang in my heart from not being able to reach out to him is overwhelming.

While rearranging the 'G's" in the fiction section at work and trying to distract myself from making a drastic move, like bursting into the compound and demanding to see Cage, a tall, clean-cut Asian man in a tailored, powder blue suit enters the alcove, searching the shelves.

"Can I help you find something?" I offer, intrigued by what this possible finance bro could be looking for in the Fiction section.

"Can you point me to where Neil Gaiman might be? I can't seem to find..." He trails off, intently looking at the book spines.

"Ah, you can't find him because I'm standing in front of where you need to be." I smile, standing aside to allow him to look at the books I was shelving. "He's one of my favorites. You have great taste." I almost wink at him.

He smiles shyly, his eyes falling to his shoes as he kicks his embarrassment away. If I'm not mistaken, he's hiding blushing cheeks under his downturned gaze.

"I read American Gods after watching the series and now I'm hooked." He says, scooting closer to look at the moderate stock we have. He has a professional haircut with a smooth side part in his straight, dark, ink-black hair.

"Oh, then have you read Good Omens? It's probably one of his best and most popular. He wrote it with a good friend of his, Terry Pratchett, and they are a hilarious duo. It's about an angel and a demon and their friendship surrounding the arrival of the antichrist."

The store happens to have both copies that feature the angel with the black cover and the demon with the white cover. I grab the black cover.

"You strike me as an angelic guy, so you might like Aziraphale." He takes the book from me, interested.

"I dunno, I can be pretty dark, sometimes." He says, introspectively.

"Don't we all?" I agree.

"I'm Peter, by the way." He holds out his hand and I shake it, happily.

"Peter...?" I probe, hoping to see if my hunch is correct.

"Lee." He says.

"Li like the Chinese Li with an "I", Korean Lee or Vietnamese Le?"

"Korean." He smiles.

"I'm Claire."

"Nice to meet you, Claire. Thanks for the recommendation. I feel like I have the inside scoop here at The Strande."

"No problem. If you ever need any more recommendations, I'm here." I beam.

He shoots back a smile of his own and turns to leave. I go back to the shelves but before a few seconds even pass, Peter rushes back.

"Claire?" He says, boldly.

"Yes?"

"Sorry if this is too forward, but would you be interested in going out on a date sometime? I'd like to know what you have to say about these books."

At the prospect of going out with someone else, flashes of Cage run through my mind. Every moment we shared pops into my thoughts, and it's painful.

I want to be rid of them.

"Yes. I'd like that very much." I say, flattered.

Peter smiles, we exchange numbers, and he's off to the register, leaving me to look at the smiley face he just texted.

After my shift, I call Jenny on my way home to tell her about the encounter after I thoroughly stalked his Insta profile.

"He kinda looks like if Jay Park was a bit older and worked at a bank." I say, unlocking my door.

"So he's a finance bro?" Jenny asks while she's checking out at Sefora.

"That is exactly what my immediate first impression was, but then he asked me about Neil Gaiman." I say, walking through my front door and taking off my shoes. I head to my sink to get a glass of water. "If he was soulless, I wouldn't think he'd connect with such an interesting, deep author, you know?"

"Totally." Jenny says before I can hear her telling the clerk thank you. "So when are you going out?"

I look at my phone and pull up his text. "He's asking if we can get dinner this Saturday."

"Oooo you should take him to Tsunami and see what Takashi has to say about him." Jenny offers, snickering.

I roll my eyes at Jenny's suggestion to take Peter to our favorite sushi place. The owner is around 70 years old and although he's very joyful, he's always asking us why we don't have boyfriends.

"Takashi will just scoff and say Peter is too thin. That old man needs another hobby other than commenting on our dating lives."

"Non-existent dating life." Jenny says with a heavy heart.

"No luck on the dating apps since I've been gone?" I ask as I sit on my plush white couch.

I can hear Jenny heave a sigh. "It's brutal, Claire. Most of these guys are just fuckboys who aren't interested in anything serious. And some of them are almost 50!"

"Bleh. Men." I gag.

"The worst." Jenny agrees.

"Hey, maybe we can go out to karaoke at Jim's this Friday and we'll scope out a nice guy for you!"

"Nice guys don't hang out at bars, Claire." Jenny laughs.

"I don't know about that. We hang out at bars and we're plenty nice."

"Well, that's debatable, and besides, I don't know if the kind of guy I'm looking for would even hang out at a bar."

"What *exactly* are you looking for? Give me the details. Maybe if we put it out into the universe, we'll manifest him!"

"You know me, a guy who's...impressive. Who works hard and wants to help people. Someone who's driven in his profession but is tender and kind when he's at home. Someone who's artistic, like me, but well-established in his field."

"So... like, a trumpet player with the New York Symphony who's also a baby hand surgeon?" I offer, trying to see if I'm picturing the same person Jenny is describing.

She laughs. "Yeah, someone like that."

"Okay." I nod, the wheels in my head turning. "That's a good place to start. We can go where musicians and baby hand surgeons hang out. Do we know anyone who can point us in the right direction? Do any of your model friends know anybody?"

"I don't know Claire, but I have to catch my train. I'll call you when I get home?"

"Sounds good. Are we still on for karaoke this Friday?" I ask quickly.

"I'll meet you at Jim's at 9:00." Jenny says in a rush.

"Okay bye, love you."

"Love you!" Jenny gives me kisses into the phone before hanging up.

Friday eventually rolls around, and although I'm having a fun time texting Peter about our favorite books and movies throughout the week and I'm excited to go out with Jenny tonight, I'm still fighting the thoughts of Cage that creep into my mind whenever I have a free moment to myself.

I drown out the memory of his smell, his strength and his eyes by taking a few shots of whiskey in my bathroom while I'm doing my hair and makeup.

Getting ready to go out has always been more enjoyable to me than actually going out, so I take my time curling my thick hair, which always takes much longer than I plan. I have fun with my makeup, using a sparkly, red eyeshadow that compliments my maroon, spaghetti-strap dress.

I check my phone for the time and it's almost 9:00 p.m.

"Shit." I'm late.

I slip on some sparkly red heels and head out the door.

Thoughts of Cage circle my mind the whole walk to the subway, the whole ride, and the entire walk to the bar. I'm annoyed with myself for allowing images and memories of him to fill me, so when I arrive, I ask Lisa behind the bar to get me two shots of tequila. I down one right after the other to hopefully chase Cage away.

I wince at the burn, but I'm grateful for the way the warmth travels down my throat.

How was I supposed to see Peter tomorrow if all I can think about is Cage?

I ask for a lemon drop shot, and down that in one go before Jenny meets me at the bar.

"Geez, slow down! How many have you had already?" She jokes, a little wide eyed at the state of me. I'm clearly further along in my night than Jenny expected, but I feel light and amazing, and the noise of Cage in my mind is quieted by the alcohol in my system.

"Jenny!" I scream, louder than necessary. "You beautiful thing, have a shot with me!"

"You're already drunk?" She laughs, surprised. "We haven't even started yet."

"Lisa! Get this girl a Moscow Mule!" I shout, a little sloppier than I'd like.

Jenny centers me, both hands on my shoulders. "Whoa, Claire, let's get you some water first." She says, gathering my purse and coat from the bar and pointing me to our favorite booth near the karaoke stage.

I hear Jenny call across the room to the bar. "Get her some water and I'll have a glass of Pinot, please, Lisa."

"Wine? We're supposed to be partying, not at book club." I slur, accusatory and a little offended she isn't sharing my same wreckless mood.

"I have an early shoot in Chelsea tomorrow, I gotta take it easy." Jenny explains, slipping off her coat to reveal a simple, black, long sleeve body-con dress that goes down to her calves. "Plus, we haven't met for book club since you got mad at the last book I chose."

"She died at the end!" I scoffed, disgusted. "What kind of romance book kills off the main character?" I shake my head, but Jenny doesn't dignify my bitterness with a response. "What are you doing working on a Saturday, anyway?" I continue.

"It's a favor for a photographer friend. She's working on a concept about the juxtaposition of starving artists living in one of the wealthiest cities in the world. I'm pretty sure we're shooting in a dumpster in an alley, but she's got a great eye, so it'll be worth it."

Even in my drunken haze, I can tell it's going to be amazing. "Send me the raw images when you get them. I *have* to see them."

Jenny nods. "You can see me with trash on my head."

I laugh, reaching up to gently caress her face. "The most gorgeous trash I've ever seen."

Jenny takes my hand off her cheek, but doesn't let go. She cradles it in her warm, delicate grasp and her face softens. "What's wrong?"

I shake my head messily, my curls falling in front of my face. "Does anything have to be wrong for me to enjoy a few drinks on a weekend?" I'm defensive, but I don't pull away.

"I haven't seen you this way since Alfonso broke up with you to date that violinist."

Oh yeah, I forgot about that lie I told Jenny years ago to cover up my parent's overbearing lifestyle. It turned out Alfonso really did date a violinist after me, I just told Jenny *he* broke up with *me* to explain why I was crying for weeks.

"He ended up marrying that violinist, you know. I remember seeing the pictures on Insta. They looked beautiful." I say, a little forlorn at the memory, but happy he found someone.

I look at Jenny's bright, concerned face. Her patience and openness, and the ever-flowing understanding we have between each other makes it impossible for me to hide my heartbreak any longer.

I start to cry silent tears so I don't attract attention. I hide my face in our clasped hands.

"Hey, it's okay." Jenny soothes, rubbing my back. "This is about that guy you met at the bookstore? I thought you weren't going out with him until tomorrow?"

Leave it to Jenny to know exactly what ails me. I can take on the entire world, whether it's professionally, or my workout goals, or cooking, but nothing truly bothers me and gets under my skin more than *men*.

I shake my head. "Someone else…" I whisper, almost unable to admit it.

"Who? You haven't mentioned anyone else to me?"

"I met him while I was…away." I struggle, trying to figure out how I can explain without revealing the parts I don't want her to know.

"When you went on vacation with your parents?"

I nod. "They introduced me to him." Which technically, was not a lie.

"And he wasn't tripping over himself from how stunning and awesome you are?"

"That's the thing…" I say, finally looking up at her. "He did." I nearly whine, desperate for her to know how much Cage has overtaken my life. I feel pathetic and nothing like the controlled boss-bitch Jenny knows me to be.

"Okay! Great! So, what's the deal? Has he been ghosting you?" Jenny is in her problem-solving mode, and she got shit done when she was like this.

"Not exactly…" I sniffle.

Jenny gets up to grab a few napkins and hands me the stack.

I blow my nose before continuing. "I can't see him right now. He's…away, and I don't have his number."

"You didn't get his number? That doesn't sound like you."

"Well...he's a bit older. I don't think he took me very seriously."

"How much older?"

I shrug. "Maybe like, 45 or 50? I didn't ask. But he's *hot,* Jenny. The hottest man I've ever seen."

Her eyebrows raise, impressed. "He's gotta be, if he's pulling those kinds of statements from you. You are not generous with compliments about men."

I grab her arm, relieved to have someone who understands me so well. "I. Know."

"What does he look like?"

"You know the actor who plays the dad in Doon? That SciFi movie we didn't like?"

Jenny's jaw drops while she nods, understanding. "You do have a thing for men with dark hair."

I swoon into her arms, and she catches me. "Oh my god, Jenny, this man looks *just* like him, just without the beard. Ugh, but he would look *so* good with one. He has the most incredible eyes, and his face is just..." *Delicious* is what I want to say. "He's such a protector, he makes me feel so safe, and his smile?" I sigh, leaning back to look her in the face. "I might have a crush." I admit sheepishly, almost guiltily, feeling like a little kid caught with her hand in a cookie jar.

"I don't think you have a crush." Jenny says.

I'm taken aback by her words, but a bit relieved. Maybe she's right. Maybe she can talk some sense into me and advise me to finally be free of Cage, forever.

"I think you're in love."

"What?! No!" I guffaw, dismissing her words. "I've only known him a few days!"

"Claire, you *hate* beards. And you've *never* been this generous when talking about any of the men from your past."

I mull over her words. "That's because none of them impressed me the way this one has."

"Exactly." Jenny points at me. "You've never been impressed by *anyone*, to the point of getting this drunk and *bothered.*"

"I'm not...bothered." I blurt out. My own ears don't believe me.

"You are."

"I'm not. I'm getting another drink." I stumble from our table and head to the bar.

"Fine, I'll put in our songs." Jenny calls over to me and heads to the DJ whose name is JD, funnily enough, to request "Cry Me A River" for her, and "Man, I Feel Like A Woman" for me.

I take both of my whiskey shots at the bar before grabbing Jenny's next glass of wine and bringing it to the table, even though she hasn't finished her first.

"You need to catch up to me." I accuse, feeling irrationally irritated that she is intentionally trying to make me think of things I want to avoid.

"How many have you had?"

I shrug. "5 or 6 shots? I can't remember."

"Claire! One glass of wine is enough to knock you out for the rest of the night, and you're out here throwing back all those shots? Don't you think you should stop?"

I shake my head as I'm sipping on her new glass of wine. "I think I need to sing."

I'm lost in the music, singing my heart out, and stumbling on the stage. The crowd loves me. They're hooting and hollering, and I'm halfway through my song when a bachelorette party comes laughing through the door.

I beckon them onto the stage and they all join me, helping me finish the song. A bridesmaid wraps a hot pink feather boa around my neck afterwards and invites me over to their table for celebratory shots.

"Alright, I'll have one, but you have to cheer for my friend Jenny, she's up next!" I clap for her as she walks up and grabs the mic. The other women shout, hoop and holler for her, too.

Jenny feels awkward from all the ruckus but waves back to us. She dazzles with her sultry rendition of the classic jazz ballad, and takes a deep bow when it's over.

The place erupts with applause, and she meets me back at our table with a bright smile.

"That was fun!" Jenny laughs.

"They love you, dahling." I say in her ear, but am unable to raise my head, so I lean on her shoulder.

"Hey, you good?" She asks, worried.

I nod. "I'm just so sleepy. I need a second…" I close my eyes, the darkness a welcome relief to my overstimulated senses.

I feel my body relax, and I feel safe here with Jenny. My limbs feel light and airy, like I'm floating away.

"Claire?" I hear Jenny's voice, but she sounds so far away. I want to tell her I'm fine, but nothing comes out.

"Oh my god, Claire!" She sounds even further away now, but I can't open my eyes to see her.

"I'm calling your dad!" I hear her say frantically.

No. I try to say. *Don't do that.*

She must have unlocked my phone with my thumb, because I can hear her through the bachelorette party gathering around me, asking if I'm okay, if I need anything, and if there was something wrong with me.

"Mister Nguyen? This is Jenny, I'm Claire's friend? She's not okay, and we're out at a bar. I think she's had too much to drink...I don't know what to do..."

Stop, Jenny. Don't talk to them. I want to say, but I drift away, deep into the darkness, and I can't fight it anymore, so I give in, letting it surround me.

Chapter Six

I wake up smelling the vinyl from the bar booth pressed against my cheek. Jenny must have laid me down.

I try to sit up, dizzy, lightheaded, and drunk beyond belief. Lisa has stepped out from behind the bar and is kneeling next to me, helping me up.

"She's awake!" Lisa calls over her shoulder, shoving a glass of water into my hands. "Do you need an ambulance, honey?"

A deep, rich voice answers behind her.

"She's good."

And then Cage is there.

Lisa's face is replaced with his in my blurry vision, but when I focus, I can see Cage is kneeling in front of me, both hands cradling my face, his palms warming my cheeks.

"What happened?" He asks me, voice rumbling and low.

"Cage..." I whisper, touching his cheek, where a short beard has grown. He looks good. *Really* good. "You're here."

"I'm here, beautiful." He gently removes my hand from his face, his fingers checking my pulse, first on my neck, then my wrists. "What happened?"

Jenny's small voice chimes in. "She drank a lot, had a ton of shots, which isn't like her at all."

"It's not." I hear Cage agree with her.

How would he know?

"I'll take her home, get her to a doctor." Cage says.

"I don'tneeda doctor." I try to sound defiant, but I can't stand up and my arms feel weak, so they just flail at my sides.

"My colleague will drive you home, Jenny." Cage orders, standing to face her. "Thank you for calling us. It's nice to meet you." I watch Cage offer his hand to her as the bar spins around me. She shakes his hand with deliberate strength.

"You must be the guy she's so...concerned about."

That catches him off guard. "Am I?"

Jenny doesn't give anything more away. I breathe a sigh at her discretion. She's always adhered to the girl code, and I'm glad to see her not break it now.

She leans down to give me a quick kiss on the cheek. "Text me the moment you feel better. Promise?"

"Promise." I respond weakly. "Love you."

"Love you."

Jenny leaves with another driver, one of Dad's men, and I'm left with Cage.

"Can you stand up?" He asks, concerned.

I shake my head, too disoriented to know which way is up, let alone how to stand there.

His sturdy arms slip beneath me, one arm under my knees, the other around my shoulders, and he's carrying me through the bar, towards the door.

I hear the bachelorette party squeal and swoon with "oh my god" and "what a hunk" and "lucky woman" and a few "take good care of her!"

"I will." Cage grumbles, a hint of possessiveness in his voice. With my head so near his chest, I can hear it vibrate beneath me. I bury my face into his neck and inhale his intoxicating and familiar scent.

He lifts me into the back seat easily. "You sure you don't need to go to the hospital?" He asks me gently, moving my hair out of my face to get a better look.

I shake my head slowly. "Ineedagohome."

"Okay." Cage closes the door softly, climbs in the driver seat and drives me back to the penthouse.

When we arrive, we're buzzed in from the garage, where Cage has parked the SUV in the designated spot for the penthouse, which usually sits empty since I don't have a car.

He carries me to the elevator and holds me the entire time, only putting me down when we get to my bed. Cage tenderly takes off my heels, tucks me in, and heads to the kitchen for some water and medication.

I bury under the covers, but can't seem to get comfortable. The sparkly fabric of my dress is itchy, so I awkwardly wrestle it off while I'm still laying down and toss it to the floor. I'm naked, except my panties. I use my duvet as the only cover I have to keep me decent before Cage comes back.

When he does return, pills and water in hand, he stops dead in his tracks, frozen by the door.

I'm sitting up now, holding the duvet to my chest to cover me, but my shoulders are exposed.

Cage walks over to my bedside table, practically prowling, and sets everything down before kneeling next to me. I sit up and face him, my legs opening to invite him closer.

He shifts forward, ever so slightly, bringing his pelvis closer to mine.

"How are you doing?" Cage asks, his voice tender.

I smile, happy to have him so close again "Good. I've never been black-out drunk before, I think it was just a shock to my system." I slur, knowing I'm barely coherent.

He grunts, but doesn't answer. Cage gently takes my face in his hands again, searching my eyes for any other signs I might be worse than I seem.

"It could be alcohol poisoning." He suggests, and I can't look away from his face. His eyes are laser focused on me, and he's so heartbreakingly handsome, I'm overwhelmed by his attention.

"You look good." I say, unable to finesse my words the way I want to. "And it's not alcohol poisoning. Wouldn't I be throwing up all over the place?"

"Symptoms can be different for everyone." He offers, unhelpfully.

I don't respond. I just take in the way the dim light of my bedroom reflects off his shiny, curly dark hair.

"Thank you. For getting me. You're on the list of saviors." I say. The chilly night air prickles my skin, and I shiver, even with Cage's furnace-of-a body in front of me.

He chuckles. "What do you mean?" He asks while he moves to lay me back down, propping my head on the pillows and tucking the duvet around me. He sits on the bed next to me, making sure I'm settled.

"My parents were always too busy to take care of me, ever since I was little. So whenever I was sick in school, or needed to go home, a nanny or babysitter or henchman would have to come fetch me from school, or after school practice, or whatever."

"That must have been lonely for you." He says quietly, unable to resist gently moving my hair from my face.

I nod. "But this time, I'm glad to see you." I smile, grabbing his hand and kissing the inside of his palm. The alcohol has taken all of my inhibitions away and I don't care if he knows I want him, or miss him, or have thought of him in every waking moment of my life since we separated.

"Claire..." He whispers, closing his eyes and enjoying the feeling of my lips in his palm. "Cameras." Is all he says, and it's all I need to know to explain why he isn't giving me more.

"There aren't any cameras in here." I whisper, watching his face to see if he's close to releasing some of his restraint.

He isn't. He pulls back, moving from the bed to kneeling on the floor beside me again.

He grabs my hand and moves it between our bodies, kisses it quickly, out of sight from any of the surveillance in the penthouse, before releasing me.

"We installed more cameras just after you got back." Cage's voice rumbles, low in his chest. "For your protection. In case anything happens."

"I said I didn't want to be watched." I knew about the cameras in the front entryway, kitchen and living room, but I distinctly said I didn't want to be seen in the bathroom or bedroom.

"You'll have to talk to upper management about that, I'm afraid." Cage jokes, but caresses my cheek gently. "It's good to see you." He admits.

"Good to see you, too." I smile, feeling more sober by the minute. "Can I have your number?"

Cage shakes his head. "They track my phone. They see and hear everything I do."

I reach past him to the drawer of my bedside table. "Take this one." I say, giving him an old phone that still manages to power up. "I bought it for Jenny when she studied abroad in Greece for a semester. The SIM card is still active." I plug in the charger and make sure some juice is getting to the phone before setting it on my table. "Take it with you before you leave. So I can text you."

His gentle huff is appreciative.

"Oh, but maybe change my name in the contact list." I yawn, feeling myself fall asleep again. "You can call me 'the sexiest woman I know' or 'karaoke queen' or 'Iron Chef,'" whatever you feel is right."

"Okay." Cage chuckles and picks up the phone, sitting beside me on the bed again and angling himself awkwardly, probably to try and cover up what he's doing from the camera's he undoubtedly knows very well, since he's the one watching them.

Does that mean he's been watching me this whole time?

He puts the phone down just before his work phone buzzes.

"It's your mom. I'll tell her you're okay."

I nod, shooing him away with my hand, fighting the pull of sleep to spend as much time with him as I can.

I can hear his low voice from the other room. I check his new phone and search my number to see what he updated my contact with, and I catch my breath.

Mi Corazón.

My Heart.

I practically toss the phone onto the bedside table when Cage returns.

"You should probably change the passcode on it, too." I slur, more embarrassed than I should be.

He looks at me suspiciously but does what he's told, tapping on the phone for a while before finishing and placing it back down to continue charging.

"What did Mom say?" I ask, snuggling further into bed, finally warming up.

Cage sits beside me again. "Just wondering how you're doing. I told her you just had too much to drink and your friend panicked, that's why she called us. It wasn't because you were in bad shape."

I nod. "Thanks. For how much they care and love me, sometimes they still don't have the time to show up, you know? Not that they should be taking care of me, anyway. I'm a grown woman."

"Everyone deserves to be taken care of, once in a while." Cage says, tenderly.

I smile at him. "I'd love to take care of you." I wink.

"I wish." Cage huffs a laugh.

I yawn, unable to stop myself. "I wish you'd stay here the rest of the night."

"I would, but they need me back at the compound." He says, tucking my hair behind my ear.

I nod, sleepily. "Make sure to take the charger with you."

"I will." He says softly.

I love hearing his voice. I'm sad to hear it go.

"Good night." I whisper.

"Good night, Claire." Cage rumbles, slowly.

I love you. Is the last thing my mind conjures before I fall into a peaceful sleep.

Chapter Seven

When I wake up, it takes me a few moments to remember the events of last night.

My head is pounding from all the alcohol, and I'm grateful to find a glass of water on my nightstand, along with some painkillers.

I toss back a few pills to tackle my headache and chug the water before remembering it was Cage who brought it to me. I look to find the old phone and the charger are gone, so he definitely took them with him.

My phone buzzes with text notifications. I open the app and find I have three unread messages, one from Mom, one from Jenny and one from Jenny Greece.

Which is Cage.

I'm filled with joy, and I open Cage's text to find a simple message.

Let me know when you're awake.
Jenny Greece

I ponder what to change his contact name to, opting for "Pussy Tamer" and immediately delete it, but not before cackling to myself. I settle on "Hot

Stuff" thinking I can always update it later, unable to come up with anything that will keep him anonymous to anyone who might see his messages.

I check myself in my phone's front camera, fluffing my hair so I look effortlessly disheveled. I snap a quick selfie, trying to look sexy and barely covering my breasts with my duvet.

I send him the picture, praying I look as enticing as I feel.

> Hungover as hell but surviving.
> Me

Jesus.
Hot Stuff

> You don't like? :(
> Me

Like it too much. You gotta
warn a man before dropping a
bombshell pic like that.
Almost choked on my coffee.
Hot Stuff

> I can think of something
> I'd like to choke on. ;)
> Me

Jesus, Claire!
Hot Stuff

I laugh, kicking my feet up like a teenage girl. This interaction throws me back to my younger days, and I'm happy to relive them. I hope I make him feel as excited as I do.

I'm mindlessly scrolling social media when Cage's next message buzzes.

You'd look beautiful on your knees.
Hot Stuff

My jaw drops. Warmth begins to unfurl between my legs, and I'm excited to see what he'll text next. But he's being careful, as always, and I get to ask him about it now.

> Are you being vague on purpose to keep the paper trail as clean as possible?
> Me

Yes.
Hot Stuff

> Then this will be a lot of me flirting and you agreeing with how hot I am?
> Me

Okay.
Hot Stuff

> I miss you. Think about you all the time. <3
> Me

Miss you, too.
Hot Stuff

    Honestly, this new arrangement is more than I can ask for, considering I had no way of contacting him before.

    His responses will be dry and unexciting, so I'll have to find a way to get him alone again so he can let down his guard, and we can talk about how we left things after the fight at the cabin.

> **We should talk.**
> **Me**

    When he doesn't respond after a while, I take the time to knock out any tasks I need to complete this morning.

    I quickly call Jenny to tell her I'm fine, I just need to rest and I'll be right as rain to head back to work on Monday.

    I call Mom with updates on how I'm feeling, and also demand she tell Dad to remove the cameras in the bedroom and bathroom of this place, as it's a violation of privacy.

A message from Cage buzzes my phone during the call.

> Going to a meeting.
> will call you next time
> I'm alone.
> Hot Stuff

My parents settle on increasing the security system with motion sensors and installing more responsive panic buttons being throughout the penthouse that I can push if I need help, in exchange for removing the cameras and microphones, to which I agree.

Mom tells me both she and Dad are in Vietnam right now and don't have any of their goons to spare, so they'll send the head of security later this afternoon to remove the cameras.

"It'll be Cage. Sorry you have to see him so often, *con*, but he should be quick. In and out." Dad says.

I swallow my squeal of delight. "Fine." I feign annoyance. "But he better not linger." I try to hide my smile.

"He won't." Mom says. We exchange our goodbyes and I hang up.

A few heartbeats pass before Cage texts me again.

See you soon. <3
Hot Stuff

 I really do squeal this time, laughing at his use of a heart. It doesn't seem his style to use emojis, but the effort is adorable and I appreciate his attempt at affection through text.
 I'm ecstatic, bolting from bed to hop into the shower before brushing my teeth and making myself decent before he arrives.
 I'm hungry, so I order enough Peruvian chicken and rice for two people from an amazing place around the corner, and it's delivered by the time I'm dressed in a cream silk slip dress with a matching robe.
 The small aluminum trays go in the oven to keep warm before I go back to the bathroom, putting on just enough makeup to make me feel confident.
 The camera doorbell rings throughout the penthouse, and I have to keep myself from sprinting to answer.
 I open the door to a vision in black.
 Cage looks refreshed, with his hair slicked back into neat, dark waves with highlights of gray around his temples. He hasn't shaved, opting to keep the

beard growing, with a neat trim around the perimeter of his cheeks and neck to keep him looking sharp.

He's wearing his signature uniform, a black dress shirt under a black suit jacket with black dress pants. He's holding a briefcase in one hand and a black bag I assume holds tools in the other.

"Hi." I breathe, unable to stifle my smile at the sight of him.

"Hello, Miss Claire. May I come in?"

I swallow a laugh. "Yes, Cage, you may, but don't take too long. I have a busy day." I wink, and step aside to let him in.

"You look like you're feeling better." He says, keeping the conversation neutral for the cameras, but still showing his concern for me in his warm tone.

"I was taken care of very well last night." I smile up at him, watching him take off his shoes by the door. I bend down to pick them up and put them away in the closet.

As I rise to stand, Cage bends down to whisper in my ear. "Not as well as I wanted to."

I can only bite my lip and look at him wide eyed, glowing from his playfulness.

"Work your magic, sir."

It's Cage's turn to wink at me before heading to the corner between the bed and the bathroom. He pulls off a panel from the wall and begins working with the wires behind it.

"Did you install these, too?"

He nods, unplugging a small camera and a connecting microphone.

"While you were at work."

I see. "So they meant for me not to know about it?"

"I believe so, yes, Miss." Cage says, moving to the wall on the other side of the bed and removing a panel from the wall there, repeating his quick disconnection.

Hmm. I'll have to talk to dad about that.

Cage makes quick work of those cameras, rolling up the wires and packing them away in his briefcase.

I watch him kneeling down, keeping the case organized, and then quickly connecting motion sensors around the perimeter of the entire place, along with panic buttons discreetly hidden in plain sight.

"Push these and we'll be here in no time." Cage says.

I nod, impressed by how quickly he finishes the job.

When he's packed everything away, Cage slowly walks towards me with his hands in his pockets. I strain my neck to look up at him, and he reaches out to grab one of my hands. Cage slowly pulls my knuckles up to his lips, but stops.

"May I?" He whispers.

I can only nod, holding my breath.

Cage gives the top of my hand a single, gentle kiss.

"This is bold, even for you." I whisper, wondering what has allowed him to slip his composure, even just the slightest bit.

He smiles. "Well..." He pulls my hand up to curl around the back of his neck. My other hand joins happily, and I'm comfortably holding on to his large, sturdy frame. "Cameras are gone, I'm not there to watch them, and the other guys are busy keeping an eye on your parents, so..."

I nod, my smile beaming, understanding that we're both free from the ever-watching eyes, at least for a while.

"Can you kiss me for real, then?"

Cage chuckles. "Yes, ma'am."

He takes his time, reaching down to gently lift my chin before hovering just the tiniest bit, enough to drive me mad. Finally, after what feels like an eternity, his lips are on mine.

Cage is slow, chaste, and warm. He takes his time, giving me soft, gentle pecks. Long, closed-mouthed, savoring kisses take over my senses, and it's simultaneously overwhelming and somehow, not enough.

Just a taste of him makes me hungry for more. I test the waters, slipping my tongue out to caress his lips, and instantly, he meets me with his own, deepening the kiss and devouring me.

Cage reaches behind my thighs and picks me up effortlessly, wrapping my legs around his back. I yelp from the sudden lift, but he gives me no time to react before his mouth is on mine again. He's hot, wet and *delicious*, a word that always comes to mind when I think of him.

He walks us over to my white dresser and gently places me down so I'm sitting, my legs still wrapped around him, and his hands are free to roam.

Cage circles my waist, caressing the softness of my hips and then down to my thighs. His grunt of approval of my body in his hands shoots straight to my pussy.

He breaks away only to trail kisses down my throat. I open to him freely, tingling at his attention.

Over the echoes of our breaths, my stomach commits the ultimate betrayal and rumbles so loudly, it stops us in our tracks.

Cage only chuckles. "Should we get you something to eat?" He pulls back, cradling my face in his hands. "I'd better stop before I get carried away and you pass out from everything I want to do to you."

"That sounds amazing, actually." I huff.

He kisses me again once more, quickly. "I'd feel better if you ate something first, considering what happened last night."

I sigh. "Oh, alright. I happened to have already ordered some chicken and rice before you got here." Cage helps me down from the dresser, but not before righting my clothes to cover my assets so I'm decent for the kitchen. "You hungry? Will you eat with me?" I ask.

Cage kisses my forehead, and the act is so sweet, I feel myself melting inside.

"I'd love to." He says.

I lead him to the kitchen and he sits on one of the stools under the island opposite the sink, watching me take out the small trays of chicken and rice to plate up. He takes his jacket off and tosses it on the back of the couch, the move so casual, I can see him doing it every night if he were to come home to me after work. I'd feed him a home cooked dinner, and we'd make slow, sweet love before falling asleep in each other's arms.

I shake the thought from my head before pulling out a stool next to him and we sit and eat, the mundane task filling me with brimming happiness.

Cage rubs my knee and thigh between bites, and he's so affectionate, it's enough to make me almost forget what has been looming in my mind this whole time we've been apart.

He looks me dead in the eyes. "I gotta apologize for saying what I said, when we were last together."

"At the cabin?" I clarify, making sure we're on the same page.

He nods. "I was outta line. Regretted it the moment I said it." He shakes his head, as if to shake the shame from his mind. "I've been looking for the right time to talk to you about it. It's all I've been thinking about."

I chase down my mouthful of seasoned rice with a few gulps of sparkling water from the can I just opened.

"I've been thinking about you, too. Only you, actually, which has been driving me insane." I laugh away the embarrassment that should be radiating from me with that kind of confession, but I'm feeling calm and comfortable. "I accept your apology." I continue, taking another quick bite of perfectly seasoned chicken thigh. "This is difficult, the situation we find ourselves in, but I think with enough maturity and communication, we can make it work. Starting with our first date."

I expect Cage to hit me with the usual 'they'd never let us' and 'what about your dad?' and 'I can't' but he says "What do you have in mind?"

I don't anticipate him being on board right away. I'm elated.

"Well, I need to have a conversation with Dad first, about a few things actually, but I thought we could get pizza, and then maybe ice cream for dessert?"

Cage nods, his eyebrows raising. "I'm impressed, Miss Nguyễn. I was expecting a fine-dining restaurant with snails and trendy, bland, circular croissants."

I laugh, throwing my head back. "Please! I take food very seriously, no matter how much it costs or how popular it is." I take another bite of chicken. "Besides, the best food in this town is not extravagant or expensive. Like the dumplings and baked buns in Chinatown?" I bring my hand to my lips and give an exaggerated chef's kiss.

Cage smiles, chuckling at his plate. "Alright. I'll leave it to you to make the big moves. Until then, my hands are tied, you know that, right?"

"Of course." I nod.

"I mean it." Cage points at me, serious. "I need you to know, I would plan the best date for you, one full of good food and dessert and karaoke. A night you'd love. If I could."

I rub his knee, reassuring. "I know."

"God, I'd be so good to you." Cage huffs, a little exasperated. "If only I...we..." He sighs.

My heart aches for him and the circumstances we find ourselves in. I stand to wiggle my way into his arms. He embraces me easily, as if the space between his thighs and arms were made perfectly for my body to rest in.

"How good would you be to me, Mister Cage, if that even is your real name?" I tease, snaking my arms behind his neck and resting comfortably there.

He chuckles, his mood lighter from my teasing. "It's not."

"It's not?!" I gasp, pulling back. "Are you serious?"

Cage only nods with a small, amused smile on his lips.

"What is it?" I demand, now feeling like an idiot for thinking and calling out a name that isn't even his when I'm alone at night.

He takes a deep breath. "My full name is Sebastián Ramón-Rodríguez Valenzuela. Your dad calls me Cage because he first found me locked in a...well, a cage, before he busted me out."

"You're kidding me!" I pull back, trying to read his face to find any teasing there, but only seeing a delighted earnest. "This whole time, I've been calling you something awful that isn't even your real name? Has it been reminding you of that horrid time in your life? This whole time?!"

"Hey, hey, hey..." Cage, no, *Sebastián*, soothes, trying to calm me down. "You can call me anything you want, *hermosa*." His small laugh puffed his breath against my lips as his nose nuzzled mine in a gentle eskimo kiss. "I really didn't mind. You can call me 'Lover', 'Servant Man' or 'Hey You' for all I care."

I frown, still unhappy about this new information. "Why were you locked in a cage?"

I'm expecting a heartbreaking, long story, but he just shrugs. "Some folks got to me before your dad did."

I nod, understanding. "Probably that asshole's henchmen?" I ask, knowing some of our wealthier clients have teams of their own to do their bidding.

"We call them 'employees' but yeah." He teases, trying to bring up the mood.

My heart aches for the man sitting in front of me. I'm sure the concern is written all over my face, but I don't try to hide it. I trace the subtle lines on his cheeks, caressing his hair and wishing I could protect him from the pain in his past, and anything else that could be coming his way in the future.

I kiss him, hard. "I'm sorry. I should've known." I pull back to get a better look at his face. "Tell me more."

"About what?" He asks, warmly.

I melt in his arms. "About you." I nudge.

Sebastián shrugs. "There isn't much more to tell."

"When you're alone, with time off, what do you do to relax? How do you enjoy yourself?"

He takes a second to think. "Jerk off to the thought of your tits bouncing in my face?"

I playfully slap his arm. "I'm serious!"

He laughs before taking a few moments to think. "When I can, which isn't often, I'll pick up a book about self-defense, or security cameras. I've been in the middle of a biography of Marie Van Brittan Brown for the past few months. Haven't had much time to finish it."

I nod, impressed. "Who was she?"

"She invented and patented CCTV."

My jaw drops. "She sounds so cool. *You're* so cool." I snuggle closer. "Maybe you can get me into reading more non-fiction."

Sebastián playfully takes a handful of my ass in his hands. "And you can show me some of those romance books you read."

My eyes grow wide at the prospect of acting out countless sex scenes from my favorite books. "Sounds like a deal to me." I kiss him with a smile on my face. "So, can I call you Sebastián, now? Or maybe Seb?"

He growls, pulling me closer. "Call me whatever you want, just kiss me again."

He doesn't have to tell me twice. My mouth takes all it wants, kissing, sucking, nibbling and gently biting his plush lips.

"Seb..." I sigh into his mouth, ready to climb on top of him.

He sharply inhales through his teeth. "Say it again."

I smile. "Seb."

His hands reach around and grab my ass, squeezing my luscious cheeks.

"You're the only one who gets to call me that, understand?"

I nod. "Your family doesn't call you that?"

"Don't have a family." Seb breathes between kisses. "Orphan. Raised by nuns, actually."

My heart breaks a little more. "Oh my god, Seb, you're killing me."

"Don't feel bad for me, Claire. Just let me take you to bed."

"Okay." I say, and he's lifting me again, his hulking arms and frame holding my softness and curves easily.

Seb tosses me onto the bed, and I yelp with surprise and laughter. He doesn't waste a second being away from my body, following me down and hovering over me.

"God, I love seeing you like this." He says, kissing me again. I don't think I'll ever get tired of his lips on mine. "The image of you under me is burned into my brain. When I close my eyes, I see your face when you're coming, and it gets me so hard." Seb's hand comes down and cups my breast as he grinds into my pussy.

I moan, almost involuntarily, the sound flowing from my throat.

That pulls a groan from him. "Fuck, you're like music. I could listen to you all day." His hand travels down to the hem of my dress. "Let me make you come." Seb breathes, his urgency hot and wanting.

His words shoot straight to my core.

I nod, enthusiastically. "Yes, please." I sigh.

Seb's fingers are practiced and quick, slipping off my silk thong, tossing it across the room and coming back to stroke my core. He grunts in approval the moment his fingertips reach my folds.

"Already so wet?" He asks, impressed.

"I was wet the moment you walked through the door." I moan into his lips, planting sloppy kisses on his perfect mouth.

"Fuck, Claire." Seb breathes, slipping a finger inside me.

The fullness makes me gasp, his tender warmth surrounding me. He languidly strokes my walls, laying next to me, watching my face.

"Seb...?" I ask, breathless, reaching for his belt. I search his eyes in my request for permission to get into his pants. He doesn't stop me, too drunk on feeling me, listening to me.

I undo his belt, and when he still doesn't stop me, I make quick work of his button and fly, pulling down his boxers and freeing his cock.

I take him in my hand. He's huge, much bigger than I imagined, and I need both hands to stroke him.

He hisses when I start working his shaft. I'm clumsy, unable to grasp him properly from my angle, a little frustrated I can't see him in my hands.

Seb is still fingering me, bringing me closer to my orgasm, clouding my mind with pleasure.

"Oh my god, Seb, I'm close..." I moan.

He pumps into me faster. "That's it Claire, come for me. Let me see you." My walls begin to clench around him, bringing me closer to my orgasm. He adds another finger, filling me to the brink, pushing through the closing walls of my pussy. Seb sucks in a fast breath. "Fuck, *estoy loco por ti, te necesito.*"

I fall over the edge, the height of my pleasure washing over me when I hear his gruff words. I'm overcome, lost in my senses, unfazed by my inability to understand what he's saying.

"Fuck, yes, yes, yes!" I cry through gritted teeth, riding his hand to chase every ounce of pleasure I can. I look up to see his gorgeous eyes hooded with pleasure as he watches me, his jaw slack, mesmerized by my orgasm.

Somehow, he pumps into me even faster, the heel of his palm hitting my clit and before I can come down from my first orgasm, my second one is washing over me, and I'm drowning in my over-wired senses.

"Oh my god, Seb!" My entire body tenses. While lost in my pleasure, I somehow have the good sense to let go of his cock to save him from my uncontrolled grip. I'm writhing beneath him, grabbing onto fistfuls of my duvet and his shirt, anything to ground myself before I float away in my heady orgasm.

Seb growls in my ear. "I'd kill to feel your nails digging into my skin."

I breathe a shaky laugh as I'm coming down, my body slowly relaxing beneath him. I run my nails through his hair, scratching his scalp. He shivers beneath my hands, and I'm filled with a small sense of triumph from eliciting even the slightest response from him. I reach for his cock and find it still achingly hard.

Seb gently slips his fingers from me and rolls onto his back leisurely beside me, bringing his hand to his mouth and licking my wetness from his fingers.

He moans, and the sound makes my pussy flutter again. "You taste as good as I remember."

"Mmm." I smile, kneeling up next to his hip and finally getting a good look at his huge cock.

He's smooth and thick, beautifully straining with arousal, his head glistening with precum. Again, he looks delicious, and my mouth is watering at the thought of finally having my lips around him.

"It's only fair I get my turn, don't you think?" I ask, looking up at him. "Please, Seb." I beg, kissing the tip of his cock. "Let me taste you?"

He moans again, unable to stop himself. "I shouldn't, Claire..."

Shouldn't is a step up from *can't* so I think I can convince him. There's no way I'm letting today happen the way it did back at the cabin. I'm determined to make him feel good.

"Please, Seb…" I kiss his tip again, gently rubbing the ridge of his cock on my tongue. "I want you." I flatten my tongue and slowly lick the length of him, stopping at the head of his cock and circling his tip, getting him wet. "I want to feel you fill up my mouth. Mmm, it would be so good. I'm drooling just thinking about it." I trail kisses down his length, never breaking eye contact. His strained look, the fight he's battling between telling me no and giving into his pleasure is so heartbreaking, it makes me want to give him all I can. "Please?" My one final plea, and I'm prepared to let him go if he says no.

But his hand, the one that wasn't in my pussy a few moments ago, comes down to stroke my hair, then gently caresses my cheek. "You look beautiful down there." He says, breathless.

I smile, measuring his eyes as I bring my lips closer to his tip, and when he doesn't stop me, I finally wrap my lips around him, taking him little by little, to make sure if he wants me to stop, I will.

He doesn't stop me, thank God. I watch his head fall back, and a soft moan escapes him. "Claire…" He breathes, covering his eyes with his forearm.

I take that as a sign to continue. I wet the head of his cock, slowly and happily, before working my way down towards the middle of his shaft.

There's no way I can fit him entirely in my mouth, so I lick my hand and grab his base, stroking the part of him my mouth can't reach. I'm sucking as I'm taking him deeper, hitting the back of my throat.

Seb's fingers tangle into my hair and he pulls slightly, the gentle tension on my scalp washing me with pleasure.

"Fuck, that's good." He moans, gently bucking his hips up to match my rhythm.

"Mmm." I moan in delight, proud I can get him to let loose, for once.

I lick and suck while moving up and down his cock, and when he's nice and slick, I rotate my hands to bring another level of pleasure to him.

Seb hisses at the move, smiling down at me. "Mmm, that's my girl. Just like that."

I quicken my pace, my eyes getting a bit watery from being filled so fully, but I keep going, wanting to make him come in my mouth.

He brings his arm behind my back and reaches to run his fingers through my exposed pussy, and it feels so good, I moan on his length.

"You're dripping." Seb says, impressed. "You like having my cock in your mouth, don't you?" He teases, a bit surprised by my continued arousal in response to giving him a blowjob.

I release the head of his cock with a soft pop. "I love it." I say, breathless, a bit of drool rolling down my chin. "I love feeling you in my mouth."

Seb looks down at me, unbelieving. "Jesus, what did I do to deserve you?"

I can only smile before going back to sucking his tip, then moving my way back down again.

I feel Cage pick up my leg and move it over his head so I'm straddling his face. "I have to taste more of you." His arms come up over my hips to pull my pussy down, forcing my legs to spread wider so he's eating me out, his tongue and lips licking and lapping at my drenched folds.

It's overwhelming, and I'm overcome with pleasure so quickly. It's a little frustrating.

Being caught up in my own enjoyment takes away my concentration for the task at hand, so I push his cock deeper in my throat and bob my head, doubling down on my work.

His hips are bucking up to meet my mouth, and it feels incredible. On my pussy, his tongue and the friction from his beard is pushing me towards another orgasm, and I practically scream on his cock, needing to take him out or I might bite him.

"Fuck, Seb, I'm coming again!" I clench, feeling my body tense from the pleasure, and I try to keep stroking him, I really do, but I lose my rhythm and become sloppy, unable to continue. I close my eyes and bury my face in his thigh to ride out my pleasure on his mouth.

My body involuntarily tries to pull away from him while my orgasm rolls over me, but his sturdy arms hold me in place while his tongue works my clit, keeping my writhing above him.

Being over him like this, having him so close to my most vulnerable parts, should feel too obscene to enjoy. But I feel as if I was made to be right where I am now.

"Jesus..." I sigh with a laugh. "I don't think I've ever come that hard. Here, let me get off you..." I try to swing my leg carefully over his head, but his arms lock me in place.

"No way." He says, muffled by my pussy. "I'm in heaven." He begins kissing my wetness again, and he nuzzles the inside of my thigh, tickling me.

I laugh. "You do feel amazing, but my knees are locking up."

Seb plants one last loud kiss on my folds and gently helps me bring my leg over. I collapse onto my back beside him, my feet by his head.

He sits up to face me, wiping off the glistening wetness left on his mouth with the cuff of his sleeve. "I'm never washing this shirt." He teases, flipping around to meet me face to face. "How are you feeling?"

I hold his face in the palm of my hand. "I don't know how you can look at me right now, I feel like I'm glowing. Blindingly blissful." I smile with a sigh. "Just give me a few minutes to bask in the afterglow of the orgasms you gave me and I'll be ready for more."

Seb kisses me gently. I can taste a hint of myself on his lips, and knowing he *likes* how I taste and smell is getting me excited again.

"Maybe we should quit while we're ahead." He whispers, tucking his impossibly hard and huge cock back into his pants. He struggles to zip over the bulge, but manages it after a few adjustments.

"What? No, Seb, that wasn't what I meant, I still want to-"

"I know you do, but we really shouldn't." He crawls to the side of the bed, kneeling on the floor, caressing my hair. "I've been away too long. I should head back, or they'll get suspicious. Plus..." He trails off, grabbing a spare washcloth from the bathroom and running it under warm water while he's talking. "I don't want to rush things."

He comes over and offers me the towel, but I don't accept it, hoping my glare will make him change his mind. "I don't want to fuck you in hiding, like we're some horny teenagers."

He continues, gently opening my legs, silently asking if he can wipe me clean. I'm hesitant, but eventually give in, opening for him. "I want to take my time with you. Make you feel how you deserve, and then fuck your brains out." Seb smiles, wiping me gently but thoroughly with the damp cloth, cleaning me of my wetness.

"The circumstances don't have to be perfect." I say, shaking my head. "You, this, what we have right now, is perfect for me."

"But you deserve to be wined and dined, spoiled, and then I want to spend the entire night with you. Teasing you. Loving you."

"But we don't know when we'll have time together like this again." I practically whine.

"Which is why I don't want to rush things."

"Seb." I say, exasperated. "You're being unreasonable."

"And you..." He tries to lighten the mood, playfully tapping my nose with his index finger. "...are thinking with your pussy."

"Of course I am!" I snap, not even denying it. I sit up fully to square myself to face him. "Do you know what it's been like for me? To want to see you, talk to you, *fix* things with you, and not be able to even text you?" I stand, fired up by my anger. "All of my days were filled with thoughts of you! And now, I finally have you in my bed and you don't want-"

"You could have come to the compound." Seb interrupts, quietly.

"What?" I ask, almost unwilling to comprehend his words.

"You could have come to the compound, anytime, and found me there."

I'm stunned. The anger in me grows. "You know I can't go back there."

"If you really wanted to talk to me, you could have."

"Seb, you *know* I can't be there!" I say, exasperated. "I left! I can't go back there, you know that!"

He releases a small sigh, and stands to meet me. "Maybe that's the problem. I'm part of that world. Hell, it's my whole life. And you don't want to be anywhere near it." Seb shoves his hands in his pockets. "Maybe this is a sign that this can't work between us."

"But, again, you aren't giving it a chance!" I say, heated.

"What chance do we have? I can't escape, and you don't want to come back. Where in the world can we go that we're not always...clashing?"

"Seb..." I warn.

"This is a mistake." He steps back.

"Fine. Maybe you're right." I tighten my robe around my body and stomp over to his briefcase and bag, snatching them up and shoving them into his hands. "This is a mistake." I rush to the living room to get his jacket and to the closet by the front door for his shoes, tossing them on the ground.

Seb slips them on, silently.

"If you don't think I'm worth the trouble, fine. Go." I say, using my anger to cover up my sadness. "I've had enough."

Seb straightens after putting on his shoes, looks at me one last time, and leaves through the front door without another word.

I'm left alone, the coldness of the penthouse in the wake of Seb's heat surrounds me.

I'm too angry to cry this time, opting to find my phone to call Jenny and tell her about the whole thing.

I see a text message from Peter.

**Hey Claire, are we still on
for dinner tonight?**
Peter Lee

I'm seething. I don't need Cage, or Seb, or whatever his name is. My life was fine before I met him, and I'll be fine after.

> **Definitely. Meet you at Tsunami on Houston at 7?**
> **Me**

Chapter Eight

Peter is wearing a dark, hunter green suit with a thin floral necktie printed on black fabric when he meets me at the restaurant. He looks sharp, which I like. His hair falls effortlessly in a flowing side part, and he looks good with a short fade on the sides and back of his head.

I stand from my seat at the bar where the chefs are making the dishes in front of us. We hug, and I do my best to keep from fidgeting in my black bodycon sweater dress.

"You look great." He says with a sheepish smile, his pristine face and skin the envy of any K-Pop boy band group member.

"Thank you." I say, blushing. "That's a great suit. So much personality."

"Oh thank you, I try to branch out of the tired blues and blacks once in a while."

He sits next to me in a moderately awkward silence before scanning the menu. "Can I order you a drink? They have a lychee cocktail that's delicious."

I smile. "That's my favorite. I get them with my friend Jenny here all the time."

Peter flags down one of the people behind the counter and orders two of the same drinks. "So you come here a lot?"

"Maybe too often." I laugh.

"I work just up the street so I'm here probably a lot more than I should be, too." He smiles.

"What do you do?" I ask, unfolding my napkin and putting it in my lap.

"I work in finance. Boring stuff, really. But it keeps me busy."

I was internally high-fiving myself. I knew my finance bro instincts were on point.

"I thought I got a finance vibe from you. Which is why I was so surprised you asked for Neil at the bookstore."

"Ah. Yes. Well, I gotta escape the drudgery of everyday life somehow, right?"

"Of course. And he's a great escape. I love how he writes his magical worlds just adjacent to our real world, you know?"

"Exactly. Sometimes I feel I can just turn a corner and stumble into an adventure."

That makes me smile. "I love that."

Our drinks are brought out and we both take a quick sip. Peter releases a quick "Mmm" of approval at the drink, and I think it's darling.

He is ready with questions. "So, tell me more about yourself. You said you bring your friend Jenny here a lot?"

I talk Peter's ear off about Jenny, my favorite books and how excited I get when I find a romance book that has the perfect balance of believable characters and plot.

We both share a sashimi platter, the signature dish of the restaurant. The pieces are light, balanced, and tasty.

Conversation flows easily after we get through our slightly awkward "tell me about you" phase. He has a younger sister who's in law school, and his parents own a nail salon.

I mention my parents also own a nail salon and leave out the details he doesn't need to know about.

Peter pays the bill, refusing to split it with me. "You can get the next one." He winks, and his boyish charm is fun, if not a little disarming, and I don't know whether I should leave my guard up or let it slip, with how comfortable it feels to be with him. We sip our second drinks as we wrap up the evening.

"Oh hey, Claire, if you're interested, I just found this app that lets you rank the restaurants you've tried and helps you find new places based on your ranks."

"That sounds amazing." I say, my eyes wide.

"Here, I'll text you the info." He pulls out his phone and sends me a quick message.

"And I have to text you the name of that zombie show. I can't believe you haven't seen it." I say, pulling out my phone as well.

"I know. I've heard nothing but good things."

"Okay, you have to watch The Last of Us and tell me how you like it."

"Deal." He says, and sends me a link to download the app. "I didn't develop this app or anything, I just eat out a lot and find it handy if I want to try something new. And since we both love food, I thought you'd like it."

His thoughtfulness is sweet. "I'm downloading it now." I say, opening my app store.

"And if you find somewhere new you like, I could take you there on our next date." Peter slips in, a little quietly. "If you're interested?"

His hopeful peek at me makes me laugh. "I'd love to. I had a great time." I say as I stand.

Peter sighs, his bright smile shining. "Me too." He helps me with my coat. "Can I call you a car? It's late."

"I appreciate that, thank you." I give him the address to the bodega around the corner from the penthouse, unsure if I'm comfortable with him knowing where I live yet.

We chat about the best dessert in town while waiting for the car, debating between some matcha shaved ice or a 20 layer slice of cake.

"We'll just have to get both of each and compare." He offers.

"Is it a fair comparison if we aren't judging the same desserts against each other."

He nods, exaggerating his seriousness. "You're right. We'll have to get shaved ice from Cha-An and Bonsai, and then cake from Lady M and Strip House and compare them."

I nod. "I think we have our next date planned."

Peter beams. "Awesome. Great. Sounds amazing."

I can't help but smile at how excited he is. The car pulls up to the curb, and he confirms my name with the driver before turning back to me. "Can I give you a hug?"

I step in and wrap my arms around him, happily. He's tall and lean. Strong. Not too bad to hold onto. "I had a great time." I say again, and I enjoy the way he respectfully gives me a tight squeeze around my shoulders.

"Text me when you get home?" He asks, stepping back and opening the door for me.

"I will. Goodnight, Peter." I say as I step into the car.

"Goodnight, Claire." He shuts the door softly and waves after me as the car pulls away.

I call Jenny immediately. She picks up after the second ring. "Tell me you're safe." She says, breathless.

"Are you on the treadmill?" I ask, checking my phone for the time. "It's almost midnight."

"I had a long day. Had to push my workout to now." She huffs, gulping a drink of water. "But was it good? Are you okay? How was he?"

"He was nice. Cute. Shy in a cute way." I offer, unsure how to sum up the events of the evening.

"You don't sound too excited about it."

"No, I really had a great time. He was…nice."

"Yes… you said that already." She huffs, and when I don't have anything else to add, she continues. "Maybe he's nice enough, but you're thinking about another certain hulking, stoic, dangerously hot man?"

I groan. "You caught me."

Jenny huffs a laugh. "There's nothing wrong with that, Claire. So you like Cage, is that a crime?"

I bury my face in my hand. "No, but it's never gonna work out with him, so I should let it go."

"Were you going to tell me your parents were filthy rich? I didn't know nail salons could make that kind of money?"

"What do you mean?" I ask, watching the streetlights shimmer off the wet pavement outside as we drive by.

"Your dad sent, like, a fleet of black SUVs to the bar the other night."

Oh shit. If I was in any state of my right mind, I would've stopped her from calling my parents, or told my dad to keep the rescue calvary to a minimum.

"Uh, my uncle owns a premiere taxi service. Basically like Oober, but with only Oober blacks." I lie.

"Damn, Claire, that could've saved us on a few drunken escapades over the years."

I shrug, leaning into my made-up story. "Yeah, well, he and my dad don't get along, so I try not to reach out." I lie again, and am internally surprised at how naturally it comes to me.

"Oh, well they took me straight home with no problems. Did anything happen with Cage after he took you back to your place?"

"Uh..." I hesitate, and it's just enough to put Jenny on high alert.

"Oh my god, something *did* happen!" She accuses. "Tell me everything!"

"Nothing! No, really, nothing happened. We just...kissed." I cringe, the memories of 69ing Seb rushing back to mind, heating my face.

Jenny squeals so loudly, I have to bring my phone away from my ear to keep from blowing out my eardrum. "Did you kiss him or did he kiss you?"

I try to remember the order of events, but it all blurs together in a sweaty, slick, heated blur. "I think I kissed him."

"Oh my god, when? Was the sexual tension through the roof?"

"Not really, I mean, we had brunch together this morning-"

"THIS *MORNING?!*" Jenny screams. "Did you sleep with him last night?!"

"No!" I cry, overwhelmed by Jenny running away with assumptions. Granted, they are accurate, but I don't want her to know that. "Really Jenny, just listen! We ate, we kissed, he went home. That was it."

I hear a "Tsk, tsk." on her end. "I don't think you're telling me the whole truth, Claire Nguyen, but you know what? That's okay. Keep your secrets. Maybe a tangle in the sheets with a giant, buff, perfect specimen-of-a-human-being will be good for you."

"Hey, no sheets were tangled." I defend, holding my hot face in my hands.

"What does he do, anyway?"

"He works for my parents." I say before I can stop myself. My hand covers my mouth, but it's too late.

"...at the nail salon?" Jenny asks, skeptically.

"Uh, yeah."

"He does nails?"

Fuck. "Uh... yeah." Damnit, I should've said he was their accountant.

"Huh." She says, and I can practically hear the gears in her head turning. "He doesn't seem the type."

"What type does he seem like?"

"Like a gym bro."

"Oh." That was not what I thought she was going to say. I thought she was going to say he was security, or something.

"Yeah, he doesn't seem like he can sit around in those rolling chairs all day." She says, logically.

"Well, he's very talented. Does a killer french tip."

Jenny makes a noise that makes her sound impressed. "I believe it." She says, honestly.

"Anyway..." I try to move the conversation away from Seb. "Did you end up going out with that guy on Tindr?"

"Nuh-uh, we are not moving on to my pathetic dating life. Tell me more about Peter. Are you even excited about him? Will you see him again?"

"Yeah, actually." I nod, going along with her dodging my question. I internally vow to come back to it later. "Peter and I have a lot in common. We like the same movies and food, and we have a really cool date planned next."

"Ooo, what are you gonna do?"

"We're getting two different chocolate cakes and two different matcha shaved ices and comparing them."

"Wow, that sounds right up your alley."

"I know. It's like, too perfect, right?"

"Do you think he's hot?"

I hesitate at the question, only because I don't really know my own answer. "I don't know, I guess so? He's cute. Like, really cute, but…"

"Do you wanna date 'cute,' or do you want hot?"

"The thing is, Peter isn't bad! He's really nice! And he looks amazing, it's just…" Jenny doesn't press me, but leaves me to torture the truth out of myself. "Cage is like, *really* hot."

"He's *really* hot." Jenny agrees. "But you're right, Peter does look nice, if he looks anything like the photos you sent me."

"He does." I defend, because Peter was a great date, and he doesn't deserve the slander I feel I'm dishing out in this conversation. "I'd like to see him again."

"But do you want to see him because you like him, or to distract you from Cage?"

And I can't answer, because she knows that's exactly what I'm doing.

Jenny continues. "Well, whatever you decide, I'm here to support you."

"Thank you. Now tell me about that Tindr date?"

"Ugh, it was hardly a date." She says, disappointed. "He asked to meet up at a coffee shop *after* it had already closed, so we walked around Harlem for a while before he asked if I was interested in a hookup, and when I said no, he said he needed to go home and take care of his dog."

"That's it?" I ask, jaw on the floor.

"That. Was. It." Jenny said coldly. "I told you, it was a total disappointment. But..."

"But?"

"Another guy did message me today and offered to take me out to dinner at Nohboo."

I gasp. "No way!"

"I know!"

"Nohboo is so expensive! And practically impossible to get a reservation."

"He says he knows a guy who works there and can get us a table."

It's my turn to squeal, only a little quieter, since I don't want to distract my driver. "What's the guy like? Is he cute? How old is he?"

"Hold on, let me check the app." Jenny takes a few seconds to pull up his profile and reads it to me. "Ravi Patel, he says he's 6 feet, 4 inches tall." She chuckles. "He works in tech, which is cool."

"Wow, he sounds great. Let's hope he has some personality."

"Yeah, I'm excited. We're going out next week. But, and tell me what you think about this, Claire, he's only 29."

I scoff, trying to minimize her hesitation. "So what? That's only a 4 or 5 year age difference. There's nothing wrong with dating younger people."

"Yeah, but am I getting myself into a situation that will just be more stressful than fun?"

"I don't know, Jenny, you'll just have to go out with the guy and find out."

"But what if he's just a little baby man? I mean, 29? That's so young. I can't even remember where I was at 29."

"You were on a solo trip to Guam."

"Oh, yeah."

"I know you want to get ahead of all of the potential bad things that could happen with someone who seems wonderful on paper, but you really will never know until you meet him. He could be the best man you've ever met and he'll sweep you off your feet, and you'll get married and make beautiful, tall, Indian children."

"Oh my god, Claire, one step at a time, please!"

I laugh. "I know. But you can't judge him before even meeting him! You'll be so focused on looking for the bad, you won't see the good if it's sitting in front of you."

"You're right, you're right. You're always right."

I shrug. "It's a curse."

My driver turns down my street and stops in front of my corner bodega. "Hey, I'm getting out of the car right now, I'll text you later?"

"Okay, text me when you get inside."

"I will. Love you."

"Love you!" Jenny says, and quickly hangs up the call so my hands can be free while I walk down the street. It's one of the ways I feel safe when walking in the city. My hands should be free, if I ever need to defend myself.

I thank my driver before gently shutting the door behind me. I walk around the corner and head to the penthouse. Once I'm in the building, I text Jenny I'm safe and she responds with a smiley and a thumbs up.

Chapter Nine

"Don't stop." Seb grunts beneath me, both hands gently caressing my hips as I ride his huge cock. My plump waist feels as if I was made perfectly for his hands to rest, and he lovingly palms my softness, encouraging me to keep up my pace.

His thickness fills every inch of my clenching walls, and each thrust down brings me closer and closer to my next orgasm.

"Fuck, Seb..." I breathe, angling forward to rest my hands on either side of his head. This change in position puts my breasts right above his face, and he buries into my bouncing tits, reaching up to grab one in his hand and taking a nipple into his hot, wet mouth.

The jolt of pleasure from his licks and kisses along with the head of his cock hitting right at my G-spot pushed me over the edge.

"Oh my god, Seb, I'm coming!" I practically scream, my voice echoing through my bedroom as my pussy tightens, almost forcing his cock out of me.

I feel him plant his feet on my mattress and drive up into me, meeting my thrusts. I'm eventually so overcome with pleasure, I can't keep my rhythm, but Seb takes over, fucking me through the height of my orgasm.

I'm seeing stars. I'm on a different celestial plane. I'm floating. I've never come so hard, or for so long. My orgasm carries me away for what feels like an eternity, but I'm nearing almost two minutes before Seb flips me onto my back, as if I'm as light as a feather, and thrusts into me just as quickly as I was riding him.

"Fuck, *estoy loco por ti, yo puedo amarte toda la noche.*" He growls, taking in every look on my face as I'm carried away. "You feel amazing, Claire. Fuck."

"Jesus, Seb, I- I-" Before I can come down from this orgasm, another one starts building, and I'm overtaken, writhing beneath him again.

He picks up the pace without missing a beat. "Again?" He asks, impressed.

I nod, flashing a breathy smile, but I can only moan into my pillow, unable to say anything else.

This drives Cage wild. He gently but firmly grasps my hair to turn my face towards him. "Let me see. Let me watch you." He whispers, hot and wanting. His thrusts are slower, but deeper, and it feels incredible when he bottoms out, filling me to my core, giving my walls something to close around.

It's magical, looking at him while I'm coming. Seb is possessive. His eyes are hooded with pleasure, from both my pussy and the satisfaction of making me come again and again.

To keep from closing my eyes, I reach for his face in an attempt to ground myself, but the tension is overwhelming my body, and I bury my face in his neck.

The hand in my hair tightens and pulls my head back onto the pillow softly and firmly. "Let me see." He demands, and the hunger in his voice pushes me over another edge, and I'm coming again, before the last orgasm leaves my body.

"I can't-" I strain, astounded by the never-ending stream of pleasure. "You're too much. I can't come again..."

"You're already coming again." Seb breathes, rising onto his knees to take my hips in his hands, slowly driving into my arousal. "You're coming and you're glorious. So tight, so wet. I'd fuck you all night. For the rest of your life, if you'd let me. God, I'd fuck you every morning, when you wake up with your hair messed up, lips swollen from sucking my cock the night before. I'd kiss you until you get so wet, you'd beg me to fuck you. And I would. All morning, until you couldn't walk." He kisses my cheek, my forehead, my lips, and I'm still coming. "Then, at night, I'd throw you onto this bed and fuck you so hard, you'll scream my name."

"Seb!" I moan, giving him exactly what he wants. I'll give him anything, if it means he can make me feel this good all the time.

"That's it Claire, just like that. I'll fuck you until you beg me to stop, and tomorrow morning, we'll do it all again." He says tenderly, a warm promise in his tone.

But then he's slipping away. Seb is further and further away. My body feels heavy, like lead sinking into my mattress.

I wake up.

I'm in my bed.

Naked.

Alone.

My clit is throbbing. The inside of my thighs are coated in my wetness.

I had an orgasm in my sleep. I'm actually impressed with myself. I didn't think that could happen.

I look around my room skeptically, searching for any sign of a man being here.

I don't find any. Everything is as it was last night when I came home after my date with Peter. I got ready for bed, and promptly fell asleep.

Then I dreamed of Cage.

"Shit…" I whisper, wiping the sleep from my eyes. I reach for my phone and click the speech to text feature, asking "orgasm in sleep question mark" and it turns out to be more common than I thought.

I get up and go through my morning routine on auto pilot, the memory of that vivid dream still haunting my thoughts.

I'm in the middle of making tea when Peter texts me.

All I can think about is
chocolate buttercream
and caramel.
Peter Lee

> Yuuum. I've been
> craving that damned
> shaved ice with red
> bean.
> Me

We have to get going
on this, or else
we'll go crazy.
Peter Lee

> Well...if you're free
> tonight...I can grab the
> shaved ice if you get
> the cakes?
> Me

Let's do it. Meet you at
Bonsai around 6? It's
the most central to
all of these places.
Peter Lee

> I can do that. It'll
> save them from
> melting, too. :)
> Me

Sounds like a plan. :D
See you then.
Peter Lee

It's Sunday, and my first day off in too long. I sip my tea as I make a quick spinach and ham omelette to use up some leftover ingredients in my fridge.

I sit on my couch to eat while I scroll TickTock, but I'm bored quickly, so I switch to the TV and put on my tried and true comfort film, Pride and Prejudice starring Keira Knightly.

I finish my quick breakfast, and when I'm clearing my plate, I have a craving for something sweet. I have enough chocolate chips for some cookies, so I reach for my favorite recipe from Laura Phan's *Dessert for Dinner.*

I listen to the film play in the background while I brown my butter, Laura's secret step to the richest cookies I've ever made. The little tricks in her book make me feel pretty accomplished, even though I've burned a good few batches of cookies and cupcakes in my time.

When the oven is finished preheating, I'm scooping out the dough onto my baking sheet lined with a silicone baking mat. The first batch is in the oven while I'm scooping the rest of the dough onto a smaller tray and putting them in the freezer. It will be great to have frozen cookie dough for later in the week when I'm craving a fresh baked cookie, and this way, I can bake one or two at a time.

I'm in the middle of Elizabeth Bennet touring Mr. Darcy's home when the timer goes off, and I hop up excited to take the cookies out.

They're perfectly golden brown. I barely let them cool before trying an unset corner, and the burning-hot glob stings my mouth, but also tastes amazing.

I look around the penthouse, warm and cozy from the cloudy day and now smelling like fresh baked cookies.

It's nice, having this peace to myself, but I can feel boredom creeping up on me. Not having a task to do is uncomfortable, and I wrestle with the internal struggle of allowing myself to relax or feeling productive.

I settle on something that always makes me feel like I can accomplish both: skin care.

I leave the cookies to cool on the counter and head to the bathroom, pulling out my various masks and serums. I start with a cleansing charcoal mask and allow it to dry on my face for a good 30 minutes. I pass the time by letting myself enjoy the rest of the film. When it ends, I put on a comfort series, The Last of Us, and enjoy a rough and tough, grumpy man guiding a young girl across the country while fighting off zombie mushroom heads.

The timer on my phone lets me know I need to wash off the charcoal mask, and I scrub it off before opening a hydrating sheet mask and gently placing it on my face. I go back to the couch and finish up the second episode, happy to begin the third, which centers on one of my top-rated romantic and heartbreaking couples, Bill and Frank.

Before I can enjoy the beauty and sadness of their older years, I fall asleep on the couch, waking to my TV on the home screen. I check my phone for the time. I slept for just under three hours. It's almost time for me to get ready to meet Peter.

In my bathroom mirror, I slowly peel off what's left of my sheet mask and toss it in the garbage. I rub in the remaining serum on my face, and when I look like a well-hydrated snail, I wash my hands and head to the kitchen to grab a cookie before facing my closet.

The chocolate chips bring hits of sweetness throughout the nearly savory dough, and the combination is insane. It's one of the better things I can make, and I bet Seb would love to taste...

I shake my head. I try to ignore the creeping thoughts of that man in my life. I don't need him. He doesn't need me. No need for any of this.

I'm renewed with energy to see Peter, looking for any reason to distract myself from the intrusive thoughts of Seb.

Inspired by Peter's hunter green suit from our last date, I find some sleek, baggy trousers in a similar color and pair it with a thin, black, turtleneck sweater. The weather app says it's going to rain tonight, so I want to be prepared. I slip on thin black socks and find my leather, waterproof ankle boots. I'm satisfied enough with the outfit before heading back to the bathroom for a leisurely amount of time to play with some makeup.

This ritual can't be complete without some music, so I find my trusty K-Pop playlist and blast the cute girl groups, baddie girl groups, and the heartbreaking talented, multi-member boy bands.

I'm going for a dark green smokey eye to compliment the outfit, but not too much that it's going overboard. I blend a deep green all over my lids with a dark gray at the outer corners of my eyes, bringing the shadow just above the crease. The effect works so well with my hooded eyes, I applaud myself quietly.

I grab my purse and tan peacoat and am just about ready to head out when Peter texts me he's ordered a car. He says it will pick me up at the same address I gave last night. I smile at the kind gesture, and get ready to head to the corner bodega.

As I'm walking through the lobby of the building, Juan whistles at my outfit.

"Hot date tonight, Claire?"

I wink at him, not missing a beat. "You know it, Juan. You'd like him."

"Who is he?" He pries, a hint of fatherly concern in his words. "Is he nice to you?"

I laugh. "He's *too* nice, you'd love him. His name is Seb...Peter. His name is Peter." Fuck, that was the biggest Freudian Slip.

"Ah, is he the big, strong man who carried you up last time?"

"What? No, I- uh, no, that's not him." I blush.

"I met Peter at work. At the bookstore."

"Hmm, okay." Juan says skeptically. "I'll be looking out for you to come back with all smiles. No tears, or else he'll answer to me."

I laugh at his teasing, but I know he means well. "You got it. Goodnight Juan!" I call behind me.

"Goodnight!" He says affectionately.

The car is already waiting for me at the corner. I apologize to the driver for making her wait, but she shoots me a bright smile and says "No problem. Looks like we have two stops tonight?"

"Oh, yes, thank you." I say before ordering the two matcha shaved ices online.

She drives me to Cha-An and waits while I run in quickly to pick-up my order. It's ready for me, thank goodness, and I rush out to where the car is parked illegally. Traffic is honking, but the driver doesn't budge, yelling "Go around!" and staying put. I laugh at her tenacity, and when I shut the door behind me and put on my seatbelt, I play along and yell "Go, go, go!"

She peels out like a maniac and shoots off to Bonsai, where the second order is also waiting for me, along with Peter.

I rate my driver five stars for her impeccable skills. "Thanks so much. You're one of the funner drivers in these streets."

"You're sweet, thank you! Have a great night."

"You, too!" I shout to her before she peels out again, disappearing into the night.

Peter is waiting for me just outside the dessert shop. He's more casual tonight, wearing a light blue polo under a rain jacket. He wraps me in a quick hug before opening the door.

"You look beautiful." He says, a little shyly with a slight tinge of a blush on his face.

"Thanks." I smiled at him. "You, too. I got the goods." I hold up the desserts as I walk inside.

The place is dimly lit, a slight change from their usual bright and natural ambiance. The place seems a bit empty on a Sunday night, but towards the back, one small, round table has a red checkered table cloth with two candles glowing next to a bouquet of flowers in a stout glass vase.

In front of each seat is a paper white to-go box.

"What's all this?" I ask in awe, looking up at him.

"I may have pulled a few strings to get us the place for the night." Peter shoves his hands into the pockets of his jeans, a little embarrassed. "Also, I wasn't sure if you wanted to fill up on desserts, but I got us my favorite hot chicken sandwich, if you're hungry?"

I'm so impressed. His consideration is unmatched. "I didn't even think about dinner. You're so smart." I beam, suddenly acutely aware of how little I actually ate today.

Peter shrugs, bashful. "I try. Plus, I was working in the office today. I'm starving."

"Let's eat, then." I smile, taking one seat as he takes the shaved ice from my hands and gives it to one of the servers to keep in the freezer.

I open the box to peek inside. It looks familiar. A fried chicken sandwich with steak fries and a special house sauce for dipping. "Where is this from?"

"Pretty Bird? In Harlem?" Peter says, opening his own box.

I nod in approval, offering my hand across the table. Peter shakes my hand hesitantly, confused.

"Good work, sir, good work. Pretty Bird is one of my favorites. The best this town has to offer, in my opinion."

He beams, proud of his choice. "I knew you'd like it. You have amazing taste."

"That is seriously such a nice compliment, thank you." I say, too earnestly, and we laugh together before diving into our dinner.

He catches me up on a project he's behind on at work, which is frustrating him a bit. He doesn't want to talk any more about it, though, excited to tell me about the first episode of The Last of Us.

"The actor who plays Joel is really good." Peter says, dipping his fries two at a time between praises.

"It'll be interesting to see how his relationship with Ellie evolves as the show goes on."

"Oh my god, Peter, it's amazing! It's paternal, but friendly, and, ugh, it's just incredible." I gush, taking a sip of sparkling water the server brought mid-meal.

"Do you want to watch it together?" He offers, finishing off his sandwich and working on the rest of his fries.

"I'd love to." I nod, excited.

"You're welcome to come to my place. I'm on the Upper East Side. Then maybe, I can finally muster up the courage to kiss you." He confesses, looking up at me through his lashes to gauge my response.

I'm a little surprised. I hadn't thought of kissing him. But what was the harm? Maybe he could take my mind off...

"I think..." I begin, leaning in closer to him. "That can be arranged, if you can pick which of these desserts is my favorite."

"A challenge I'll gladly take." He smiles, his voice low.

The servers kindly clear the table and bring out all four desserts, managing to keep the shaved ice from the previous place from melting.

Peter and I both take a bite from one slice of cake, and then the other.

Both are rich and tantalizing. I softly moan after the second bite, dancing a bit in my seat at how delicious they are.

I move on to taking a bite of the snowy shaved ice from Cha-An, but Peter doesn't follow. He's staring at me, his mouth slightly agape, spoon suspended in mid air.

"Do you always make noises like that when you eat?" He practically whispers, a teasing smile on his lips.

"When it's dessert, yeah." I say quietly, unsure if he's trying to say if it bothers him or not.

"It's hot." Peter says, his eyes heating.

It's my turn to blush. I lick my lips, suddenly embarrassed, but I manage to say "Thank you."

"I want to make you sound like that." He continues, taking another bite of cake.

"Oh my god, Peter!" I whisper, playfully hitting his arm. I'm covering my mouth, hoping to hide the heat in my face.

His mischievous look and laughter makes me think he knows exactly what he's doing, and I don't hate it.

I'm having fun. I can't believe myself.

"You don't want to? I haven't wiggled my way into your favor with all this sugar?" He asks, leaning in to hear my response with a playful look of hope on his face.

"I want to." I manage through my blush.

Those simple words are a breakthrough, and he relaxes, sprawling his long legs around me and resting both of his hands on the back of his head. "Good." He smiles. "I wasn't sure if you were into me the same way I'm into you."

"How are you into me?" I ask, wanting to both tease him and clarify how he sees me.

"Well I can't stop thinking about kissing you, for one. Your lips are..." He gives me a thumbs up before reaching for my hand. I let him hold me, his gentle thumb caressing my knuckles. "And if you come back to my place, I promise to be the perfect gentleman, unless you make a move?" A small laugh huffs from his lips. "What I really mean is I hope you make a move. Please make a move."

I laugh at how forward and honest he's being. "I think I'd like that."

"Yeah?" He's hopeful, a sparkle in his eye glimmering.

I nod, and that makes him very happy. His smile is broad, and he almost leaps from his chair.

"Okay, cool. Awesome. So, uh, what do you think about the desserts? Which do you like better?"

"I don't really care anymore. I kinda want to go back to your place?"

He smiles. "Good plan." Peter has the staff pack up everything for us to take, and he gives them an extra tip for going above and beyond to make this evening special.

We're holding hands while waiting for a car to take us to his apartment, all the while chatting about catching a broadway show and sneaking blushing looks at each other.

We're too old for these chuckles and peeks and blushes, but we're both leaning in, allowing our mature masks to slip.

While in the car, he's silent, but gently caressing my knee. His hands are lean and long, much like the rest of him, and I can feel his heat through my pants.

We make it to his apartment, which is in an updated building with an elevator. He's on the top floor, and once we're inside, we both take off our shoes and Peter takes all of the leftovers to put the shaved ice in the freezer, and the cakes in the fridge. He takes my coat and hangs it on a hook by the front door, next to his rain jacket. I snoop around while he's getting the show on the TV.

He has a black leather sectional that fills up the entire living room. His tiny kitchen has all black appliances, matching the rest of the place. The exposed red brick throughout the space is undeniably charming, and I peek into his bedroom to find a decent-sized mattress on a simple iron bed frame. His navy blue sheets scream bachelor, and I find his place endearing.

I meet him in the living room as he's scrolling through the shows, trying to find the right one. One hand is on his hip, and the look is so casual, yet authoritative, I find it pretty attractive.

I stand right in front of him. "Sorry, it should be easier to find…" He mumbles.

I gently take the remote from his hand and toss it onto the couch. Peter looks down at me, intrigued, but goes along with my moves.

"I think I want to kiss you now." I whisper, resting my hands on his forearms. "Is that okay?"

He nods, not saying anything, too enthralled with my closeness to speak.

I have to lean up on my toes, but when he finally reaches down slightly to meet me, our lips touch, and it's sweet, soft, and chaste.

Chapter Ten

"Wow." Peter whispers when I pull away. His stunned awe makes me smile.

"What do you think?" I ask, gauging his expression.

He wraps his arms behind me, pulling my body flush against his. "I think I want to kiss you again." He bends down to press his lips to mine, a little bolder this time.

His lips are a little cold and thin. It's difficult for my lips to find purchase on his, and I have to lean in closer to smoosh our faces together.

I pull back again, wrestling with the thought in my head that I don't really like kissing Peter. "Maybe we should put the show on?" I want to slow things down. I need time to think.

He nods, a shy smile on his face. "Sure. Yeah, awesome."

We cuddle on the couch while the show plays, but I'm not paying attention. Peter's arm is around my shoulders, and I'm holding his hand, but his fingers are thin and they feel a little delicate. There shouldn't be anything wrong with that, I've dated men much less masculine than Peter, but there's an uneasiness in my gut about how much work I'm putting in to convince myself to stay.

I want to go. I want to see Seb. I want to feel warm and safe and effortless.

But I can't. He's not an option for me anymore. So I stay.

Peter and I finish my favorite episode which centers on Bill and Frank's love story, and I feel myself putting on the mask of interest while I gush and aww and squeal with delight at the lovely parts, and shed a few tears towards the end. I really do love this episode, but I've seen it at least a dozen times already. I still want Peter to know I love it though, so I play up my reaction.

"It's really good." He agrees. "It's awesome how they showed Frank's declining health by letting the audience see how detailed his paintings were in the beginning, and how abstract they became the worse he got."

I nod, thoughtful. "I never noticed that before. You're so astute."

He shrugs. "Maybe I just pay attention better than you." Peter says offhandedly.

Wow. Okay. That was uncalled for. Whatever.

"Uh, it's late. I'd better head home."

"You sure you don't wanna stay? We can watch another episode. I don't want you feeling like you can't stay, is what I mean to say." He offers, trying to sound welcoming.

"That's sweet of you, but I'd better go. I have to work early tomorrow."

"Okay. Let me call you a car."

I smile at his thoughtfulness. Again, there's so much about him that's so good, but I'm finding more that I don't like.

"Thank you. I'll have to invite you to my neighborhood so I can call you a car for once and start returning the favor." I tease.

Peter smiles. "It's no trouble. I don't like the idea of a woman like you out there alone at night. It's dangerous."

I prickle at his comment. I can hold my own out there in the streets at night. I was born and raised here, so I know how to take care of myself. And even though I know he means to sound chivalrous, I'm a little offended.

We say our goodbyes when the car is close and he walks me down to the lobby.

"Text me when you get home safe?" He says after we share a quick hug.

"I will. Thank you so much for tonight. It's the most fun I've had in a long time."

"Can't wait to see you again."

I smile, but don't answer, because I don't know if I am looking forward to seeing him again.

Peter shuts the door behind me and I wave goodbye through the window.

It doesn't even occur to me to kiss him goodbye.

But, I do see Peter again.

And again.

And again. Many more times in the next few months. He takes me on elaborate Broadway dates where he talks to me for hours afterwards about the actors and the story and the staging. Our conversation bounces back and forth easily, but it still takes so much effort on my part to care about everything he has to say.

Peter is very well-known in the local food scene and finds us impossible reservations to the trendiest places. We eat well and talk, and get along relatively easily.

I trust him enough to invite him over to the penthouse, using my 'rich uncle works in real estate and found me a good deal' excuse I gave to Jenny.

Peter and I watch movies and cuddle, and it's decently pleasant. I secretly hope Seb is watching on the cameras and is angry and jealous out of his mind.

We make out a few times on the couch, but I'm clear with him that I want to take things slow, so he never pushes past some heavy petting.

One weekend afternoon, Peter texts if we can get brunch. I respond that I'm heading to my pilates class but can meet with him afterwards.

He texts 'I didn't know you worked out' and I am immediately hit with what feels like judgment on my body.

It's been a long time, maybe years, since I engaged with anyone that had anything to say about my body.

I message Jenny right away to hear her thoughts. Was I being overly sensitive, looking for anything negative as a sign I should cut things off, or was he being a jerk?

Jenny doesn't text, but calls me.

She's livid. "He. Did. NOT. Say that." She can't believe what I'm telling her.

"Am I crazy? Am I freaking out, reading too much into what he said? Or does he really mean he thinks I'm too big to work out?"

"I think he really means that. What an asshole. You should drop him. Come to brunch with me instead."

I laugh. "I just might take you up on that offer."

"I mean it. I have an editorial meeting soon, but I'm free after."

Fuck it. "Let's do it. I'll tell him I'm busy."

"Cool. Dim sum at Nam Wah or biscuits at Gracie's?" Jenny asks, already on the ball of making plans.

"Let's do dim sum. I'll head there after my workout. The line might be insane in the afternoon."

"I'll meet you there. You'd think they'd take reservations with how popular they always are." Jenny says.

"Yeah, you'd think. Okay, I'll call you when I'm done." I say, slipping on my shoes and heading out the door.

"Okay, see you soon. Love you."

"Love you." I reply quickly before hanging up. I text Peter, saying I have plans with Jenny afterwards, and he's sad, but says we can meet up sometime this week.

"We'll see about that." I say to myself, still a little stung by his comment.

Pilates is brutal, as always. The reformers are a great burn, but they leave me feeling exhausted after every class.

I love how strong I feel after, so I keep going week after week.

When we're finally done, I hop on the subway to Chinatown and make my way to the colorful street Nam Wah calls home. They have the best dim sum in the city. I only know because one summer in college, Jenny and I tried all the ones we could that had an "A" health rating.

I arrive to a relatively long line, about 15 people deep, and text Jenny that we'll have to wait about an hour.

She's running late, but says she'll be here in 40 minutes.

I'm prepared, putting on my headphones and turning on my audiobook, a spicy Scottish romance about an American woman traveling to Glasgow and falling in love with a previously famous singer who fell out of the good graces of the media, and now lives a humble life in his hometown.

After 40 minutes on the dot, Jenny meets me, and we're next in line to be seated. The timing is perfect.

She hugs me hello. "Oh my god, tell me everything. He's got some nerve."

I roll my eyes, astounded at the situation. "Do I text him back?"

Jenny shakes her head, zipping up her leather jacket. She's in matching leather leggings and looks amazing, as always, her long dark hair tied up into a high ponytail. "You should confront him. Face to face. Don't give him the chance to cower behind a phone."

"Shouldn't I ask him what he meant? Clarify? We could be reading way too much into this."

She shakes her head again. "What else could he have meant? God, I'm so mad. Who does he think he is, talking to my Claire that way?"

"I appreciate your fierceness about this whole thing, I really do, but shouldn't we be adults about this?"

"I thought it was pretty immature of him to text that, to be honest." Jenny shrugs. "Why should we be the responsible adults? You should go to his place and scream at him. How dare he make you question your worth? As if you aren't the hottest babe he could ever get. He should be groveling at your feet, kissing the ground you walk on, dedicate the rest of his life-"

"Jenny, alright, I got it." I try to bring her down from her growing tirade just before we're beckoned into the restaurant towards a booth at the back. We order our usual barbecue steamed buns, har gow, shu mai and green tea.

"I don't want to talk about him anymore." I say, resolved to deal with this in my own time. "Tell me about you. What was your meeting about?"

"We were hammering out details for a shoot next week. They were stuck on whether or not they wanted to find another model with a complexion as dark as mine or lighter, and I said if the concept is good, it doesn't matter what color the model is. Not that it mattered. They never listen to me. I just do my job, pose, and go home." Jenny sighs, taking a sip of green tea.

"Sounds bleak." I say, feeling like she hasn't felt inspired in her last few projects. "Does it bother you, not having any say?"

"Sometimes. Sometimes I feel like I should dedicate my time to something better, you know?"

"Of course. You have your incredible idea of opening a crisis center for refugee women and helping them assimilate into our communities." I say, remembering the way Jenny's eyes sparkle whenever she mentions it.

She smiles. "Yeah, but we need money to do all that. And that's something we ain't got." Jenny jokes, but we both feel the pang of truth in her words.

I try to sound hopeful. "We'll both be filthy rich one day. Just watch. I'll have my bookstore, you'll have your crisis center. We'll be dead exhausted working everyday but we'll be living the dream."

Jenny laughs. "Leave it to us to dream of working ourselves to death. Maybe finding a rich

Indian husband who will make me a trophy wife is in the cards for me."

"Speaking of Indian men, how did that date go with that guy, Ravi?"

"Ugh, awful. He talked about his income and his watch the whole time." She gags.

"Oh no, one of those?"

Jenny nods. "Maybe I'm just meant to be alone."

"Please. You are meant to be someone's entire world." I really believe my own words. "Or maybe we're both meant to be alone."

"There's no way that's true. You're batting off guys left and right." She says.

I scoff. "Yeah, getting one to stay is the problem."

"Still no luck with Cage?" Jenny asks just as our food is brought out. The mention of his name startles me, and I feel a slight pang in my heart.

"I'm off his radar, I think." I try to smile, but I can never hide anything from Jenny. She reaches across the table and grabs my hand, trying to comfort me.

"I can actually feel my heart breaking for you." She says, as attuned as ever to my emotions. "You know I'm the last one to suggest chasing after a guy, but if you're this upset over him, maybe call him? Try to clear the air? You have his number now right?"

I nod solemnly, my frustration brimming, threatening to spill over. "I don't know, Jenny, I don't know! He might not answer if I call him. I don't even know if he'll text me back."

"Is he mad at you?" She asks, putting a few dumplings on my plate and pouring soy sauce onto each of our dipping dishes.

"We had a fight." I finally admit, unable to hide from her any longer.

"A fight?" Jenny asks, a bit astounded.

I nod, shoving one whole shu mai into my mouth.

"Wow." Jenny says, a little impressed. "The Claire I know does *not* fight. She burns every bridge to protect her peace."

"I know." I say, still chewing on my food. I rub the frustration from my eyes, trying to clear my head. "He wanted to take things slow. Take me out. Date me. And I just wanted to fuck him."

"And he said no?" Jenny gasps.

"Not exactly. He said he wanted to wine and dine me, spoil me, and then have sex with me."

"Damnit Claire, that sounds perfect. Exactly how you deserve to be treated." She's beaming, but pulls back when she sees the glooming shadow on my face. "But...you had a problem with that?"

I nod, tormented. "The thing is...up until that morning, we had been...dabbling with each other."

Jenny's eyebrows raise, but she doesn't interrupt.

"We had been kissing and touching, and...doing other things." I drop my voice to avoid other tables from eavesdropping. "And we basically had done everything except...you know."

"Sex? Penetration?" She fills in, trying to help.

I wince at her choice of words, but nod.

"I knew it. I knew you weren't telling me everything." Jenny says with a smile, but keeping her voice hushed.

"And he'd say all of these wonderful things, like, how beautiful I look and how..." I look around, making sure no one is listening, and lean in closer to whisper. "How good I taste."

Jenny squeals silently, shaking with excitement. "Oh my god, he would." She nods, proud of herself and her accurate judgment of him. "He seems like a very generous lover."

My face gets hot at the memory, but I somehow manage to continue. "Yes. He is. Anyway. We've been getting *extremely* close but everytime, when we're just about to go for it, he brings up all of these excuses and explanations on why we should wait, or we shouldn't be doing this, or yada, yada, yada." I take a sip of my tea.

"Maybe he has a micropenis and he's insecure?"

I choke on my cup, nearly spitting it everywhere.

Jenny laughs, but hands me wads of napkins to wipe myself up and the table around us. It takes a while for me to compose myself, but after downing a glass of water, I'm teary-eyed, but back to normal.

"He doesn't have a micropenis." I defend, shooting down her theory before she gets too carried away.

"How do you know?"

"I've...seen him..."

Jenny's eyes grow wide, her mouth turning into an understanding 'O' before she has another dumpling. "You've..." She makes a lewd gesture for a couple of strokes and quickly moves it up to her mouth, pantomiming a blowjob.

"Jenny!" I practically screech, throwing my wad of napkins at her.

She laughs but tries to move the conversation along. "Okay, okay. No micropenis."

"No. He's very much the opposite." I say, still red in the face.

"Noted."

"No, don't note that. That's not the point."

"Okay, okay. So he wanted to date you and you wanted to have sex with him?" Jenny tries to sum up the conflict

"No, I also want to date him."

"So what's the problem? It sounds like a great plan." She says, breaking open her steamed barbecue pork bun and putting a small piece in her mouth.

"It was the excuses he made."

"Did they seem valid?"

"Well, yes, I guess."

"Then, Claire, don't you think you're being a little stubborn about this whole thing?" Jenny offers in a level-headed tone.

"No, I don't, because he keeps saying how he wants my parents permission to be with me."

"That sounds like a good excuse to me. He's respectful."

I'm starting to get frustrated that Jenny sounds so reasonable, and she isn't agreeing with how ludicrous Cage is. "But, then! Get this, he basically claimed that because we have an unbalanced power dynamic, that it's probably best we take it slow!" I say exasperated, hoping she'll come around on my side with this new information. "If he loved me, wouldn't he throw caution to the wind, consequences be damned, and just take me? Ravish me? Do everything we always say a man should do for us?"

I look at Jenny, expecting her to match my outrage, but she has a soft, surprised look. "I didn't realize you wanted him to love you."

"I don't! I..." Did I? I guess that is what I said.

If he loved me...

"Oh, Claire." Her words are warm, hopeful. "Give me his number. I'll call him for you. We'll clear all this up. Because if it's love, then there's not a moment to lose."

"No. I can do it myself."

"Alright. But just so you know. You should reach out to him. He has valid points. I think you were just upset because he didn't want to do what you asked, and you don't take it well when someone tells you no." Jenny teases, but she's only speaking the truth.

I nod, digesting her words. "You may be right. But in my defense, I don't think I make unreasonable demands."

"You don't." Jenny agrees.

I take a bite of my pork bun. "Okay. So. I'll text Cage? Or call him?"

Jenny nods. "I think that's what's best. You'll be happier. And you can deal with Peter whenever."

"Okay. I'll try next weekend. I might call you if it all goes badly."

"I'll be waiting by the phone." Jenny smiles, and I finish our meal feeling more at peace than I have in weeks.

Chapter Eleven

I spend the next week working at the bookstore and drafting what I'm going to text or say to Seb if I end up calling him. I pace my kitchen, bedroom, and bathroom all week, unable to make my thoughts as concise as I'd like.

I want to get to the bottom of things with Peter as well. I text him, asking if he can call me when he's free tonight. He's finishing up a late Friday meeting near the penthouse and asks if he can stop by instead.

It's raining outside, and I don't want to get dressed and brave the wet streets, so I say yes. It's probably best we have this conversation in person, anyway.

I stay in my cozy dusty pink velvet sweatsuit and pull on some fuzzy white socks to keep the cold away.

It's nearly 8 o'clock when Peter buzzes the penthouse, and I'm more nervous than I thought I'd be when I walk to the front door to let him in.

Peter is considerate enough to whip his jacket outside of the front door to get as much of the rain off as possible. He takes his shoes off and comes into the living room, sitting down, as attentive as ever.

"Is everything okay?" He asks, all ears and a heartbreakingly sweet look on his face.

I nod. "Yeah, I have a few things to talk to you about."

"Oh geez, you're making me nervous." He laughs, a little jokingly and uncomfortably.

I bring up our text messages and scroll up to his 'I didn't know you worked out' and show it to him. "Can you tell me what you meant by this?"

He has a look of shock and surprise. "Uh, I meant that, you never mentioned working out before, so I didn't know you worked out." He smiles, a bit confused. "If I had known, I would've invited you to my work's private gym. It has great amenities."

I'm relieved, and a little sad to still have to follow through with my plan. "Thank you, Peter. You're very considerate. I've always liked that about you. I have to be honest, I thought you were saying something about my weight."

"Claire!" He nearly gasps. "I would never. I wouldn't change a thing about you." He stands, desperate for me to understand he never had any bad intentions.

"Thank you. It was all me. My insecurities and what not. I'm sorry for thinking so badly of you."

"I should say so. You gotta give me more credit than that." Peter says, a little exasperated.

"Exactly. You deserve the best. You've been nothing but a total sweetheart to me, but... I have something to admit." I breathe, sitting down and inviting him to join me. Peter scoots closer to me, still a little confused. "I've been...in love... with someone else. Someone I knew before I met you. And I've been debating with myself about whether I should let him go or give it another chance, and I think I decided to try again with him." I take a deep breath, but push through. "I'm sorry, but I can't keep seeing you. Truly though, you're one of the best men I know, and if you're up for it, I'd still love to be friends."

Peter takes a few moments to process my words. He nods, a little defeated, but tries throwing me a shy smile. "I can't say I'm not totally heartbroken, but if you know, you know, you know?" He chuckles, tears welling up in his eyes. "I think I'd still like to have you in my life. Who else will go eat with me at all these amazing places?"

A quiet laugh escapes me, despite the bittersweet moment. "I will eat with you anytime. And there are plenty of women in this city who would kill to go on these elaborate dinner dates with you. My friend Jenny is single, and she lives in an apartment filled with models, so I can set you up with any of them-"

"But none of them will be you." He interrupts, the pain in his voice now apparent.

That shoots a pang through my heart. "I'm sorry, Peter."

He wipes away a single tear. "It's okay. I mean, it's not, but it'll take some time for me to get over it."

Peter stands, offering his hand. "Friends?"

I reach up to shake his hand but when he steps forward, his sock slips on my polished marble floor, catapulting him onto my body and knocking me flat on my back onto the couch.

I laugh. He laughs. We're both laughing at this hilariously embarrassing tussle.

He braces both hands by my head, hovering over me. "Geez, I'm so sorry. Are you okay?"

"I'm fine." I laugh, playfully holding his face between my hands as we both work to stand up. I walk him to the door, and we're in high spirits. "I'll see you soon?"

Peter nods while he's slipping on his shoes. "Maybe we can still check out that Korean barbecue place next week? And maybe, you can bring Jenny? Introduce us? If you think I'm good enough for her, of course."

I nod. "I'll make sure she's there."

We hug goodbye. "I'll see you soon." Peter confirms. He slips on his jacket and turns to go, but quickly turns back. "Oh. Good luck with that, uh, other guy. I hope it works out. You deserve it."

My heart melts a little at this sweetheart in front of me. "Thank you. I need all the good vibes I can get."

Peter smiles, waves a small goodbye, and heads down the hall.

I sigh. One hurdle done.

Now to the bigger, more difficult obstacle.

I pull out my phone and text Seb. I type out my message, take another deep breath, and hit send.

> **Hello.**
> **I need to talk to you.**
> **Me**

I don't know what to expect. I've played this scenario over and over in my head.

Maybe he'll call.

Maybe he'll text.

Maybe he'll ignore me.

Maybe he's still mad at me.

Maybe he still doesn't see a future with me.

Maybe he's lost interest.

Maybe he doesn't find me attractive.

Maybe, he never did.

Maybe…he doesn't love me.

Maybe he can't ever love me.

I sit. I wait. I stare at my phone.

Three minutes pass.

Then 10.

Then 15.

My heart begins to sink. It's nearly shattering.

My insecurities are running wild. I've never let a man make me feel this way. So cloying, so pathetic, so wrapped up in the response or approval of *one* man.

17 minutes pass.

I panic. He's not going to respond. He's ignoring me. He's blocked me.

It's okay. He's probably working. He's probably busy. He's an important man. He can't be on his phone all day. I can't expect him to drop everything at the drop of a dime and respond. That isn't a fair expectation to set on someone I haven't talked to in months.

31 minutes pass.

46 minutes pass.

Alright. This is it. One last attempt. One final moment of wearing my heart on my sleeve.

I need you.
Me

I sigh. Okay. I did it. I reached out. He didn't respond. I made an honest attempt, and he isn't interested.

A sinking feeling fills my gut.

I'm heartbroken.

I'm unwanted.

I thought if I did this, I'd feel relieved.

But I don't.

I'm sad. So, so sad. I feel my eyes strain, tears filling, and then overflowing, running down my cheeks.

Seb doesn't want me.

It wasn't the same for him as it was for me.

My front door flies open.

"Claire!" I hear a voice shout.

It's Seb.

Chapter Twelve

I stand. In shock. It's him.

Sebastián.

In my hallway.

He's heated. Furious.

"Where is he?" Seb snarls, locking the front door behind him. He's scoping out the place, checking closet doors and slamming them shut when he doesn't find what he's looking for.

I watch him, taking in every detail of the massive man in front of me. He's sleek in his uniform, looking like a handsome devil all in black.

He let his beard grow, the lush, dark curls bringing a sultry dimension to his already stunning face.

Seb looks amazing.

My heart skips a beat. I don't notice I'm crying while I watch him search the place.

He checks the kitchen, then the bedroom and bathroom. When he finds it all empty, he comes to the living room and towers over me. He grabs my face, both hands on my cheeks and burns his eyes into mine.

"Don't cry, *hermosa*, I'll get him." His voice rumbles low in his chest, and my heart aches at the sound. He wipes away my tears with his thumbs and checks me over, as if looking for a gaping wound he needs to mend.

"Who?" I eventually ask quietly, still astounded by his warmth, body and voice filling my senses.

"That guy, that...boy who jumped you on this couch." He pulls all of the pillows off, as if a man could be hiding behind them.

"Oh...Peter?"

"Whatever." He dismisses, still angry. "I'll find him and I'll kill him."

"Wait, why?" I ask, slowly coming back to my senses and finally processing his words.

"I watched him jump on you! I saw it through the cameras. And look, he made you cry." He cracks his knuckles. "It's enough to kill him." He says, more to himself.

"Whoa, whoa, whoa, no one is killing anyone." I say, trying to calm him down. "Peter tripped. Or, I mean, he slipped, and then fell. Onto me. He didn't jump me." I try to explain, but it doesn't come out nearly as tantalizing and mature as I'd like.

That stops Seb in his tracks. "He didn't force himself on you?"

"No!" I say, a little flustered. "He...we... didn't you see us laughing? I walked him to the door. It was a very amicable separation."

"I didn't see that, no. I saw him jump you so I left the cameras and came as soon as I could."

"You came...here?"

"Yes, I thought you needed help."

"You did?"

"Yes, Claire!" Seb huffs, exasperated and frustrated. "You texted me!" He reaches into the breast pocket of his suit and pulls out his phone, pulling up our text thread. "See?" He shows my last text.

**I need you.
Mi Corazón**

I inhale sharply, finally getting on the same page as him. He didn't receive my other messages. He was away from his cameras, rushing here, and then getting my one message? No wonder he's so riled up.

"Oh. Seb, I'm sorry. This is a misunderstanding." I step closer, hoping to diffuse him.

"It better be, Claire, because I nearly ran over an elderly couple and a lady pushing a stroller to get here."

"I didn't text you to save me from Peter." I try to explain. When I planned our conversation in my head, I didn't take this series of events into account. "I broke up with him, and wanted to talk to you about-"

"You broke up?" Seb interrupts, coming off the tail-end of his rampage. He's still a little heated, both hands sternly on his hips, but his breath is slowing.

"I..uh, yes. We, uh, we broke up." I stumble, suddenly bashful and unsure of what I want to say.

"Why?"

"Uh, well..." Damnit, I didn't account for his questions, either. "Um, I wanted to talk to you about-"

"Because if he doesn't see what an incredible woman you are, it's his loss. You shouldn't be shedding any tears for that moron-"

"Seb!" I shout, a little louder than intended.

That halts him to a standstill.

"I don't want to talk about him. I want to talk about you."

"Me?" He straightens, a little taken aback at my harsh tone.

"I wanted to apologize, for one." I say, looking up into his stunning eyes. "I'm sorry about how I reacted the last time we were together. Frankly, it was pretty immature and horny of me, and you didn't deserve it."

His eyes soften, and when he doesn't try to interrupt me again, I continue. "Second, I wanted you to know I'd come back to the compound, if it meant we could be together."

"Claire..." He begins.

"Let me finish." I put up my hand so he can't say what I know he'll say to try to stop me. "I realized I first thought you didn't care for me the same way I cared for you because you wouldn't throw caution to the wind and go against your contract to have sex with me. But I realized I wasn't willing to sacrifice my freedom to be with you. But being out in the world, without you..." I struggle to find my next words. "It's worse. Out here. Without you." I try to read his face, but I can't make out what he's feeling about it all, so I continue.

"And I broke up with Peter because I realized I was in love with you." I can't look at Seb when I say this, so I keep my eyes on the white carpet under his shoes. "And I wanted to talk to you about, maybe, if you still felt the same way, we could try to be...together." This isn't how I want to say things, but it's what comes out. I wanted to ask him if he loved me the same way I love him? Does he think of me as much as I do him? If he does, then we could belong to each other.

Seb is silent.

He doesn't respond.

A lifetime passes. An eternity more. I try to give him the time and space to think, but another painfully long moment passes, and he still doesn't say anything.

I look at his face for any sign of a decision, but he looks as if he's at war with himself.

I panic.

I backtrack. "But if you don't feel the same way, I understand, I-"

"I've loved you for years." Seb grumbles, and I'm unsure I hear him correctly. I don't have time to respond before he rushes towards me and kisses me so deeply, he's bending me backwards. His lush, hot lips feel so good on mine, and I kiss back, already intoxicated by his taste.

He's just as I remember. Sturdy, firm and solid. He tastes like the same masculine orange and bourbon as he did before, but mixed with a clean cologne.

Seb is the first to pull away, bringing me back up to stand on my own two feet. "I have a confession." He says slowly, his hot breath warming my lips.

It's my turn to be silent. I don't know what to say, so I stay in his arms and look into his eyes, giving him the patience he gave me.

He doesn't wait for my response. "You might not like what I'm going to say, but since you're laying everything out, I should too."

I nod, eager to hear what he's been holding back.

"It's best if I show you." He pulls out his phone, taps around a few screens, and puts it in my hands.

It's us. Right now. From the security cameras. I see us standing in the living room of the penthouse. Me holding his phone, Seb standing in front of me.

"You have a live feed of the penthouse on your phone?" I ask, not as scandalized as I prepared myself to be. I was thinking he was going to show me he had a kink for feet, or something.

"I have a live feed of anywhere and everywhere you are." He taps down a menu on the top of his screen. Saved under "Most Frequent" cameras are the ones labeled:

'CLAIRE STRANDE'
'CLAIRE HOME'
'CLAIRE JENNY'
'CLAIRE BAR'
'CLAIRE KARAOKE'
'CLAIRE BOBA 1'
'CLAIRE BOBA 2'
'CLAIRE BOBA 3'
'CLAIRE SUBWAY'
"CLAIR RIPPED BODICE"
'CLAIRE DOCTOR'
'CLAIRE BRUNCH'
'CLAIRE DIM SUM'
'CLAIRE WORKOUT'
'CLAIRE BODEGA'
'CLAIRE HAIR'

'CLAIRE PETER'

And the list goes on, and on. My whole life, from my favorite restaurants, to my favorite bookstores, Seb has saved the cameras for everywhere I go.

"You've been watching me?" I say, slowly understanding.

He nods grimly. "For years. Ever since I started at the compound. Ever since your dad charged me with making sure you were safe." He sits on the armrest of the couch, folding his arms. "When we're fully staffed, and the other guys are watching the other cameras, I'm watching you."

I'm stunned into silence. I click through the cameras, and sure enough, the security systems of all of my favorite stores, my friend's apartments, my subway route, are all saved.

I say nothing, so Seb lays out even more. "When your dad first asked me to keep tabs on you, I figured you were some spoiled post-grad who was playing commoner, drinking and partying like the rest of them. But you were calm. Quiet. A reader. My first day on the job, I found you crying just inside your front door here." He points his thumb behind him towards the door he just barged through. "You started taking off your clothes to shower and I was stunned. I'd never seen a woman as beautiful as you." His eyes are dark and guilty, but smoldering. "That was the beginning of my obsession. I watched you, telling myself it was for work, that you were so important to your parents, they needed to keep an eye on you 24/7 but really, I couldn't get enough of you. I watched you eat alone, read alone, go out with Jenny, spend hours in bookstores, buy boba, sit in the park, finally get the job you wanted for so long. I memorized your smile, your face, your hair, your clothes. I memorized everything about you. You became my life."

I look at him now, no longer interested in the cameras on his phone, and see the pain on his face twisting his features.

He sighs. "And you were doing okay. Lonely, a little lost, but fine. Safe. I could watch you and know you wouldn't get yourself into trouble. Until the night of Jenny's birthday, when you slapped that piece of shit. God, I was so proud of you, but I could see the fallout as it was happening. The idiot calling his parents, their decision to kill you, everything. I showed your parents right away. They panicked, sent me and everyone who was free to get you from work."

Seb sighs. "And I finally saw you. Not on a screen. Not through the cameras, but with my own eyes. Damn you were beautiful." He smiles at the memory. "And shorter than I thought."

"Hey." I interject, in a slightly playful tone, resenting his last words.

He just shoots me the smallest, regretful smile. "But I had you in my hands."

I remember that. When he took me into the back alley the first day we met, he was holding my hand.

Seb looks at me knowingly. "And then, well, you know the rest. I finally had you, and I could protect you in real life, not through a screen, and I was determined to do that. I told myself I could do my job. Keep things professional." He sighs. "Until you started looking at me the way you do."

Seb stands cautiously, slowly coming towards my planted body in the middle of the room.

"In the years I watched you, you never looked at anyone the way you look at me. And it drove me crazy." He chuckles, laughing more to himself. "I still don't know how I managed to keep you as far away as I did."

"Well, not *that* far." I say, surprisingly playful.

He smiles, a small laugh huffing from his chest. "Yeah." Seb reaches down and gently grabs my hands. "So. You have a regular old stalker on your hands." He brings both of my hands up and kisses the back of each. "I thought you should know. That it might change your mind."

I hold his large, warm hands, taking long moments to feel every inch of him.

I want to feel more.

My hands slide up to his wrists. They're thick and strong. The hair on his forearms go all the way down and peek past his sleeve, and I want to take his jacket and shirt off to feel it beneath my fingers.

"Claire?" He whispers, asking for my answer.

His voice saying my name sounds so right. I close my eyes, committing it to memory.

"So… you *do* love me?" I ask, hesitantly.

Seb laughs, my words surprising him. "Yes."

I nod, sliding my hands up his arms, over his jacket and snaking them behind his neck. "I was worried you didn't love me."

"I've loved nothing *but* you for the better part of two years."

My heart skips. "How come I've never seen you, even when I went to the compound to visit my parents?"

Seb shrugs. "I didn't have a reason to leave the surveillance room until that night. I stayed there watching the cameras, out of sight. We were so short staffed that night of Jenny's birthday, they needed me to find you and bring you back."

I nod again, understanding.

I should be upset. I should be put-off, but I feel myself settling into the comfortable existence of being *known.*

He knows me. Better than anyone. Better than I know myself. I don't have to convince him to love me.

He already does.

I smile at him. "I know I should be creeped out, but honestly, I'm more relieved I don't have to give you my rehearsed speech about why you should be with me."

Seb wraps his arms around my waist, and I feel warm, supported, and at home. "I'd still like to hear it." He says tenderly.

I feign a sigh, pretending to be *so* put out by listing off my reasons. "It mostly consists of how good I'd be to you. How good you'd eat if you were with me. How much I love having your cock in my mouth."

"Fuck, Claire." Seb groans, rolling his head back with a smile.

"I'm not finished!" I laugh, shushing him. "I was going to say I love having your cock in my mouth and I know I could ride you so well if you gave me the chance. I'd fuck you so good, you'd be craving my pussy."

Seb grinds his bulge into me, growling.

"Mmm, I like that. I like what I feel." I say, reaching to palm his hardening cock in my hand. "I had the best dream about you."

"Oh?" He breathes, his eyes smoldering.

Chapter Thirteen

I bite my lip. "Yeah. I was fucking you, you were fucking me, and you made me come over and over again. I woke up from an actual orgasm in my sleep. My clit was throbbing." I hiss, wanting him to know how much he has taken over my life.

Seb slams his mouth onto mine, devouring me. His hand comes up and palms my breast through my velvet top, kneading my softness.

The pressure on my nipple is wonderful, and I moan into his mouth.

"Fuck, you don't know how many times I've thought about you in the shower." He breathes, breaking away for air.

"Yeah?" I sigh, desperate for him.

Seb nods. "I've come thinking about you more times than I can count."

"Oh my god, Seb, you're driving me crazy." I breathe, practically climbing him.

"Now you know how it feels." He growls, tickling me.

I yelp at the jolt to my senses, laughing at his fingers prodding my sides. "Stop it!"

Seb pulls me to sit on the couch. I bounce into my seat just as he kneels on the floor in front of me. At this height, we're closer to being face-to-face.

He gently puts his hands on my knees and slowly pushes my legs open, making room for him to come closer. He settles near my center, taking my face in his hands and kisses me, sweetly.

I reach for the button on his jacket, and he leans back to let me slide it off his shoulders. He watches my sure fingers reach for his shirt, and when I'm certain he isn't going to stop me, I push the black buttons through their holes, one by one, to reveal his hard, built chest beneath a black undershirt.

Seb does me the favor of slipping his shirts off for me, and I feel my eyes grow wide at the sight of him.

He's so fucking hot. Jesus Christ. His olive skin stretching across his shoulders, his giant arms, and the smattering of hair across his chest instantly makes me wet. I want to close my legs together to relieve the pressure building there, but a giant man is in my way, so I can't.

He lets me trace my fingers on his muscles, taking him in my hands. I squeeze anywhere I like, and he watches me enjoy him. I bend forward to kiss his chest and pepper my lips across his shoulders, neck, and everywhere else I can reach.

Seb gently pulls back and I feel his hands come to the hem of my top. "My turn." He grumbles, and I lift my arms to let him pull off my pink velvet top.

He hisses in his next breath when his eyes fall to my breasts in a sheer, lace pink bra. My nipples are hard, showing through the lace, and they're even more wired from the cold air and his burning eyes.

"Fuck." He whispers, his eyes full of the sight of my ample breasts in front of him. He looks like he's at a buffet and doesn't know where to start. "You're even more beautiful than I imagined."

"They aren't anything you haven't seen before." I smile, squeezing them together by bringing my arms towards my center.

He shakes his head slowly, eyes piercing mine. "Not like this, Claire. Not through the cameras, or in a hurried rush." He looks back down at his feast.

Both of his hands come up to palm my breasts, his thumbs running over my nipples, pulling a quick moan from me. "You're perfect like this." He gives my tits a good squeeze before coming in to kiss me, slipping off my bra straps from my shoulders.

He reaches around and unclasps my bra. Seb pulls it off, tossing it aside and revealing my breasts completely.

"Fuck." He breathes, squeezing my softness before bending down and taking one nipple into his mouth while firmly rolling the other between his fingers.

I squirm beneath him, luxuriating in the pleasure that fires through me. He moves from one nipple to the other, kissing, nipping, licking and sucking me until I'm so near my first orgasm, I moan in frustrated pleasure.

Seb gently lays me down on my wide, deep couch, hovering over me to grind his hard cock into my pussy, giving me the slightest sense of relief. I wrap my legs around his hips and match him, moving to rub my clit against his pants.

"Are you gonna come so easily for me?" He whispers, kissing my neck and still teasing one nipple with his firm, nimble fingers. "So hot for me you'll come without me even touching your sweet, wet pussy?"

"Seb..." I moan, trying to reach for him, lost in my pleasure. "I'm close."

"I know." He breathes in my ear. "I know when you touch yourself, your body tenses up and your head rolls back just as you're about to come." He grinds his hips harder into me to get me closer. "I watch you with your vibrator. The way you shake and close your eyes. You're so fucking sexy. I wanted to be the one to make you come. To get you there."

"You do!" I whine, so close to the edge, I'm teetering on falling.

"I will, beautiful. I'm going to make you come, and then I'm going to get my mouth on you, so wet and slick, and fuck you with my tongue until you come all over my face. And then I'm going to give you my cock and fuck you until you beg me to stop."

His words push me over the edge and I'm coming, writhing beneath him, my wetness slicking my panties as I rub up into his hard cock. My breathy moans echo through the room.

Seb loves it. He watches me, taking in my face as I'm lost in my orgasm. He kisses my breasts, licks and sucks my nipples and buries his face between my softness, inhaling, tasting, and enjoying me.

As my pleasure slowly fades, I'm renewed with purpose. I reach for Seb's belt and tear it loose, freeing his button and pulling his zipper down quickly. He stands to shuck off his pants, boxers and socks, now completely naked and gloriously baring himself to me.

I reach down and throw off my pants and panties as well. I'm naked, too, enthralled by the anticipation of feeling his chiseled body on top of me.

Seb's eyes roam over me slowly, taking every moment he can to enjoy my body.

He kneels back down on the plush white rug and slowly crawls to me. "Open your legs."

"No." I smile playfully, clamping my legs together to shield my pussy from him.

His eyes grow wide, rising to the challenge. "Oh, you don't want to listen?" He clamps my knees together with one hand and rolls me onto my side, exposing my ass. He gives me one firm spank, which pulls a laughing yelp from me. I surrender by rolling onto my back again and opening my legs for him.

"That's my girl." He smirks, kissing me and nestling his large body between my legs again.

"Fuck, I love it when you call me that." I moan, burying my fingers in his hair.

"Yeah?" He smiles, kissing me again.

I nod.

"Well if you're good, I'll say it again." He teases, heartbreakingly handsome above me.

"What do I need to do to be good?" I ask, playing along.

"Let me taste your juicy pussy."

"Oh my god, Seb! You're so crude." I playfully slap his arm, but also open my knees more for him to have better access to my wet core.

"I'm just getting started, honey." He winks before trailing kisses down my neck, my chest, and licking and sucking my nipples, pulling more moans from me before moving lower. He kisses my soft stomach and inhales deeply when he gets to my curls, not hesitating to flatten his tongue against my slick lips and catapulting me towards my next orgasm.

It comes quickly, jolting through my nerves. I bury my fingers in Seb's hair while he tongues my clit, already a master at finding my most sensitive spots. He slips a finger into me, pushing me further into my pleasure, and I ride his hand and face as I'm overcome, his beard bringing an even more inviting friction to my folds.

"Oh god, that's good. Fuck. You're amazing, yes, yes, yes!" I moan, nearly incoherent in my ramblings as I'm lost in the height of my pleasure.

"That's it, that's my girl, keep coming. Fuck." Seb growls while his fingers keep working inside me. His rapid pace keeps me going, and my body stays tense while I ride out my delectable orgasm.

As I'm coming down, Seb slows, coming up for air and wiping his mouth on his arm before kissing me hotly and tenderly.

"I have to have you. *Te querido entera.*" His breath hits my mouth.

"But can I..." I reach for his cock to try to pay back the favor, but he grabs my wrist, stopping me.

"I'm so close to coming. I don't want this to be over too fast. Let me inside you?" Seb breathes, and his voice is so rough and strained, I can only do everything and anything he asks.

I nod, reaching down to grab his cock, and this time, he lets me. I stroke him a few times before lining him up, urging him to push in.

"We don't need a condom." I tell him, and he nods. He's watched me go to my doctor once every 3 months for my birth control shot, so he knows we're covered.

Seb tries to be slow, but I'm dripping wet, so he slides his huge, thick cock into me easily.

I'm ready, but not ready enough for him. He's too big for my walls to handle, and I wince a little at how far he's stretching me, despite being so hot and open for him.

But he feels incredible. I'm so full, and he reaches every inch inside me.

Seb doesn't move yet. He lets me get used to his size, so I breathe through it, trying to relax into him. He props himself on his elbows on either side of my head and kisses me slowly.

"How's this?" He whispers, still unmoving, but keeping himself buried deep inside me.

I sigh, trying to adjust. "You're huge. I knew you wouldn't fit." I nearly moan, because it feels so good just having him in me.

"You can take it." He encourages, kissing my temple. "Fuck, how are you so tight?"

I lean up to kiss him, and he gently coaxes my mouth open to caress my tongue with his. "Am I as tight as you imagined?" I strain.

My words stir something in him. His arms tighten around me. His body tenses above me. Seb tangles his fingers in my hair, gently pulling, giving me the most thrilling sensation.

He growls in my ear. "Tighter. Better. Everything about you is better than anything my tiny brain can think of." He pulls his cock out slightly, then slowly pushes in. "Fuck." He breathes, burying his face in my neck. "Fuck, you feel so good."

"Mmm." I bite my lip, running my hands down his back. "Again." I ask, but it comes out more like a demand. "But slow."

Seb obliges, pulling his hips back to draw his cock through my walls and he slowly, oh so slowly, pushes in again.

The sensation is amazing, but his thickness is still stretching me towards a teetering pain, and my breath hitches at the feeling.

"Too much?" He asks, in tune with my every breath.

I nod quickly, trying to move things along. "It's okay. I'm okay." My voice is tense, and Seb hears it. He stops moving immediately.

"Oh Claire, I knew you'd be good, but this good?" He kisses my lips, unbothered by our pace. "How can a man stand it? How does every man not come at the sight of you? The smell of you? Fuck." He kisses my throat. "We'll go as slow as you want. I want you to come on this cock so hard, you won't be able to walk tomorrow."

I moan. "Seb..."

"That's it, *hermosa*, I can stay like this all night. Buried in you all night." He gently bites the skin on my shoulder, and the sensation shocks through my entire system.

"I'm so full." I whine, loving his words. My hips glide on their own, slowly moving back to pull off his shaft, and coming forward to take him in again.

"Fuck Claire, that's it. As slow as you need."

I do it again. And again. "I don't want to go slow, I want to fuck you."

Seb chuckles. "Not if it hurts you."

"I think..." I buck my hips up to meet him, and the movement stretches me to a point it feels good. Really good. I'm hungry for more. "I think I'm okay."

"You're perfect." Seb smiles, kissing me. He tests the waters, pulling back and cautiously driving into me. His pace is slow, languid, and it's deliciously decadent.

"Oh fuck, that's good." I moan, looking up into his heated eyes. "Just like that."

"Like this?" His hips make slow waves above me, and my body is gradually overtaken with pleasure.

"Yes, oh my god, yes." I reach for his cheek, holding his face. Seb's beard is coarse on my palm and having him so close, exactly where I want him to be, fills me with warmth. "You're so hot, do you know that?"

He chuckles, turning his head to kiss the inside of my palm. "If you say so."

"I do." I strain, reaching up to kiss him. "Fuck, you're hot. I love the beard. Did I tell you how much I love the beard?"

"You didn't." Seb kisses my cheek, then trailing kisses down my neck.

"It makes you look even more handsome. And fuckable."

He huffs a laugh against my skin. "Anything that makes you want to fuck me, I'll do." Seb swirls his hips, and the change in motion gives me another jolt of pleasure.

"Seb, oh my god." I'm tense, arching up from the pleasure. "You're amazing. You fill me up so-" I gasp when he does it again.

"I love how you sound." He rasps in my ear, picking up the pace. " Like music. I could listen to you for the rest of my life and never get used to how your voice makes my cock hard."

That drives me crazy. "Fuck, I'm coming again." I moan just before a few more slow pumps push me over the edge.

This time, it's slow. The pleasure unfurls throughout my center to my limbs, warming and numbing my arms and legs. I keep my attention on Seb, sharing this orgasm with him, our eyes locked.

I'm filled with love. He's making love to me, I'm making love to him, and we're making magic.

My walls are clenching while I ride my gentle high and Seb is forced to push harder through the resistance. I'm almost too tight again, but he's focused on staying slow, holding the reins on his control.

"Fuuuuck." He breathes through clenched teeth. "Fuck Claire, that's it. Give it to me. Come all over this cock. That's my girl." Seb sits up to grab my hips but keeps thrusting, watching my folds take his length with his lust-filled eyes.

Suddenly, he snaps. When Seb feels my walls begin to relax as I'm coming down from an orgasm that has taken over all of my senses, he begins to pound me faster, finally taking his full pleasure in my wanting folds.

"Oh my god, Seb, yes!" I scream as I'm being pushed towards my next orgasm sooner than I expected, barely coming down from the last one. He's pounding into me relentlessly, a wild animal bucking into my core, and the fierce, unbridled chase of his own pleasure shoots me towards my own. I'm coming again, and he knows, and I'm tighter than ever again, clamping around his glorious cock.

Seb bends down, resting on his elbows to wrap his arms underneath my shoulders, caging me while he fucks me into the cushions. "Fuck, Claire. *Estoy enloquecido por ti. Te amo más que a nada. Te amo* Claire."

With one final, long thrust deep into my center, Seb pulls out his cock and comes all over my stomach. One hand is pumping himself, the other comes to my clit and rubs me so I can ride out my pleasure with him.

His lips are wet and parted slightly. His eyes, hooded and dark, burn into me as he watches himself finish across my soft skin. It's the first time I can feel myself coming at the same time as someone else, and it's satisfying beyond measure to share this with Seb.

"Fuck." He breathes, leaning down to kiss me quickly. "Fuck." He breathes into my neck, reaching to kiss the inside of my breasts before standing. "You're amazing."

"You are." I smile, sleepily.

Seb walks to my bathroom and runs a washcloth under warm water before sauntering back to me. I reach up to try and take it from him but he pulls his hand back, silently asking if he can clean me off.

I'm weak, too tired to fight, so I let my arm go limp at my side and allow him to clean me up.

When he goes back to the bathroom to take care of himself, I pounce in bed, hiding my cold body under the covers.

Seb finds me, and I grab his hand to pull him into bed, unwilling to let him go.

He doesn't protest or try to leave. He settles in, spooning me from behind, and falls asleep.

Chapter Fourteen

It's still dark when I feel Seb's hand slide down my front, getting lost in my curls. His warm fingers languidly rub my folds and I'm instantly wet, pulled from sleep in the most tantalizing way. Only a few hours must have passed since our last fuck, but he's ready again, and I'm easily convinced.

His cock is hot and hard against my back. I try to reach around to stroke him, but the angle and his closeness keeps me from grabbing him the way I want.

It doesn't matter though because in an instant, Seb flips me around and lifts me above him, forcing me to straddle his hardness.

I gasp, my system shocked by the sudden change, but a breathy laugh falls from my lips.

"Jesus, Seb." I plant my hands on his firm chest as I'm grinding my wetness onto his cock, slicking him up and down. "You wanna be in me?" I slur from the sleep that is already fading from my mind.

Seb grunts, but doesn't respond. He only massages my hips, urging me to keep going.

I lift one knee up to align his tip with my center. I wobble, having to come higher than comfortable due to his length, but he keeps me steady, his firm grasp on my waist holding me above him.

I finally get him right where I want him and slide down his cock slowly.

I'm stretched, filled to the brim. His thickness knocks the wind out of me, and I have to gasp to remind myself to breathe. The fullness in my core is too much and I collapse over him, hands coming down on either side of his head.

Being this close, I can finally see his face in the dark. His eyes are closed and his features are entirely relaxed, not twisted with pleasure like they were earlier tonight.

"Seb?" I try to whisper, but it comes out more like a moan.

He doesn't respond. I kiss his cheek, but he doesn't move an inch.

Oh my god, I think he's asleep.

"Seb..." I kiss him again, a little more forcefully this time.

His grip tightens on my hips when he stirs beneath me, and his eyes shoot open, meeting mine.

"Oh my god!" I nearly scream.

"Mmm..." Seb grumbles, looking around the room, then back up to me. "Claire..."

"I- I..." I try to explain. "You..."

"Did I...?" He tries to remember the last few moments, slowly waking. "Am I...in you?" He moves his hips to thrust into me, trying to find his bearings.

The movement feels incredible, if not a little painful, and I bury my head in his neck as I'm overcome by the feeling.

"Yes..." I moan, trying to breathe through the pleasurable pain. "You lifted me up and..."

"I thought I was dreaming." His hand comes up to cradle my head as he kisses my temple. "God, you feel incredible. Do you want to get off?" Seb asks, his voice rough in my ear.

"Do you want me off?" I whisper, rocking above him slowly and already feeling myself nearing my next orgasm.

"Fuck no." He growls, urging me to keep lifting up and sliding down his cock. He plants his feet on the mattress and begins to meet my thrusts.

He's slow, at first. Being on top gives my body more control, and I adjust to his size more quickly. Seb is eager, though, and picks up his pace within the next few strokes. He throws me off my rhythm so I'm not really riding him, he's fucking up into me, and it's glorious.

His strength, size and control fills my senses, and I can let loose under the cloak of darkness. I allow myself to get lost in the pleasure as it swallows me, moaning and grinding without holding back.

Seb slows, allowing me to take over, and I move above him in every way that feels incredible. I lean forward to place my hands on the headboard, hovering my breasts above his face while I pull my pleasure from his cock.

"Holy fuck." Seb hisses, burying his face between my breasts. He feasts, kissing, licking, and gently biting my nipples. When his hands come up to pinch my sensitive tips, the sensation shoots through my nerves and I throw my head back in pleasure.

"Oh god, that's good." I say, the words barely coherent as my orgasm draws closer, clouding my mind.

"Fuck yes. Fuck, Claire, come on this cock." He growls, thrusting his hips and driving up into me again.

My walls tighten, my muscles tense and I'm close, so close to coming, I moan in frustration.

"Fucking god, *mi amor*, you're perfect. You feel so hot. So fucking tight."

His words cut through my hazy pleasure. "What did you say?" I breathe, still chasing my high.

"Your pussy is so tight around my cock. Fuck, you're..." He grunts, planting his feet again and thrusting into me at full speed, taking his pleasure.

"You called me... you said-" I can't finish my thought. I'm coming, hard and fast above his pounding hips.

My walls are so tight, Seb's cock slips out, but he wrestles himself back in to fuck me through my orgasm.

The climax rushes through me, overtaking my senses. My muscles are tense, and I'm writhing, desperate for anything to ground me, so I reach for his shoulders, his arms, his hands, anything.

Seb's grip on my waist tightens when I grab onto his forearms. He's fucking me so hard and fast, his pelvis is thrusting against my inner thighs, creating the most obscene and delicious smacking sound.

Seb pounds a few final times deep into my core, and the intensity feels so wonderful, I almost come again.

His movements stop, and he's coming inside me, spilling himself in my walls. I feel his thick cum drip down my thighs, and the sensation is so deliciously indecent, it makes me feel like I own his pleasure, and he owns mine.

"Fuck." Seb breathes, sitting up to kiss me. "Fuck, let me stay here." He wraps his arms around my shoulders and gently flips me onto my back, his cock still inside me. "I'll be the happiest man in the world if you let me stay inside you."

I huff a laugh. "Stay." I smile up at him, locking my ankles behind his back to trap him in place. "Don't ever go."

"Mmm, never." He says against my lips, his lazy kisses filling me with butterflies. "Let me clean you up."

"I think there might be a lot more to clean up than a washcloth can handle."

Seb nods, proudly apologetic. "I'll take you to the shower."

I nod, still groggy from our impromptu fucking.

He slips out of me, and even though he's technically soft after coming in me, he's still impressive, and the loss of him from my core pulls a small gasp from my lips.

He warms the shower while I clip up my hair to keep it from getting wet, and we both step in. The wide cascade is enough to keep our bodies under the running stream. Seb grabs my white loofah and squeezes some lemon body wash skillfully, as if we've done this for each other thousands of times before. He lathers it up between his hands, and when it's nice and bubbly, he places it on my chest, silently asking my permission to clean me.

I play along, opening my arms wide to let him do his thing. Seb smiles before he begins his ministrations, first lathering up my shoulders, then going down each arm.

When he gets to my breasts, his playfulness becomes more heated. His eyes darken with desire, and he's watching the soap run down my curves. My nipples are already hard from his attention, but when he gently brushes the sensitive tips with his hand, I gasp, getting excited once again.

A mischievous smile pulls at his lips, but he doesn't say anything. He continues down my body, lathering up my back and stomach. He kneels on the marble floor to reach down the length of my legs.

Seb smirks up at me, his head now level with my pelvis. "Do you want to take over?" He asks, resting the loofah on my hip to give me the choice to either allow him near my pussy, or wash myself.

I bend down and plant a quick kiss on his forehead before dramatically leaning my back against the shower wall and hooking one knee over his shoulder. The marble is shockingly cold on my skin, but I don't let it bother me.

"You might as well finish the job." I smile, wiggling my toes behind his ear.

His laugh is hearty and echoes through the bathroom. "Don't have to tell me twice."

He's gentle but thorough on my folds, taking his time to clean what is left of our mess on the inside of my thighs.

Seb tosses the loofah over his shoulder and rinses the rest of the suds from me, his fingers softly running the length of my slit. He's so big and warm, I feel pussy getting wet again.

His eyes shoot up to mine when he realizes his fingers are slick with my arousal. "Already?" He asks, impressed.

"With you? Always." I say.

He grunts with approval, the sound rumbling in his chest. "You look so good, I gotta have a taste." Seb breathes, but he's asking for permission again, and my stomach flutters at his consideration and the genuine choice he offers me every time.

"Okay." I smile, running my fingers through his wet hair and gently pulling his face towards my center.

Seb dives in, his thumb immediately on my clit while his mouth kisses and laps at my wetness. A soft moan vibrates from his mouth through my core, and I know he loves how I taste.

"*Exquisito.* Like dessert." He rumbles, winking up at me before bringing his other hand up to slide two fingers into my folds.

I gasp from being filled with him again. He curves his fingers and finds my G-Spot easily, hitting me in all the right places. I attempt to control my voice, but it's shaky from how good he makes me feel. "Oh stop it, you'll make me blush." I huff, trying to smile through the pleasure.

"I'll make you come." He teases, but there's a hint of serious determination in his tone.

"Mmm, you're very good at that." I try to say, feeling myself nearly coming again.

"Thank you." Seb tries hiding his pride but his smile makes me laugh, and before I know it, I'm coming on his hand.

I hold onto his arms to steady myself as I'm tensing above him, my orgasm shooting through me.

Seb is a sturdy, unmovable piller as he fingers me into oblivion. "That's my girl. Fuck yes." He growls, working my clit with his thumb at the same time he's fingering me.

I writhe and moan and cry through it all, and he's right there at my feet giving it to me.

When I finally begin coming down from my high, I pull Seb up, urging him to stand. He lets me kiss him slowly while my mind is still clouded from the orgasm.

"That was incredible." I say against his lips.

He smiles. "I had a pretty great view down there." He says, his hands gently coming to give my breasts a firm squeeze.

I reach down to find his cock and he's hard. Fuck, he's really hard. He just came a few moments ago and he's hard again? I try to figure it out, knowing most men need at least a few more moments to recover, but he's long and thick in my hands, straining with desire. I begin stroking him and I have to use both hands to reach most of him.

"This is your fault." Seb grumbles, his voice catching in his throat from my attention to his cock.

"I was going to say I'm very impressed by your rebound time."

He huffs out a laugh. "Don't get used to it. It's not every day a man has the woman of his dreams in his hands. Give me some time to get used to it."

"I hope you never do." I tease, reaching for my body wash and squeezing a generous stream onto his cock. It slicks him up, and I can stroke him more easily.

I love watching the suds form on his length. The head of his cock is covered with tiny bubbles, and my mouth starts to water from the thought of rinsing him clean and licking his tip.

He grunts. "Fuck, the way you look at me…" He grabs my face and pulls me up to kiss my lips, hard. "Like you wanna fuck me. Like you want this cock in your mouth."

"I do. I'm craving it." My words are nothing but desperate moans as I stroke him faster.

Seb grabs my hands and pulls them free. "Stop, stop, stop." He leans down to kiss me quickly. "I'm about to come, and I want to fuck you again, so let me stop for a second."

I nod. "Okay."

He wraps his arms around me, pressing his cock into my soft stomach. "I'll finish showering. You dry off and get into bed. I'll find you." He smacks my ass, pulling a yelp from me.

I laugh. "Okay. I hate shower sex, anyway. The water washes away my...excitement."

"Mmm, and I want you wet for me."

I smile before giving him a quick kiss. "I will be." When I turn to reach for my towel, Seb gives my ass another playful smack, making me laugh again.

I'm drying myself while standing on the plush bath mat in front of my sink, watching him wash his hair. Then quickly, Seb lathers up to run the loofah over his body. He's so big and cut, the suds seem to almost get stuck on his abs and bulging arms.

When he's finished washing his face, he turns to rinse his back and finally sees me watching him. He quirks his head, silently asking *'what's up?'*

I lick my lips and lean back against my sink, unclipping my hair to let it fall around my face. "Just enjoying the view."

His smile is shy when he looks at his feet, but he's happy and proud. It's written all over his face.

"You're unbelievable." He shouts over the sound of the running water. As he's finishing up, I head to my bathroom cabinet to grab a spare towel to leave it on the warmer next to the shower for him.

I quickly moisturize my face and toss my towel in my hamper, diving into bed naked. The room is a bit cold, so I bury under the covers to try and warm up.

The sound of the water turning off squeaks through the room, and my heart skips a beat. I poke my head out from under my duvet, excited to see what he looks like after a shower. A few short moments pass while he's finishing up.

Then suddenly, he's there, stepping around the corner and heading towards me, hair damp, with a towel tied low on his hips.

I shake my head, trying to look stern, but I can't help but smile.

"What?" He chuckles, crawling up the length of the bed to lay next to me.

I feign a dramatic sigh. "You're just a little too hot. Too sexy. I almost can't handle it."

Seb throws off his towel before gently pulling back the covers and crawling over me to nestle between my legs. I'm open and ready for him, and he's already starting to feel like home. His heavy body, hot at the core and cool to the touch from the shower, fits perfectly on top of me.

I sigh again, but this time, from comfort. "I can get used to this."

"So can I." He's leaning on his elbows, propping himself up on either side of my head. Seb leans down and plants a gentle kiss on my lips. "How are you? You done with me yet?"

I wrap my legs around his thick waist and grind my wet pussy up against his still-hard cock. "Does this feel done to you?"

He grinds down into my folds, swirling his hips into me. "Thank god." Seb growls. "You're too good to stay away."

"M'yeah? You like how I feel?" I tease, gently running the length of my slit against the underside of his hardness.

"Fuck yeah." He breathes, his hot words warming my lips.

"You like how my wet pussy feels on your huge, hard cock?"

He moans. "You feel amazing."

"I bet you love making me wet. When I think about you, how you smell, how you sound, how you taste..." I shudder. "Oh god, my pussy starts dripping."

Seb grunts as he thrusts a little harder into me. "Yeah, I know how much you like sucking my cock."

I moan. "I love it."

"Watching you work your pretty little mouth all over the tip. You take it so good, honey, so open and wet and hot. And when you take me to the back of your throat, and you're choking and sucking, I know your pussy is drenched from how much you love it."

My moan sounds more like a whine, but I don't care. "Seb..." I desperately grind my pussy against his cock, slicking his length completely, but he doesn't push into me. He lets me hump his length, and the pressure from his impressive shaft coated in my wetness gives the most glorious friction.

"And you love having my cock stretch you out." He growls in my ear, sending shivers down my spine. "Your wet, little pussy. So tight, I barely push in and you're coming."

I almost climax from his words alone, but Seb is slowly and firmly rubbing his cock along my slit, the pleasure almost pushing me over the edge.

"Two strokes and you're coming. Fuck, it's enough to drive me out of my mind. You're beautiful when you come, tight on my cock. And when you scream my name…" He kisses my temple. "Fuck, I can come just thinking about it."

"Seb!" I cry, edging towards my peak.

"Fuuuck, just like that. You close, *hermosa*? You gonna let me make you come?"

"I'm so close, but I want you in me." I beg.

He smirks. "You want my cock to fill you up again?"

I nod in desperation.

"You want me to come inside you again?"

"Yes!" I say, breathless.

Seb suddenly stops grinding into me. "Tell me how much you want me." He growls, and his dominating tone gives me shivers.

"I want you to fuck me so hard, I see stars. I want my pussy to make you feel good. Take me however you want, as hard and as fast as you want. I want it all."

"You want me to fuck you any way I want?" He demands softly, his voice commanding.

"Yes, whatever you want." I strain from pleasurable frustration.

"I can flip you on all fours and fuck your pretty little pussy from behind, watching your sweet, round ass bouncing while I pound into you?"

"Oh my god, yes, that sounds amazing."

His fingers come down to pinch my nipple, making me cry out from the shock of pleasure rushing through me. "You'll squeeze your perfect tits together and let me fuck them?"

"Yes, yes!"

He holds my chin, lifting my face so I can watch him stare into my eyes. "You'll let me fuck this pretty little mouth until I come in your hot, tight throat?"

"I'll take it all. Every inch. I'll swallow every last drop."

This makes Seb moan. "Fuck, Claire. I can't believe I have you."

I bring my hips up to find the tip of his cock and reach down to align him with my core. After finding my entrance, I push up to finally have his cock fill me again, and his hiss of pleasure gives me chills.

I kiss him. "I'm the one who gets to have you. God, you feel so good. So deep." I moan.

Seb kneels up to get a better view, grabbing my hips to pound into me quickly.

His pace slaps his pelvis into mine and the sound is delicious. It's indecent and slutty and gorgeously dirty, and he makes me feel coveted.

The hard fucking shakes the headboard, and my breasts bounce from his efforts. He's looking down at me, eye-fucking my tits, and one hand reaches up to greedily squeeze one in his hand.

My overflowing chest is too much to fit in one of his hands, so he's squeezing, releasing, and massaging all he can hold until a growl escapes his throat.

He has to release my hips to take both of my breasts in his hands, fondling them hungrily before slowing his thrusts and bending down to bury his face in my softness.

"Fuck, I love your tits." His words are muffled in my boobs. "Delicious." Seb squeezes, his hands massaging and rubbing while his tongue licks my nipples. He takes one into his mouth, sucking and devouring and making me feel incredible before giving the same attention to the other.

I bring my hands above me and brace myself against the headboard to give some resistance, and it's enough for Seb to pick up his pace again.

"Fuck, that's good. That's my girl." One hand stays on my breast and the other comes down to my hip. "Fuck you're so good, taking my cock just right." He squeezes my nipple. "You like that?"

I moan, the shot of pleasure from his pinch overtakes my senses.

For some reason, with Seb asking so pointedly, I'm embarrassed to tell him I *do* like it. It feels indecent and unrespectable, but I can't hide how good it feels. "Yes, it's amazing." I say, my honesty wrapped in a hint of bashfulness.

He brings his other hand down to roll my neglected nipple between his fingers. "So beautiful." Seb begins to rub his thumbs over the hardness of each tip, sending me into a frenzy. "What's wrong?" He senses my slight reluctance, and I don't know how to tell him I want it rougher, dirtier, nastier.

"I feel like a bad girl."

"A bad girl? For wanting me to play with your tits?"

I nod.

"Your huge, gorgeous, fuckable tits? You feel bad, because I want to tease your nipples until you come on my cock?"

I nod again.

Seb understands quickly. I want to be dominated, and he picks it back up without dropping a beat.

"Well, you are a bad girl."

I'm surprised, but pleased. "What?"

"So bad. Naughty. You're a dirty little thing." He gently smacks my ass. "You're a bad girl, and you need to be punished."

He rolls both nipples between his fingers, squeezing them just enough to drive me wild. "Look at you, look at your tits, so hard. You're wicked, wanting this."

"I'm a little slut." I whine, unable to help myself.

"You are. My nasty little slut, taking my cock so good, letting me fuck you." Seb comes down onto his elbows, cradling my head in his hands while he pounds into me faster. "You're my delicious little slut. Dripping wet pussy, nipples so hard, they're begging me to suck them. Fuck, you're bad." He pounds into me, hard. "You better take my cock."

I'm coming, and Seb doesn't stop. "Are you my dirty little slut?" He asks in my ear.

"Yes!" I cry.

"Are you a bad girl, wanting me to play with your tits?"

"Fuck, Seb, yes." My moans are loud and they echo through the room.

He reaches down to pinch my nipple again. "You naughty thing. Fuck, you're perfect." Seb kneels up to grab my hips, keeping up his thrusts. "I love watching them bounce. Beautiful."

In my orgasm, I still feel the heat of his gaze on my breasts, and I half-consciously try to cover myself up.

"No." Seb commands, taking my wrists and pinning them down on either side of my head. "Let me see."

"It's too much."

"You let me watch your tits bounce until I come. You understand?"

I nod, but still attempt to whine in protest.

"That's my girl."

I'm still coming, and he continues to pump into me, pinning me down on the mattress. When my body relaxes from the intense orgasm, I open my eyes, meeting his gaze.

Seb moves to loosen his grip from my wrists, but I stop him. "I like this."

He looks at me with a playful inquiry pulling at his eyebrow. "You like this? You want it rough?"

I nod. "A little."

"You like me pinning you down?"

"Yes." I breathe.

He laughs, low and breathless, as if he can't believe his luck. "Fuck, you're a dream come true." His full lips crash onto mine, devouring me.

My moan vibrates against his mouth. "I know you can give it to me the way I want."

"Anything. Whatever you want." Seb breathes.

"I want you."

His hard thrusts knock the wind out of my lungs. "You got me, honey."

"Fuck!" I yelp. "Oh my god, just like that. Fuck me until you come. I want you to come all over me."

"You want me to come all over those perfect tits?"

"Yes!"

Seb snarls, finally releasing his control, and he fucks me wildly.

His hands are tight around my wrists, keeping my hands locked to the bed. He's pounding into me and I come again, screaming and wild beneath him.

"Fuuuck, that's it, you slut, keep coming." He pushes through my narrow walls, greedily taking his pleasure.

Seb pumps a few more hard, deep thrusts into me before pulling out, simultaneously stroking himself to come on my chest and rubbing my clit to bring me to the end of my orgasm.

We're both breathless. He smiles down at me, immediately going to the bathroom to grab another warm washcloth, but he pauses when he returns.

"God, I'd love a picture of you looking like that. Well fucked with my come on your tits."

I laugh sleepily. "We can do that."

He kneels on the bed, wiping me gently until I'm spotless. "Nah, next time. We gotta get you to sleep."

I nod and yawn, agreeing.

Seb tosses the cloth towards my hamper, unfazed by making it in, and lays next to me to pull me in his arms.

"How was that? Too rough?" He cradles me, his giant body hard and warm against my soft curves.

I yawn again. "It was good. Excellent. I can handle rougher, next time." I turn my head to plant a small kiss on his lips. "We can test the waters, find an intensity that works best for us."

"Can't wait to see what else you want." His words are promising. "I can get you some toys, if you're into that?" I'm pulled down further into bed, and we're both adjusting to be more comfortable. "A paddle, for your glorious ass?" His mouth comes to my ear. "Nipple clamps, but only if you beg."

Despite almost being washed away by sleep, I moan in his ear. "I'd love that. Honestly, I'm still trying to figure out what I like, and how much, but I feel like we can talk it out as we go along?"

"Always." Seb nods reassuringly. "Anytime, whenever you want, we'll plan, and even if we're in the middle of fucking and you want to stop and check in, tell me. We'll find a safe word."

"Okay." I smile, happy with his unwavering support. "Can I call you *Papi*?" I tease, but only half-joking.

Seb laughs a quiet, hearty shake that vibrates in his chest. "Don't tease me, *hermosa*, that's my job."

"I mean it. But maybe, only in bed. Not when we're out to brunch or on dates."

"Oh, are you taking me on brunch dates?"

I nod, as if it's obvious. "You're mine now. I'm officially taking you off the payroll as head of security and promoting you to my personal sex doll."

His face shines, total happiness brightening his eyes and making his smile glow. He barks a laugh, then looks down at me with warmth. "Anything for you." He leans down to kiss me gently. "Now what do you want me to call you?"

"Now that you mention it, I wanted to ask you something."

He turns to face me. "Anything."

"You called me *mi amor*. Did you mean it?"

His face alights with mischief. "Was this while we were fucking on the couch, or after I woke up to your pussy wrapped around my cock?"

"Between all the orgasms, I really don't remember." I smile, planting a kiss on the corner of his handsome mouth. "You call me a lot of things, but that was the first time you called me that. Did you mean it?"

"I mean everything I say." His eyes are fierce. Serious.

"I'm really your love?"

"Yes. Did you think I could feel anything less? After watching you? Caring for you? Experiencing you?" He's searching my face, looking for any signs of misunderstanding. "You're not just *mi amor*, Claire, *eres mi vida*."

His words send a blooming warmth throughout my chest, and a schoolgirl blush creeps up my cheeks. "Well, damn." I kiss him, shyly. "That's all I wanted to know." I kissed him again. "Thank you."

"You're welcome."

"I guess I'll have to start learning Spanish."

"I'll give you lessons." Seb says, playing along.

"We'll play 'hot for teacher.' You can wear glasses."

"We'll start with the dirty words." He winks.

"Start with what you've been calling me all this time." I say.

"What do you mean?"

"The Spanish you've been saying to me. Besides the basic *amor, hermosa* and *donde está la biblioteca* from my one semester of Spanish in high school, I don't know much else. I want to know what you've been saying."

Seb takes a moment to think. "I can't remember specifically, but I'm sure it's a mixture of how much I want you, you're beautiful, you're my life, I could fuck you all night." His smile is mischievous. "That sort of thing."

I chuckle before kissing him sweetly. "I want you to teach me. I didn't know your words were so hot."

"You got it." He kisses me back. "Let me ask you, now. What do you want me to call you in bed? Do you like 'baby?'"

"Ew, no thank you. Too infantilizing." I take a few moments to remember what words he's been using during our entanglements, but it's difficult to recall while in the throes of passion. "Hmm... You'll have to call me 'Miss Nguyễn' if we're out there in the world together, at least until I get everything between us settled. I love *mi amor* for every day, but I think 'honey' was a pleasant surprise to hear in bed. It makes me feel like a tasty treat."

"And you're definitely tasty." Seb melds his mouth onto mine, sneaking his hot, wet tongue between my lips.

I sigh before pulling away. "What do you want me to call you? Is *papi* really off the table, because I kinda love it."

Seb chuckles. "You're a literal dream come true, you know that? My dream woman." He leans back to look me square in the face. "I fantasize about you calling me *papi*, but only when we're together, and we're alone. I don't like it in public."

I nod. "I can do that."

"And I don't like 'daddy,' it makes me uneasy."

"Good, me neither." I wrap my arms around his neck. "What about when we are in public?"

"You'll have to call me Cage. Sebastián doesn't exist anymore. On paper, anyway."

"Okay. Sounds reasonable." I nod. "How are you away from the cameras tonight, anyway?"

"One of the guys took over when I rushed here. I texted the others. Someone else should be covering until tomorrow."

"Good. I want you with me at least until after breakfast." I kiss him tenderly.

"Whatever you say, boss." He smiles. "But hey, if you're not too sleepy, can I ask you something?"

"Of course, *papi*." I wink, and when a broad smile spreads across his lips, I'm filled with a glowing sense of pride from learning what makes him tick.

"*Dios, ayúdame...*" He pauses, trying to hide his smile. "I almost came. Just from hearing you say that."

"Sorry." I laugh, kissing his cheek. "I'll only say it when we're fucking."

"Thank you for your consideration." He teases, still recovering from the shock.

"Sorry for distracting you. What were you asking?"

"I wanna know what you like. How you want me to fuck you? It's been a while since I've been active in that way, but I can brush up real quick."

"Oh, well..." I barely know what I want for myself, so I stay as honest as possible. "I'm relatively new to the idea of BDSM, but I was feeling like I wasn't getting what I needed from my past sexual experiences, so I looked it up. I realized I *love* dirty talk. A bit of degradation, a bit of praise. I like being held down and roughed around a bit, but not too much, and not to the point it's painful." I lean back a little to watch his face, trying to read if he's put off or on board with what I'm saying. "I think being a woman who's always in control, and being under pressure to be such an important person to my family and friends, makes me want to be submissive in bed. I want to be taken care of, to be told what to do, and to be used, sometimes."

Seb nods, keeping up with my thoughts. "And you love being called a slut? That's not pushing too far?"

"I normally wouldn't, but when you say it, it drives me crazy. I love it. Only in bed, of course. I'd be livid if you called me that in real life."

He understands. "And 'dirty,' 'nasty,' and 'fucking filthy' are all okay?"

"Fuck yes."

"The softest degradation. Mix in a bit of praise, and you've got a sexy cocktail." He smiles. "You were incredible when I got to your tits. Are you into nipple play?"

I almost moan at the memory. "I didn't know I was until you started torturing me the way you did. I loved it. I could come just from you pinching and rubbing me there."

"I'll take that challenge." He smiles. "There's a lot we can do and explore. We can have fun with spanking, I think you'd like that, and we can spend hours on your nipples." He reaches down to give my breast a firm squeeze, making the tip instantly hard. "They're gorgeous and perfect, and so sensitive. I could lick them for days, but you might like some nipple clamps. I'll get you some."

I'm getting excited. "Maybe, if you want, we can get some handcuffs? Or rope? It's something I've always wanted to try."

Seb actually moans, leaning in to kiss my neck. "Fuck, you'd look so good tied up. I'd fuck the shit out of you."

"You'd like that? To do that to me?" I ask.

"God, yes. You have no idea what I want to do to you."

"You don't think I'm...dirty, for wanting it?"

He encircles his arm around my waist and draws me closer to him. "I think you're very dirty for wanting it, my dirty, nasty little slut, my-"

"Seb!" I laugh, trying to get him back on track.

"Sorry, sorry. Of course you're not dirty, Claire. You're not wrong for wanting good, fun sex. It's common, and not as taboo as we might think. And I'm still willing to call you dirty, even though we both know you're not."

I kiss him, indebted to his acceptance and celebration of this part of me I'm still struggling to understand.

"How do you know so much about all this, anyway?"

Seb shrugs. "I dabbled, in my youth, years ago, but I never found anyone who made it feel right. And my work took me away a lot, so it wasn't like I had a lot of chances to play as much as I liked." He kisses my cheek. "But with you, I can let loose. And you don't just tolerate it. You want it."

"I *crave* it." I correct. "Whatever you want to show me, I'll do. If there's something you want to try, some roleplay or toys, I'm willing to try anything once."

Excitement at the prospect spreads across his face. "You'll be the little schoolgirl to my perverted teacher?"

I put on an innocent look, playing along. "Oh no, Mr. Sebastián, I forgot my bra at home. You'll have to punish me."

He chuckles, planting a quick kiss on my temple. "Let's continue tomorrow. We really need some sleep."

I yawn. "Good idea."

"Goodnight, *mi amor*."

"Goodnight, *Papi*."

Chapter Fifteen

The sound of my espresso machine wakes me up, and I hear the sizzling of breakfast being made. I feel around the bed and sure enough, it's empty, leaving my exposed skin to prickle with goosebumps in the cool, morning air.

I groggily stumble to my closet and slip on a plush, dusty rose-colored robe and matching socks. Knowing Seb is making breakfast excites me, but nature calls, and I have to run to the bathroom to wash my face and brush my teeth before I can face him.

Feeling clean, but still tired, I slump to the kitchen and my jaw nearly drops at the sight.

Seb is wearing his undershirt and black pants with a rag tossed easily over his shoulder. He's frying eggs, and the scene is so domestic and sexy, it feels like one of my dreams has come to life.

When he sees me walking towards him, Seb smiles. "Good morning." He puts the pan back down on the burner and pulls me in his arms.

"It's better with you here." I mumble, burying my face in his chest.

"You're not a morning person." He says, more like a knowing statement than a question.

I shake my head. "Never have been."

Seb chuckles, kissing the top of my head. "Maybe some coffee and breakfast will make you feel better?"

I turn my head to look at what he's prepared. There's some eggs and bacon, but on my marble breakfast tray is a small bowl of raspberries, an iced latte in a tall glass and half an everything bagel with whipped cream cheese.

"My favorite." I say, touched by his effort, and by his amazing ability to catalog everything about my life.

As I break away to grab a few berries, Seb shrugs, almost sheepishly. "I saw you eating it every morning."

"Perks of having a stalker." I wink at him with a smile as I pop some berries into my mouth. "You know everything I like. Saves me the trouble of having to explain."

Seb laughs. "Maybe not everything." He brings the bacon from the pan onto a plate lined with paper towels. "I hope you don't mind me making up a protein plate. After last night, I need to replenish my energy."

"And you'll need more for what I plan to do to you after breakfast." I tease, coming back to snake my arms around his thick waist.

He chuckles. "What did you have in mind, Miss Nguyen?"

I shrug. "Haven't decided yet." I reach up to kiss him quickly. "And, of course, eat anything you want. Do you need some toast? I have this great French butter that is just heaven on some whole wheat I got at the bakery down the street."

"That sounds great." Seb says, plating up the rest of his food and setting it on the other side of the island.

I pop two slices into my toaster and join him, bringing the tray he lovingly prepared to the seat next to him.

"I planned to bring that to you in bed." He offers.

I kiss his gorgeous lips before taking the seat beside him. "Appreciate the thought, but I'd like to eat out here with you. I like the view."

"Of the skyline?"

I shake my head. "Of you in my kitchen."

Seb tries hiding his blush, but I see it anyway, even when he turns away towards the back counter to grab the toast and butter.

We eat in comfortable silence, and I slowly feel myself waking up. I take a sip of the coffee and it's almost perfect, just a little bitter.

"How is it?" Seb asks, watching me take a drink.

"Nearly there. Just a splash of more milk."

Seb snaps his fingers. "Damn, so close." He heads to the fridge and grabs my oat milk.

"No one's perfect." I smile, sliding my cup so he can pour a bit in. I give it a quick taste. "Much better."

"I'll get it right next time." Seb says, kissing my forehead before returning to his seat and finishing his plate.

As if he couldn't get any hotter, he rinses off the dishes and puts them in the dishwasher. I nearly come right where I sit, watching him.

"Thanks. I hate doing dishes." I slip from my seat and walk around the island to stand in front of him.

Seb smiles while he's drying his hands before hugging me. "I'll do the dishes for the rest of your life if it means I get to kiss you anytime I want."

I wrap my hands behind his neck. "That sounds like a deal."

We kiss, and it's warm and tender and sends shivers down my spine.

He pulls away, his hot breath fanning across my lips. "I have a fantasy. Ever since I first saw you in this kitchen."

"Ooo, what is it?" I whisper, shimmying my shoulders in excitement.

Seb wraps his hands beneath my thighs and carries me to my large dining table, plopping my supple bottom onto the cold marble. I gasp at the sudden shift, bracing myself on his shoulders.

"You let me lay you down and eat you out until you're pretty pussy is coming on my face."

I blush. "But, I..." I don't know how to say I feel too exposed up here on my own. My plush robe is giving me enough cushion against the table, but I'm worried it will be too uncomfortable to enjoy.

"*Por favor, hermosa,* give a delusional man his dream?" He cradles my head, kissing me wildly, devouring my mouth as if to show me what his lips and tongue can promise.

"I'm worried my head will..." I pant, trying to tell him I might hit the back of my skull on the marble when he makes me come.

Seb pulls away quickly to rush to the couch, grabbing a fluffy square throw pillow.

His consideration makes my heart skip, and I accept it happily. I lie down, adjusting the pillow under my head, but yelp in surprise when Seb hooks his arms under my knees to pull my center closer to the edge. I reach up and bring the pillow with me, settling it under my head.

With him already spreading my legs, my robe falls loose, barely staying closed by the plush tie around my thick waist. I keep the bow secure to keep me warm, and Seb doesn't mind. He's kissing up my thighs slowly, taking his time, as if I'm the most delicious meal in front of him and he intends to savor every bite.

He pauses only to quickly pull a chair out to sit in front of me, bringing his face lower to my folds.

"Fuck, seeing you wet makes me so hard, honey." He kisses my glistening lips. "Delicious. Sweet, better than the best honey in the world." Seb flattens his tongue against my opening, swirling my clit.

The pleasure shooting through me takes over, and I'm lost to his mouth and attention. He takes one long, languid trail with his wide tongue from the bottom of my slit to the top, ending at my clit and circling the sensitive bud.

I cry out. His mouth knows just how to lick and tease me, and he's lapping it all up, sucking and taking every last drop.

Seb inserts one finger inside my folds and the pressure forces me to arch my back, my walls working to accommodate his thickness. Just one finger is enough to make me feel full, and he has a hard time drawing his hand back from my walls wanting to pull him in deeper.

"Look at your tight pussy. So small, I can't..." He tries to push in another finger, but it stretches me nearly too far, and I gasp and the fullness inside me.

Seb's eyes lock on his fingers disappearing inside me and coming out coated in my wetness.

He grunts in approval, and the guttural sound makes me shiver. "How does your tight pussy take my cock so well, Claire? You're so tight. Fuck, honey, you feel so good." Seb keeps pumping his fingers inside me, and I feel myself nearly coming already.

"I want your cock, *Papi*." I strain, losing my breath as I'm chasing my high.

"No, you come on my fingers. You take what I give you."

I moan, but it comes out more like a whine. "But-"

"No, you come on my face. Understand?" He lowers back down and teases my clit with the tip of his tongue. When his fingers fuck me faster to take me over the edge, he moves his mouth back and forth against my throbbing center.

I come. Hard. It washes over me like a violent wave, and I feel my body tense as I'm electrified by my orgasm. My body writhes beneath Seb's face, but his arms are clutching my thighs, holding me in place while he fingers me through my high.

"Fuck, Seb, Fuck!" I scream, straining to look down at his stunning face between my thighs. I run my hands through his curls before bringing them up to cover his, grasping his fingers while they dig into my supple thighs. "Oh my god!"

"That's it, that's my girl. Come for me." Seb moans, standing now to watch me break and writh on the counter. "Fuck, keep coming on my fingers, Claire." His wicked grin is almost blinding, and I barely register his words as I'm riding his hand. "You like that? You like my fingers fucking you?"

"Yes!" I cry, my voice echoing throughout the penthouse.

"You like being up there so I can watch you come? My dirty little slut." His free thumb comes to rub my clit, and it drives me insane. His words hit me exactly where I need them to.

I plummet into another orgasm.

"Seb!"

"You feel so good, squeezing my fingers." Seb moans softly, his hooded eyes burning into me. "You're coming again?"

"Yes, *papi*, yes!"

He growls, leaning up to tear my robe open, exposing one of my breasts.

"Jesus, you're perfect. So perfect." He squeezes one of my mounds before pinching my exposed nipple, hard.

I yelp, overwhelmed by the pleasure.

"That's my girl. Look at me while you come."

I try to keep my eyes on him, but my orgasm overtakes my focus, and I squeeze my eyes shut. Seb squeezes my nipple again, and it goes straight to my core.

"Look at me." He demands, his voice thick.

I manage to open my eyes, unable to hide my desperation for him. My mouth hangs loose while I come, and I feel too good to be embarrassed.

"Fuck, that's it, honey, let me see you come. I want to watch you, burn the sight of you into my brain." He leans down to cup my face. "So wherever I sit down to eat, I'll remember what it feels like, *tastes* like, to have your pussy in front of me." Seb kisses my panting lips, trailing kisses up to my ear. "So I can imagine how good it feels to eat you out, any time I want."

When Seb pulls back to gaze into my eyes, I reach up, kissing him desperately. "I'm yours. Whenever you want." I moan into his mouth.

"Whenever?" He whispers, a sly smile blooming on his lips as he rubs himself through the front of his pants.

I nod, watching him, clarity slowly returning to my lust-filled mind.

"Now?" His free hand unzips his pants while his other fingers continue to pump into me.

I nod again, entranced by his movements.

Seb only removes his fingers from my core to replace them with his cock. He pushes in hungrily, sinking in slowly.

I feel so full, my breath hitches.

"Fuck, I'll never get used to how tight you are." Seb growls, pumping into me.

"You feel so good." I strain, still adjusting to his size.

"You like how my cock feels inside your tight little pussy?"

I can only nod, unable to find my words as Seb fucks me towards another orgasm.

He slams his hips into mine. "Tell me."

"Fuck, yes, Seb! I love it!"

"You love what?" He slams into me again, staying buried deep inside, denying me the pleasure of the friction of his cock until I answer him properly.

"I love your cock inside me. I love how deep you are."

Seb picks up his pace, satisfied with my response. "That's right, good girl."

He fucks me into oblivion. I'm coming on his cock in record time, tensing and writhing around his hot, strong body.

Seb comes shortly after, pulling out and coming all over my soft stomach and robe.

I reach up for his hands and he takes them in his sturdy grasp, helping me sit up. Seb kisses me softly before helping me down from the table, walking us both to the shower to quickly rinse off.

We end up lounging in bed, my feet in his lap and both of us laying under the covers naked.

He's rubbing my feet, and the relaxation that flows through my body is intoxicating.

I smile at him. "You'll have to keep a few extra sets of clothes here, so you have something to wear when you're over."

Seb tickles my arch, making me yelp and kick him away. "Hey!" I laugh.

"Sorry." He chuckles, but grabs my feet to settle back into his lap to keep the massage going. "Do you feel bad for me being naked, exposed and vulnerable in your bed?"

I shake my head. "I quite like the view, actually." I wink.

I'm about to offer a shoulder rub in exchange when my phone rings. I reach to see the caller ID says HELEN, my mom's assistant, and my stomach immediately drops. She never calls me, so this can't be good.

"Hello?" I answer, sitting up.

"Miss. It's your parents." Helen says, her tone steady and distant. "They were killed. I'm so sorry."

Chapter Sixteen

I'm numb.

Sitting at the head of the conference table at the compound, I barely register my world crumbling around me.

My happy, warm, sunshine-of-a-father is gone.

My cool, calm, collected mother, gone.

Who am I without them?

The compound is in shambles. Chaos ensues around me. Some of our employees are running around, trying to maintain some level of organization.

I'm told some have escaped, running from their contracts.

Some have stayed, looking to me for a plan that will secure their future.

Seb blames himself, of course. He was away from the cameras. He was with me. He wasn't there to watch the screens when the guy covering for him fell asleep, not seeing an unmarked black car pull up on my parents eating at a phở restaurant in Đà Lạt, gunning them down, along with their extensive security detail and a few unfortunate bystanders.

Despite me saying countless times that it wasn't his fault and that I don't blame him, he's still riddled with guilt.

We never found who did it.

It was quick. My parents didn't suffer too much for too long. That's what Helen tells me, but I can't process any of it.

I'm alone. I'm lost.

Seb keeps the place together, quietly giving orders to our staff in order to keep some sort of semblance of normalcy.

My grief renders me immobile for the next few days. I see no one, speak to no one. Only Seb brings me food and sparkling water, alternating between hearty salad plates and warm, protein-packed congee bowls. He makes sure I'm taken care of, and when he's cradling me in his strong arms while I sob, he makes sure I'm settled before leaving me in my old room at the compound to continue the work that needs to be done.

I quit my job at the bookstore.

I text Jenny the news. She leaves me to grieve, telling me to call her the moment I'm ready.

When I finally emerge from my cave of sorrow, I barely look presentable, slapping on a quick face of makeup and wearing a cream sweater lounge set to meet with my parent's lawyers, both the legal and under-the-table ones.

The legal ones are first. They tell me my parent's Will states everything goes to me, all of their businesses, all of their millions of dollars, and every asset of theirs is now in my name.

The under-the-table lawyers tell me the same. The 3.4 billion dollars from the wealthy elite men who bid on our stock of young, Vietnamese women is now mine. All of the routes and safehouses in place to shelter the women are all in my control. There are people working for us to keep things flowing, and I won't have to change anything if I want to keep the work easy, keep my hands off the steering wheel and let the whole system continue to run itself.

The lawyers leave, and I'm alone again.

But, through the fog of my grief, an idea sparks.

What if I *do* want things to change?

What if we don't sell the girls, but invest in their education, pay for their schooling, and then employ them in all of the businesses we own? Or help them to open their own? We can let them stay in the boutique apartment buildings we own, charge them rent that is a fair percentage of their income, like the other rent-stabilized buildings in the city?

Sure, we'd lose millions of dollars, but I now have more money than I know what to do with, and I'd rather clean up our organization, make it ethical, than continue with how things are.

I also want to make our employees legal. No more contracts. No more enslaving those who are forced to be here because Dad bought their freedom, only to trap them here.

I go to Dad's office and pull up every contract we have on file.

Then, I ask Cage to round up all of our goons, and one by one, I ask them if they want to stay, or if they want me to release them, marking their contract filled.

About a third of them leave, but most of them stay, accepting my offer of a clean slate, free housing at the compound in exchange for their employment. They would legally be working for us for $30 an hour.

After a few days, some of them come back, realizing it's tough out there in the world without a stable support system, and they accept my terms.

When that's settled, I turn my attention towards the young women waiting to be sold.

Cage drives me to one of the safehouses that is holding our ladies, an updated apartment building in Bed-Stuy, and I visit each and every one, offering them a new deal.

I'll pay for their college and send money to their families while they're in school. When they graduate, they can work for one of our nail salons, restaurants, jewelry stores, or any of the others, and begin to build a life of their own while making enough money to send to their families back home.

Only a handful of the women take me up on my offer. Most of them have already prepared themselves for their future, and no matter how bleak, how awful their potential husband could be, they can't afford to stray from the plan set out for them. So I allow it, respecting their wishes, but I cut off the scouting process in Vietnam, refusing to take in any more young women into our system.

One woman in particular, Mai, is a little older than our usual batch of ladies. She speaks English a little more fluently as well, having been a professor back in Vietnam, and tells me she's worked hard enough in recent years and just wants to marry rich so she can live a less-stressful life.

I laugh when she tells me this, bonding with her quickly and telling her she has an understandable outlook towards her future.

I smile at her over the hot jasmine tea she's offered me at her small table. "You're sure? You can come work for me instead, be my assistant. You won't have to be stuck with some smelly old man."

Mai laughs. "Old men are the best ones. They forget about you quickly, so I'll be able to read in peace. I've worked enough through the years to know I don't want to keep doing it."

My laugh joins hers. "Alright. Here, take my business card, and if you get bored and want an easy job to keep the hours of your day occupied, call me."

"I will, thank you."

I give her a quick wave goodbye and meet Seb in the hallway. He wraps his arm around my shoulder as we head to the elevator.

"Was she the last one?"

I nod with a sigh. "Yes, thank goodness."

He squeezes me into his side. "Your strength is impressive. Now all that's left is the funeral tomorrow."

"Promise me you won't leave my side? I'll be a wreck all day."

"Nothing could tear me away." Seb says, pulling me into a hug as the elevator doors open to take us to the parking garage.

I fall asleep while Seb drives us back to the compound.

Chapter Seventeen

The funeral is awful.

It's beautiful, covered in thousands of fresh, white flowers, but agonizing.

It's filled with distant aunts, cousins, uncles, business clients, partners, well-wishers, and all sorts of people filling a giant castle on Long Island.

It's one of my parent's favorite places they found in their youth while looking for wedding venues.

Dad and Mom are cremated, their bodies too torn up by the bullets to be preserved for an open casket funeral.

There are so many people. Too many people. They all shake my hand and offer their condolences, but it's all overwhelming, and I'm too heartbroken to stand more than a few dozen minutes in the crowd.

Seb holds me while I sob in a glamorous bedroom upstairs. When my body can't physically produce another tear, he sweeps me away, putting me in his car and driving me back to the comfort of the penthouse.

He warms the shower while I strip, too dazed out of my mind to care about anything or anyone. Seb holds my head and kisses my forehead before heading to the kitchen.

"I'll warm up that Thai coconut curry soup you love."

I pull him down to kiss his sweet lips. "Thank you."

"Any time."

While in the shower, my mind can't help going through my checklist. I've completed everything, except one last, tragic meeting.

I'm going to ask Seb if he wants to cancel his contract and finally have the freedom he deserves.

I don't know what he's going to say. I don't know if he'll stay to be with me, or if he'll leave. He's worked for so long. If he wants to leave, he should go.

The thought of him leaving makes me cry, but I wipe away the tears before rinsing my body and stepping out of the shower, preparing myself for the conversation ahead.

I'm throwing on a thick pajama set when I hear Seb shouting my name from the kitchen.

"What is it?" I call from my closet, wrapping up my wet hair in a towel.

Seb rushes into the bedroom. "They found them. The men who shot your parents." He's quickly reading something on his phone. "My team confirms it was the *Lê* family."

"Those bastards..." I snarl, finally feeling a sense of relief knowing who to blame.

"What do you want to do?" Seb offers, ready to spring into action.

My head swims with all the possibilities:

Bring them in, let me question them about why they killed Mom and Dad.

Send a team out to kill them.

Bring them to the compound so we can torture them, make them regret ever taking any orders from the Lê family.

"I want them dead." I finally say. "All of them. The men who shot my parents, the *Lê* family, everyone."

Seb smirks. "That can be arranged."

"Wait." I stop him. "I don't want you to do it."

"What?"

I walk up to stand just a few inches away from his startled, gorgeous face. "We need to talk."

"Claire, we can't wait on this, we need to move fast, or they'll get away."

I huff in frustration. "Fine, tell your guys to bring them to the compound. Keep them in the holding room until we get there."

"Okay." He types his message and then sends it, but is confused by my lack of urgency. "We gotta run, Claire, let's go."

"Seb, wait." I grab his hand and sit him next to me on the bed. "I have one last thing I need to take care of."

"We have a lot of things to take care of in the next few hours-"

"Sebastián." I say, a little more firmly this time. "This is an official meeting between us."

He loses his momentum, finally understanding and settling in his seat. "What is it?"

"Would you like your contract canceled? You'd be free from your obligations to the *Nguyễn* family, you'll have a clean slate, we won't come after you-"

"Wait, stop, stop, why are you giving me your goon spiel?" He stands, facing me. "Get dressed, Claire, we have to go."

"I'm serious." I stand. "Do you want to leave? I'm giving you the choice."

He stares at me, dumbfounded. "Are you seriously asking me this right now? What, do you think I'm only here because of some stupid contract?"

I ignore him, steeling myself against the heartbreak I know will come. "You'll be free, Cage."

He growls. "Don't call me that. Why are you calling me that when we're alone?"

"To remind you where you came from. Dad bought your freedom when you were locked up, but now, you have the resources to start a new life. You can begin all over again. You can buy a house in California. Get a tech job in Silicon Valley. Live the life you want."

"The only thing I want right now is to get justice for what happened to your family." Seb grabs my shoulders. "Then afterwards, I want to marry you and spend the rest of my days by your side. Grabbing your boba, fetching your soup, rubbing your feet." He huffs. "When have I ever said I want to move away from the city?"

I feel tears begin stinging my eyes. "But, you can leave."

"I don't want to leave." He says, pointedly.

"What if you do, eventually?" I take a step away from him. "What if, deep down, or in a few months, you realize you stayed with me through obligation and in a few years, when the dust settles, you'll realize you've been living a life of duty?"

"Claire, I love you." Seb exasperates. "That's why I'm with you." He huffs, running his hands through his hair. "I can't believe we're having this conversation right now. I tell you I want to marry you, that I'm in love with you, and you're pushing me away."

"I love you, too." I try to smile through the tears rolling down my cheeks. "But I could never live with myself if I was the one keeping you from a better life. A free life. Free from contracts and obligations and blood and killing." I wipe the tears away. "It's too late for me. All those people in my care? They're relying on me to build a foundation they can live on. But I don't want that for you. I want you out."

"What can I do to convince you I want to stay with you? Do you want me to marry you? I'll get down on one knee right now, I have the ring-"

"You can leave." I say quickly, my voice shaking with grief.

He stops, shocked. "What?"

"Leave. Just for a week or two. Go out. Eat what you want, go wherever you want. Travel the world." I grab his large, warm hands in my small, cold ones. "Then, if you really want to come back, I'll lock you by my side and never let you go."

"That's what I already want." He leans his forehead against mine.

"Please. Do this for me?" I break away from our tender, fragile embrace to get my wallet. "Take my card. Let my money spoil you for once."

Seb hesitates, but he slowly takes the card from my hand. "I'll be back in exactly seven days."

I can only offer a small smile. "I'll always love you. If you decide not to come back, I'll understand."

"I *will* be back." Seb says firmly.

I don't want to let him go.

I want him to go.
I want him to stay.
I want him to be mine.
I want him to be free.

When I don't say anything, Seb kisses my forehead and leaves me in the penthouse.

Alone.

Chapter Eighteen

I expect to lose all contact with Seb, but he's texting me photos of the food he's eating on his travels and the sights he's been seeing.

In Queens. An hour away.

Sometimes he ventures north to The Bronx, but mostly, he stays in Brooklyn, sending me pics of the various pizzas he's eating and the bookstores he spends hours in, sipping coffee and reading.

One bar called Fiction In Brooklyn has become one of his particular favorites. He sends me photos of the place that's a cafe by day and a bar by night, with live music on the weekends.

He's excited to send me photos of The Ripped Bodice, a romance bookstore, though he doesn't spend much time browsing. He tells me he plans to take me there on a shopping spree.

Seb tries calling me, but I'm stuck in countless meetings in order to implement my new plans within the structure of our existing business system, so I always miss his calls and can never find the time to respond at a decent hour.

When facing the decision about how to handle the men who killed my parents, I order our assistant security officer, Caleb Phan, to kill them.

He's stoic and silent, a little shorter than Seb, with black hair cropped short with a geometric pattern carved into the sides. He never says much, but when I tell him to kill our captured and dispose of their bodies, a slow smile forms on his face, and he reaches out to offer me a fist bump.

"You got it, Miss." He grunts, and leaves my office to carry out his duties.

A few days into Seb's week of freedom, he stops texting.

He stops calling.

My heart drops, and the glimmer of hope I keep stamped down in my heart, not wanting it to grow, takes a painful hit.

I want him to leave this life I'm trapped in, but a part of me was starting to hope he'd come back, even though I told myself to let him go.

When he doesn't respond to my laughing emoji at a picture of him with an ice cream cone, my heart sinks.

But I don't have much time to wallow in my heartbreak, since Jenny is on her way to my office right now, and I plan to confess everything.

When Helen, who is now my assistant, walks Jenny to the office I've taken over from Dad, my best friend's eyes are wide with wonder.

"Claire, what the fuck?" She's breathless, unable to take it all in. We hug, and it feels amazing to have her back after not seeing her for so long. "You look amazing in this white blazer."

"Thanks." I smile. She comes with me to the black velvet couch that sits in the corner of my black marble office, and when Helen brings us tea and coffee, I lay everything out.

Jenny is silent while I explain who my parents were, the work they did, how they died, how I felt about them dying, and the work I'm doing now to recover and alter the structure of our business.

I'm still tender from Seb leaving, but I fill Jenny in on everything with him, too. How I love him, all the amazing sex we've been having, how he says he wants to marry me but I sent him away, giving him the choice to leave or come back after he's had a taste of freedom..

"Plus..." I add, finishing my drink. "I'm ridiculously wealthy now, so I can fund the crisis center you've always dreamed about opening!" I try to end my rant on a good note. "I can also finally open my bookstore, which you can help run!"

"Claire..." Jenny puts her teacup down and wraps me in a hug. "You've been through so much. I'm sorry. I had no idea." She rubs my back affectionately. "Cage- I mean, *Sebastián* will come back. I'm sure of it. He loves you."

"A part of me hopes he doesn't come back." I sigh, wiping away a tear.

"Well the part of me that knows you deserve to be happy hopes he does." She flashes her dazzling smile. "I wish I could've met your parents. They sound like they loved you very much."

"They did." I nod. I'm unsure about so much in my life, but I'm certain they loved me more than anything.

"Since we're laying things bare, I have a confession." Jenny squirms, an apology written across her face.

"If you can forgive me for keeping all this from you, then there's nothing you can tell me that would change how much I love you." I say, reaching out to squeeze her hand reassuringly.

"Umm, I also come from a wealthy family." Jenny confesses, hanging her head in shame.

I gasp, surprised and wanting to lighten the mood. "No!"

"Yes!" Jenny shouts, burying her face in her hands. "My family deals in oil, and they gave me an ultimatum. Either I find a husband on my own in one year, or I have to agree to the arranged marriage they've set up for me."

I gasp again. "That's why you've been dating all of these clowns!"

She laughs. "Yes, exactly. But my one year is almost up, and I haven't found anyone remotely close to husband material."

"Most of them never are." I shake my head. "How long do you have left?"

"Nine weeks, then I have to go back to Kolkata."

I take a moment to process all of this new information. "Who's the guy your parents are setting you up with?"

"Some oil tycoon's son. I've never met him." Jenny dismisses, waving off the thought.

I shrug. "Maybe he's cute?" I offer.

Jenny scoffs. "He can't be anything more than a spoiled brat. People born in that world lack any sort of personality or humanity."

"Yeah, you may be right. But, could he be the answer to all of your problems?" I ask, the gears in my head beginning to spin on this new project of finding love for Jenny.

"What problems? I have a billionaire for a best friend! Together, we can rule the world!" Jenny throws her arms around me in a tight hug, and we fall on the couch together, laughing.

When our glee subsides, I squeeze her tighter. "I can always marry you. Then you won't have to stress." I tease, but my offer is genuine.

"Pshaw. You're marrying Sebastián. I can't take you away from him."

The mention of him stings my heart. I try to laugh, but I sit up, enveloped by heartbreak all over again.

Jenny pulls out her phone. "I know it feels hopeless right now, but I saw how he cared for you that night at the bar. I know he'll come back." She taps open a new window on her phone. "I'm already looking for bridesmaid dresses."

I huff a small laugh, always reassured by her words. "You mean Maid of Honor dresses." I correct.

Jenny's head whips over to look at me. "You mean it?!" She squeals, jumping to a seated position.

"Of course! But forget I said anything. I want to make one of those cute "will you be my maid of honor" boxes with jewelry and little sparkling rosé bottles."

Jenny squeals again. "Oh my god Claire, you're going to be a beautiful bride! Oh I can't wait. We'll have to plan your dress fittings, tour venues, taste test cakes, and find caterers. But don't worry, I'll handle all of that."

"Pump the brakes, Jenny. I need to have a fiancé before we can start planning the wedding."

Jenny dismisses my words, waving them away. "I already told you, he'll be back."

I roll my eyes, grabbing my phone to pull up some wedding gown silhouettes I want to consider.

Suddenly, my phone is flooded with social media notifications.

Local murder, mass murder, NYC family killed, all murdered in one night.

Helen rushes into the office, breathless. "Miss, did you hear? The *Lê* family is dead. Every single one. Our sources suspect gang activity. Was this your order?"

I stand, shaking my head. "I only ordered Caleb to kill the men we took hostage."

"What's going on?" Jenny asks, standing next to me.

"Someone killed the family who murdered my parents." I explain before turning back to Helen. "You said everyone?"

Helen nods. "Not one was left alive." A notification beeps on her phone. Helen checks it quickly. "The news is now reporting it was a gang war. Multiple deaths, at least two dozen, they say."

I turn to Jenny. "You should probably go so I can figure out what's going on. If this is a war, they could be after us next, and I want you safe."

Jenny nods, grabbing her coat and purse before hugging me goodbye. "Call me the next time we can meet up. We have a lot to talk about."

I nod and send her out the door quickly with one of our most trusted bodyguards, Kevin.

I rush to my desk and begin calling everyone, all of our business managers and liaisons, to confirm our people are safe and away from harm. They all say everyone is fine, but they'll look out for any danger and will keep me updated.

All of my sleuthing and connections to our security system doesn't find any imminent threats, but I'm not convinced.

I scour and look for any person, any sign of danger, but I find nothing.

Then it hits me.

Seb.

He's out there, unprotected and vulnerable.

I panic, scared and petrified that he could be hurt. I fumble for my phone and call him.

I hear a phone vibrate by the elevator. I look up, and he's there.

Seb is in black jeans and a black jacket. There's a smattering of a few drops of blood across his cheek, but he looks otherwise unharmed.

He's wearing black gloves to keep his fingerprints untraceable.

I hang up the phone.

I understand.

Silly of me to believe he was in danger. Silly of me to not consider *he* was the danger.

"Seb..." I breathe, rounding my desk to meet him in the middle of the office.

"I'm a few days early." He teases, shrugging. Seb goes to hug me, but I can see more blood on his clothing now that I'm up close, and he hesitates, not wanting to dirty my white suit.

"So, I take it that the 'gang activity' the news is reporting is actually just you?"

"I think they blew it out of proportion." He smiles, and his handsome face makes my heart skip.

I lean against my desk, folding my arms. "But you got them?"

He nods. "I got 'em."

"Thank you." I smile, my heart pounding at the sight of him.

"Anything for you. And I owe it to them." He says, taking off his gloves. "I want to kiss you, but I should shower."

I nod. "You don't owe them anything, you know. It wasn't your fault."

He nods, too. "I know." Seb takes a step forward. "Let me take you to dinner."

"Okay." I beam. "But we need to talk, first."

Chapter Nineteen

Seb returns to my office freshly showered and smoking hot. His dark curls are slicked back and he's looking perfect in his signature black suit.

He sits in one of the sleek black leather armchairs facing my desk. He's serious, ready for our highly-anticipated conversation about our relationship.

I round my desk to stand in front of him. His hands come up to rest on my hips easily, as if they were made for him. He lets me hold his face, cradling his strong features in my hands.

"You came back." I whisper, unable to hide my smile.

"Did you think I wouldn't?"

I nod slowly. "A part of me wanted you to go." I gently run my fingers through his hair. "But I'm happy you're here."

Seb pulls me down for a kiss, and I eagerly let him. "I missed you." He says, hot against my lips.

"I missed you, too." I breathe, coming up to kneel on the cushion outside of his muscular thigh. This brings me closer to him, and I deepen our kiss.

Seb growls into my mouth, gently nudging my other knee up so I'm straddling him. I gasp at how close he is now, and I revel in his warmth against my chest. His plush lips taste like home, and he's devouring me, eating me up as if he hasn't had a meal in days. His hands travel up my sides, coming up to cup my breasts and giving them a firm squeeze through my white shirt.

"You feel better than I remember." Seb says, pulling away to trail kisses down my neck. "God, I missed you. Your smell…" He buries his nose behind my ear and takes in a deep breath. "You drive me crazy." He stands easily, picking me up by my ass so I have to wrap my legs behind his back. "Let's go to dinner."

"Okay." I huff, but don't stop kissing him. He's just as delicious as I remember, and I can't get enough.

"I made reservations-" He says between kisses. "At this place that has great barbecued duck." He puts me on my desk, the resistance giving him better access to grind his cock against my aching core. "You'll love it."

"Sounds great." I huff, too hot and bothered to focus. "Let's go." I wrap my legs around him tighter, grinding up against him. This ignites him, and he grinds his cock into me even harder, the friction shooting a jolt of pleasure through my body.

Seb growls in my ear, giving my earlobe a gentle nibble. "Your words say to go, but your body is telling me a different story, Claire." He smashes his lips against mine, hungrier than ever. "Which is it? Do you want to leave, or do you want to stay and let me fuck you the way I've wanted to since I left?"

I moan. His words are exactly what I want to hear. "Fuck me, *papi*. Please."

"Fuuuck..." Seb growls, standing to unbuckle his belt. He digs his cock free from his pants, and he's rock hard, his erection bobbing up and down while he hooks his fingers into the waistband of my pants and thong, pulling them both down together and exposing my pussy to the cool air of the office.

Seb gently hooks his arms under my knees and pulls me a little closer to the edge, lining me up with his cock perfectly. He gives me a heated look, silently asking me if he can continue. I nod, enthusiastically urging him closer with my feet behind his back.

He rubs the head of his swollen cock up the slit of my entrance, coating himself with my slickness. Seb finally pushes into me slowly, and I sigh from how full he makes me, leaning back to lie flat on the desk.

"Oh my god, Seb." I moan, unable to keep my eyes open. "That feels so good."

He hisses from the pleasure. "Oh honey, you're so tight." Seb pulls out before pushing in again at an agonizingly slow pace. He remembers to ease me open, stretch me out, but I'm so hungry for him, I don't have the patience to wait. "Fuck me, *papi*. I want it."

"Yeah? You want my cock?"

I nod frantically. "Yes, please. Fuck me. Hard."

My words light a fire in him and he quickens his pace immediately. "You're too tight, Claire. Fuck, I can barely fit." He slows down, working his way deeper into me. "Am I hurting you?"

I shake my head. "No, you feel amazing." I dig my heels into the small of his back to urge him into me. "I have to have you, please." I try to get comfortable, but I'm laying on a stapler, and I try to dig it out of my hair before we continue.

"You got me, honey." He buries himself deep inside me, bottoming out. "Let's get you used to me, before someone gets hurt." He smiles before leaning down to kiss me. "You're tense, is everything okay?"

I moan, choking out my words from the pleasure radiating through my body. "The desk is kinda hurting my head. Can we move to the couch?"

Seb kisses me tenderly. "Of course." He kicks off his pants and shoes while staying inside me, gently helping me sit up so he can work his hands under my ass to lift me easily, walking us over to the couch.

I don't care if anyone walks by or can see us. Everyone should know he's mine by now and since I'm the boss, they should leave us alone, if they know what's good for them.

Seb lays me down on the couch, kneeling comfortably between my legs and keeping his cock enveloped in my hot, wet folds. My slickness is making it easy for him to pump inside me, and it's getting difficult for him to keep his restraint steady. He starts up again, slowly picking up his pace, but when my walls begin to tighten around him as my orgasm starts to overcome me, he loses it.

"That's it, honey. Fuck, you come so easily, I forgot how fast you can be."

I moan. "It's because your cock is so big." I strain, almost unable to speak while I'm coming around his length, tense and writhing.

"Oh Claire, you know just what to say." Seb grabs my hips and pounds into me. "Fuck, that's it, come on this cock, Claire. You're so beautiful when you come."

He pushes through my walls that are working to force him out of me, but Seb stays true, pumping into me the whole time I'm riding my high.

When I'm slowly coming down, he gives me a few harsh, ragged pumps before pulling out and coming on my belly and part of my shirt.

He's smiling when he leans down to kiss me sweetly before walking to the coffee table for a tissue. He wipes me up, not allowing me to clean myself, and leaves me laying on the couch while he quickly puts himself back in his pants. Seb then waltzes to my desk to fetch my pants and hands them to me.

I slip them on but go back to laying down, pulling him closer to snuggle with me.

"Maybe we can cancel the reservation and go another time." I say, kissing his shoulder. "I want you back home with me."

"I can get something delivered to the penthouse?" He offers, pulling out his phone while absentmindedly rubbing my thigh.

I snake my arm through his and snuggle his hulking bicep. "That sounds good. Maybe some Pad Thai? And drunken noodles?"

"That sounds good." He takes a few moments to order from my favorite place. "Done. Should be there in an hour. Plenty of time for us to get home."

I smile, reaching up to kiss him. "I can't wait." Before I can pull away, Seb gently grabs my wrist to keep me in my seat.

"I have something for you, before we go." He moves to face me, bent down on one knee. He reaches into the pocket of his jacket and pulls out a small red velvet box and opens it, offering me a simple, gold engagement ring with a giant marquise-shaped diamond.

"This didn't go how I planned. I meant for this to happen at the restaurant, and then we'd fuck each other's brains out *after* you said yes."

I laugh, happy tears spilling down my cheeks.

"But I wanted to tell you, the moment I left, all I thought about was coming back. Not one moment passed that I didn't think of you, and I know, beyond a shadow of a doubt, that I want to spend the rest of my life with you. Will you marry me?"

I'm a tearful, squealing mess, and somehow, through all the kisses and incoherent words of love, I manage a "Yes!"

Chapter Twenty

"I, Sebastián Ramón-Rodríguez Valenzuela, promise to cherish you through your moments of clarity, and your bouts of erratic passion. I hope to nurture all of your ideas that make the world a better place, and will always support the projects that bring the sparkle to your eyes. I'll love you always, and even on the days we're fighting, I promise to apologize first, and always kiss you goodnight."

"I, Claire Nguyễn, promise to treat every day with you as a gift. I promise to keep you busy and bring excitement to your life, even when it feels like you can't get away from me sometimes."

The small crowd of our closest friends and family laugh. The warm sound reverberates through the private library in a castle just a few hours outside of the city.

"I miss you when you're not by my side, and I'm excited when you return back to me, as if we're still in our honeymoon phase. I promise to stay in our honeymoon phase forever, and love you as much as I did when I first fell in love with you in that cabin."

Helen, in her stoic way, returns to the center of the ceremony. Jenny is wiping away a tear behind me, her hands full from holding her bouquet and mine.

She's stunning in a sleek, black silk gown. All of the guests are in black, and Seb and I stand out in our white. He's in a custom white suit with black, satin lapels as an homage to Dad, and I'm in a form-fitting mermaid gown to show off my curves.

"By the power vested in me by the state of New York, I now pronounce you husband and wife. You both may now kiss." Helen says with a slight smile, the biggest I've ever seen from her.

Seb brings my veil over my head and wraps me in a tight embrace, kissing me gently. I bring my arms around his neck and pull him in for a kiss more fierce, making our audience hoop and holler.

The string quartet plays our exit song, and we're both beaming as we make our way down the aisle, our photographer and videographer capturing our best moments.

We barely have a second to ourselves for a single kiss before we're swept away by our guests for photos, well-wishes, and toasts. Dinner is in the greenhouse on the estate, and we hardly have a couple bites before we're ushered to the dance floor for our first dance.

Seb places a chair in the middle of the dance floor and has me sit to face him and the DJ for a surprise karaoke performance of Shania Twain's "Whatever You Do! Don't!"

I'm elated, reminded of the first night I sang to him in the cabin and laughing at his inability to carry a tune. When he's done, I jump up and wrap my arms around him. "Thank you, you're my favorite." I kiss him.

"My last time singing for you." He teases, kissing me back.

We spend all night talking to everyone, most of them asking about the various businesses I'm still keeping open. The majority of our small businesses are still functioning, and I even opened my dream bookstore, which is run by Trang, one of the women who chose not to follow through with the marriage auction and is going to NYU for her bachelor's degree.

After mingling for the better part of an hour, we dedicate a moment of silence to my parents and everyone else we lost. I think about sharing this special day with them, and wipe away a tear before heading over to cut the elaborate, eight-tiered cake.

By the time we say our goodbyes to the stragglers, both Seb and I are exhausted. Jenny signs our marriage certificate, a detail we forgot during the ceremony, and hugs me goodbye, reassuring me she's wrapping up all of the post-wedding details, like sending thank you cards and making sure our vendors are paid.

"Have fun in Scotland!" Jenny squeals. "Don't worry, I'll take care of everything."

"Thank you, Jenny. I love you so much. I'll send you all the pictures."

"We'll bring you back some whiskey." Seb smiles, pulling her in for a quick hug. "Or a nice Scottish guy." He teases.

"Oh my god, please do! Find some Scottish Lord to whisk me away." Jenny laughs, grabbing her bag and heading to her car. She waves from her driver window as she pulls away and finally, Seb and I are alone.

"Ready to spend our wedding night in a castle?" I ask him, wrapping my arms around his thick waist.

"Ready to spend our wedding night anywhere you are." He leans down to kiss me and slides his arm under my knees, carrying me over the threshold.

I laugh as he heads upstairs. "I'm pretty sure that tradition is meant to be over the threshold of our home."

"We can do that too, when we come back." Seb smiles, kissing me. When we reach our room, he gently puts me down and helps me out of my dress.

We both shower in the decadent, gold bathroom with brass swan faucets and climb into bed wrapped in matching white robes.

"I love you." I say, admiring his warm, inviting eyes.

"I love you, too." He says, his large hand caressing my hip.

Before I can reach over to pull him into a heated kiss, I fall asleep.

Epilogue

In the luxury suite of a castle in Fort William, three hours north of Edinburgh, Seb is railing me in front of an elaborately-styled fireplace over the back of a red velvet couch. We have the entire property booked and plan on having sex in every room.

Besides the castle staff, Seb and I are completely alone.

We haven't stopped fucking since we arrived last night on our company's private jet. The moment I step off the plane in a delirious, travel-induced stupor, I head to the bathroom and wash my hair before climbing into bed, ready to be lost to the world.

But Seb has other ideas, spooning me under the red tartan quilt. His large body warms me up before his hand travels down my plush stomach, his fingers raking through the curls above my core and slowly circling my clit.

It feels amazing, and I'm pulled from sleep by the pleasure growing throughout my body.

"Mmmm, Seb..." I sigh, opening my legs so his large, nimble fingers can play with my wet folds. He runs his hand across my slit before slowly sliding in one finger, gently filling me.

I hiss at the feeling, turning towards him to give him better access. He lowers his lips onto mine and kisses me tenderly. Seb quickly pulls his fingers from my core and puts them in his mouth, tasting me.

"Sweet as honey." He says, going back to rub my clit and taking me towards my first orgasm in the castle, which is different from my first orgasm of the day, which was on the plane.

I come quickly, burying my face into his shoulder to keep my moans from bothering the castle staff, but Seb doesn't like that. He pulls his shoulder away but keeps pumping his fingers into me, leaving me with nowhere to hide.

"*Mi amor*, let me hear you." Seb growls, kneeling up between my legs to keep his work on my pussy at an optimal angle.

"They'll hear me." I moan, too far gone in my orgasm to say much else.

"Let them." He demands, bringing his free hand up to pinch one of my nipples. "I want them to know I love fucking my wife."

His dirty words shoot me towards another orgasm, and I can't hold in my lewd cries. I'm tense and at the mercy of his nimble fingers.

When I come down from my high, Seb slips his fingers from my folds to reach into his bedside table.

He pulls out a thick gold chain with attachments on either end.

Nipple clamps.

"You're gonna love these." He breathes, kissing me before silently asking if he could put them on. My eyes grew wide at the prospect of the added pleasure, and I nod wantingly.

He pinches one clamp on, then the other, and I'm in heaven. The pleasure courses through my limbs and I'm nearly coming again.

Seb pushes his throbbing length through my tight folds. He is slow and sweet, taking his time with me, and when he feels I'm comfortable and my walls are stretched to accommodate his girth, he hovers above me, putting his weight on his forearms, cradling my head.

Seb kisses me tenderly while his pumps are languid and easy, taking his time to feel every inch of my fluttering walls. When he reaches between us to gently tug on the gold chain, pleasure pulls from my tits, and I cry out from the exquisite torture.

I come over and over again. He talks me through each orgasm and enjoys my body through it all, caressing my full breasts, supple hips and luscious ass.

When it's his turn to come, Seb tries pulling out, but I lock my ankles behind his back to keep him inside me, relishing in the warmth of his come spilling in my walls.

We both fall asleep wrapped in each other's arms.

It's late the next morning when I find my new husband fast asleep next to me in the plush red, king-sized bed. I take a few moments to enjoy his features at rest, when his brow isn't so furled and his jaw is a little slack. I rub my palm against his chest, running my nails through the attractive smattering of salt and pepper curls on his broad muscles.

Even in my sleepy, morning haze, I'm feeling mischievous, so I lift up the covers to find his impressive morning wood. I'm torn between waking him up and *then* playing with his cock, or waking him up with one of the best surprises I can give him.

I go with the latter, slowly climbing down under the covers between his legs, trying not to wake him up. When my mouth is aligned with his cock, I grab him lightly and start licking his tip until he's nice and wet. I wrap my lips around him and move down, taking him more into my throat.

Seb's thick thighs stir around me before I feel him waking up.

"What the..." I hear his raspy voice when he throws back the covers, revealing me with his cock deep in my throat.

My blowjob is sloppy as I pull off, looking up at him while flattening my tongue against the underside of his veiny length, finally catching his eye.

"Morning." I smile, licking at the precum oozing from his tip.

"Fuck, Claire..." Seb hisses, throwing his head back onto his pillow. "I thought I was dreaming." His hands come down to caress my hair. "God, you look good down there. Your pretty little mouth sucking my cock." His hips start pumping up into my mouth. "You like that?"

"Mmm-hmm!" I try to nod, almost choking on his girth. I suck as I bring my mouth off him, but my hands continue to stroke. "I love it. Love feeling your huge cock in my mouth. *Me encanta.*" I say, using some of the Spanish he's been teaching me before going back for more.

He chuckles at my attempt. "That's right, *mi amor*, keep sucking. Fuck, you're so good at that. I know you love it. Feeling my cock in your hot, sloppy mouth gets you wet, doesn't it?"

I nod, unable to talk, but I try to give an enthusiastic "Uh-huh!" again.

"I bet you're so wet right now. Bring your pussy over here so I can feel how wet you are."

I moan against his cock from his words, but do as I'm told, keeping him in my mouth and climbing over his thigh to bring my ass towards his hand. His fingers move through my dripping folds, and I scream against his length when he drives two fingers into me.

He only needs to pump into me a few times before I come, gagging on his cock and loving every moment.

Seb pulls me up to straddle his hips and in one swift movement, he's inside me, and I'm riding him to bring us both to our next orgasm together.

We're both spent. I collapse against his chest.

"I need a shower." I breathe, crawling up to kiss him. "I need food."

Seb playfully slaps my ass. "Me too, *amor*. I'll call room service."

As we clean up in the bathroom, one of the staff members wheels our food in on a cart, each plate under gold cloches.

Both Seb and I eat by the window happily, sharing in a traditional Scottish breakfast, with tea and coffee.

"This sausage is *ngon*." Seb offers, using some of the basic Vietnamese I've been teaching him to help his work move more smoothly, and because he's so tender and loving, he just wants to learn my language.

"Yes it is." I smile, happy to see him put in the effort to tell me the sausage is delicious. I can't stop myself from leaning across the small table and giving him a sweet kiss.

We've been having mini language sessions since being away from work, now having the time and energy to dedicate to the exchange. He's teaching me dirty words in Spanish, I'm teaching him the names of dishes and food-related words because that's what we want to learn first.

The view from the castle is amazing, and we plan on touring the grounds, but I'm still exhausted from our flight, so I take a nap while Seb reads by the fire.

The day passes without us even realizing it while we enjoy each other in the room, and before we know it, it's dinner time, and we're both chowing down on local Scottish salmon. When dinner is finished, Seb rolls the food cart into the hallway while I freshen up.

Taking my time in the bathroom, I use this moment of being alone to change into a cute white lingerie set, complete with a sheer bra with matching panties and a garter belt holding up sheer white stockings. I throw on a matching sheer robe and go back to the bedroom, a little embarrassed but still excited to see how Seb will react.

He's reading by the fireplace when I walk in, his head looking up when he sees me. He looks back down to his book before his eyes snap up again, raking over me from head to toe. Seb smiles as he places his book on the side table, standing up to meet me. His hands come to my waist, his natural resting place when it comes to my body.

"*Ay dios mio...*" Seb rumbles lowly in his chest. "Claire..." His eyes are wide, unbelieving as he grabs my hand and twirls me around to get an eyeful off my sultry frame.

I laugh, feeling beautiful and playful. Seb leads me by the hand towards the back of the red velvet couch and gently places his palm on the nape of my neck.

"Bend over."

Made in United States
Troutdale, OR
11/07/2023